THE GOLDEN WHIP

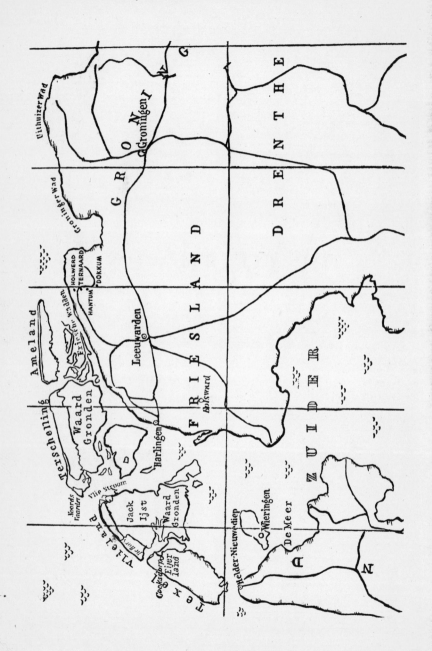

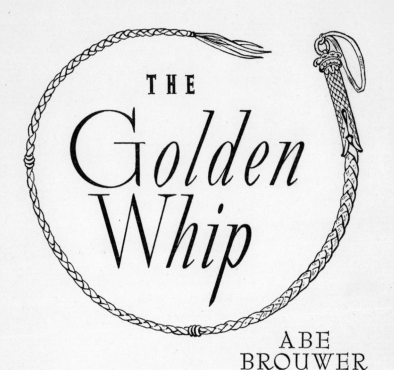

THE
Golden Whip

ABE
BROUWER

*Translated from the Frisian
by Albert Hyma*

❧

Zondervan Publishing House
GRAND RAPIDS, MICHIGAN

Preface

The English translation of *De Gouden Swipe* appears at an appropriate time, for the year 1947 marks the celebration by the Dutch in Michigan of the centennial festival commemorating the founding of Holland in the wilderness near the shores of Lake Michigan. A large percentage of these Dutch people are of Frisian stock; they can bear witness to the exactitude with which Abe Brouwer has depicted life in Friesland during the first three decades of the twentieth century. Many of them have visited Dokkum, Hantum, Holwerd and Ferwerd, where the heroes of this story spent much of their time. Both author and translator have lived more than a decade in Leeuwarden, the provincial capital of Friesland. It was the translator's grandfather who built the railroad from Leeuwarden to Dokkum.

To familiarize the reader with the locale of the narrative this volume contains a simple map of Friesland and a picture of a typical Frisian farmhouse with attached barn. Since the English vocabulary does not contain the exact translation of the Frisian word *boer*, except in connection with discussions of the Boers in South Africa, the term has been preserved in its original form. A boer is the proprietor of a large farm and enjoys a peculiar degree of social prestige which has been well described in the following pages.

ALBERT HYMA

Ann Arbor, Michigan

PART ONE

Mrs J. Moereloui Sr

1

IT HAD been market day in Dokkum. Early in the morning the cattle wagons had rattled over the cobblestones, and the drivers had come from the villages in the neighborhood with sheep and lambs, with cows and horses, to take their cattle to the market place, the "Old Churchyard."

Wagons and carts had been backed against the old school, and then the trading had begun, the negotiations, the sale of cattle, the handclasps — finally the toast and the settlements.

About noon the first buggies had arrived, and within an hour the entire place had been crowded with carriages. Near the gate that led to the wooded country there had been fewer than elsewhere, because most of the farmers from the sandy regions did not have horses and buggies; they had been compelled to walk or ride in dog-drawn carts.

On such a day the town was completely changed; everybody tried hard to please the people from the country. The dealer in mats told his wife to bring the big coffee pot; the grocer opened a box of candy, for he knew that the women loved to grab a few pieces now and then; the baker prepared more cake than on other days.

Peace and quiet were restored as soon as the outsiders had left the town. In the evening only a few farmers were still sitting in the inns, and with the long whips between their knees, they discussed their land and cattle, while, amid loud chatter, their wives drank coffee.

Finally even these farmers, one after the other, went home.

But the carriage of Douwe Ates Wallinga, a young boer from Hantum, was still standing in front of the inn.

The servant had his hands full with the black mare which had been harnessed, and he looked eagerly at the door. There they came at last, Douwe and his young wife Liesbeth, who was a head shorter than he.

With a supple swing he helped her across the wheel, put the whip in the socket, seized the reins and shouted, "Gid-up." Hardly had he uttered these words than with a start the black horse, neighing merrily, shot forward, onward to Hantum. Jouke, the servant, was barely able to step aside in time.

At the first bridge they overtook one of the buggies. Douwe said "Good evening" and raised his hand.

This evening Douwe Ates was in a strange, excited mood. As they passed another buggy he put his arm around Liesbeth's neck and gave her a kiss. "That is one, that is two." Then he sat straight again and called to the horse: "Forward, Wardy, my black girl, go ahead!"

Liesbeth checked him a little, but she did not mean to hold him at a distance, for she enjoyed riding thus with her husband on a bright spring evening, with Wardy at the front, Wardy, who seemed to be dancing on the road.

Presently they passed another carriage, and as they were next to it the other driver said, and Douwe heard him laugh, "True, you can easily pass this old beast, but the little sorrel of Wilco, that is another matter!"

Douwe suddenly raised himself and as he stared sullenly Liesbeth heard him say in a threatening voice: "Wilco Heerema."

Liesbeth felt at once the suspense in these words; she put her warm hand upon Douwe's arm and said, "We don't need to go faster, do we?"

Only two words came from his mouth, but they were pronounced so fiercely that Liesbeth understood what they would mean.

"Yes, indeed," said Douwe, and then to his horse, "Wardy, do you hear that? Wilco Heerema is ahead of us and another is laughing about it. That won't do, will it?"

It looked as if Wardy understood exactly what was wanted of her. The animal's ears were flattened against her head, her legs and back seemed to get longer, and even faster than a moment ago she ran along the gravel road.

The glow of the candle fell upon Douwe's face, and Liesbeth saw the passion that had mastered her husband.

Unconsciously he bent farther and farther forward, and then he put his head out of the buggy, but otherwise the boer and his horse seemed to be one. With the rhythm of the horse as it ran Douwe also went up and down . . . up and down. Now his wife did not count. *Boer and horse* . . . she thought, *boer and horse* . . . But unwittingly she also came under the spell, and she looked out of the buggy to see how fast they ran.

This way they rode, yard after yard, and not a word was spoken. Then suddenly Liesbeth felt a pull on her arm and she heard her husband say, "Gid-up, Wardy, we are catching up with him!" Wardy ran as fast as she could, and when they were but a few yards from the carriage ahead of them, Douwe Ates threw his blanket aside, stood straight and shouted, "Wilco Heerema, may we pass? I am getting tired of your dawdling!"

Liesbeth smiled gently, but Douwe laughed; he had enough pleasure for two. Then he heard suddenly, "Whoever wants to pass me, let him go ahead. I don't have to make room for anybody." Douwe grit his teeth. "The road is too narrow, as that fellow knows full well," he said to Liesbeth, "but I shall pass him for sure!"

He held Wardy in check until they reached a crossroad

which led to Hantum-huizen. There he said sharply, "Hold tight, Liesbeth," grabbed the whip from the socket, gave Wardy a gentle stroke and shouted wildly, "Gid-up!"

Before Wilco realized it the other buggy was next to his. For one moment they drove together, then Douwe shouted, "Now for home, Blacky!" And to Wilco in a contemptuous vein, "Shall I tell them, boy, that you will be coming along soon?" The next moment they passed him.

Wilco seized his whip and beat his horse with all his might, but in vain. He could hear only Douwe's laughing as with one arm he pulled Liesbeth to his strong chest and kissed her passionately. Then he heard him call, "Douwe, Douwe Ates!" Douwe released Liesbeth and put his head out of the buggy. Liesbeth heard Wilco say in a threatening voice: "We are still alive, the two of us, you boer of the Free Estate! When you are ready to go out alone without your wife, we shall see each other again!"

That was a challenge! Douwe checked Wardy's course, but now Liesbeth was frightened. She seized his arm and whispered, "Don't listen, Douwe; be sure not to listen. I want to go home!"

What was he to do? Stop and ask Wilco what he meant or . . . and he looked at Liesbeth. In the pale light he saw that her eyes were full of fear, and he felt her trembling hand.

He gave Wardy free rein and pulled his wife closely to him. They sped through the village, where all was quiet, followed the road to Brantgum till they reached the gates of the Free Estate, and then they turned slowly at their road, where Gelf the servant was waiting for them at the big doors of the barn.

Liesbeth and Douwe alighted, and as she entered the house Douwe listened at the barn door.

"Do you hear that buggy, Gelf?" he asked the servant. "That is Wilco Heerema, who thought that we could not pass him. But," and he walked to Wardy and stroked her, "we showed him something quite different, didn't we, Wardy?"

"You must dry her off carefully, boy," he said, and then he followed Liesbeth through the long cow barn to the house.

They sat a long time together, the young boer and his wife, and they were thinking about what had happened.

True, Douwe was pleased, but deep in his heart he was restless, for those last words of Wilco annoyed him: "We are still alive, boer of the Free Estate!" That was a challenge, and Douwe knew that the man meant something. If only he knew what that was!

And Liesbeth? She had wanted desperately to tell him something. . . . If only a great danger had not threatened, she would have. . . . They had been married for two years, and she knew the tense situation here. Old Man Ate could not have suspected what was to happen when he deeded the farm to his son. After his death it had seemed as if a strong pillar had been torn down. The honeymoon had been one series of parties. Douwe had paid no attention to the farm, and his mind had been preoccupied with racing and festivities. With both horses, Kol and Wardy, he went to all the races, and it seemed as if he were gone whole days and nights.

In the drawing room he had set up an oaken cabinet, and there hung his many prizes: silver bridles, headgear and whips; only Liesbeth knew how much they had cost. And the last few months he had been mastered by one great passion, which had become all the more fierce because the son for whom he had waited so ardently did not come. He must for once in his life win the chief of all trophies: the Golden Whip of Friesland!

And Liesbeth was afraid. . . .

Would that which lived in her be worth while? But still she had to tell him. And suddenly she suggested that they go outside for a moment.

"What?" asked Douwe, surprised. "Outside?"

"Yes, I. . . ." How could she explain it to him? "I wanted to go out for a minute in the evening air."

Queer idea, thought Douwe . . . *Let her have her way.* Walking through the cow barn, he went outside and stood immovable, while she went past him up the yard to the little gate that led to a plot of land. There she laid her arms upon the gate and looked up at the sky, where millions of stars sparkled.

Behind the tower of Hantum the moon was rising and threw a silvery light on the houses and the church. She heard the soft, melancholy hooting of two owls behind her; in front of her lay the cows in the pasture, and beyond them walked the horses.

In a moment Douwe stood at her side; she pressed her head against his shoulder, and then he heard her say softly, "Douwe, if everything goes right, then . . . a year from now we shall no longer be just the two of us."

Douwe, the strong Douwe, trembled like a child. . . . He lifted her head, and looked into her eyes for a long time. Finally he said with difficulty, "Is that true, Liesbeth? How glad I am!" He wanted to say more, wanted to shout, sing, but it was impossible. He could not express his joy in words. "My wife . . . a boy. . . ." That was all he could stammer. He said it so softly, so happily that the tears welled in Liesbeth's eyes.

They walked into the house, filled with happy thoughts about that great new thing which was to come to them, which would enrich them so much, and which, so prayed Liesbeth, might bring them together again.

Inside of Douwe there was a song — *My son — My son!* It seemed as if those simple words held for him a magic charm.

Neither Douwe nor his wife saw the dark cloud that moved in front of the moon, which cast a black shadow over the Free Estate. The farm was quiet. There was no sound except the hooting of the owls high on the weathervane.

2

Bouke Hemminga was the oldest workman on the Free Estate. Everybody knew and could see that he was unable to do much more work, but no wise person told him that! Douwe's father had desired that when he himself stopped working Bouke would also quit, but, no, he would not hear of such a thing!

"Thousands of times," he would say, "I have crawled over the Free Estate, and Douwe can receive from me plenty of assistance." That was true enough, and Douwe could not get along without the old man. Douwe was master only in name, for Bouke was the person who put the people to work.

Every morning at five o'clock, no matter what the weather, he arrived from the village and immediately he started operations, regardless of the presence or absence of the boer. Most of the time the boer was not there. Somebody else might say that Douwe was a worthless fellow, a spendthrift, a boer with a poverty-stricken place, but Bouke had a very different opinion. Bouke knew the Wallingas! They did things uniquely. They lived differently. But real boers they were, with heart and soul. For that reason he figured that his business was to preserve the Estate intact.

This morning when he appeared at the farm he saw that Douwe had been helping with the milking. Such a thing had not happened in half a year! That pleased old Bouke, and he mumbled, "He is coming back! Ate Douwes, your son is coming back!" The days that followed were like festival days, but nobody knew the reason, except the two young people.

For Douwe it seemed as if he had begun anew. When at four in the morning Gelf was about to take the milk cans off the rack, Douwe was already at work washing himself under the pump, and all day long he labored as hard as he could.

After tea he went on the land, and with the new mowing machine he cut the grass on two pieces of meadow. Bouke now had little to do, which pleased him. It looked as if Ate, the father, had returned! That promised a bright future, all the more because the haying season was at hand. That was a wild but wonderful time for the farm population, when everybody had to work from early morning until late at night to transform the huge, hungry barn into a peaceful and safe storehouse.

This feverish season passed without mishaps, and in four weeks the work was finished. The two men from the wooded country near Dokkum who helped with the haying had gone again; workmen and horses had a chance to rest. The boer could take time to saunter to the village, apparently in order to see the blacksmith or the carpenter, but actually to have a pleasant chat at the corner.

Now he had time to let his thoughts run freely. They concerned, in the first place, his son. That it would be a son he took for granted. Among the Wallingas the first-born child had always been a son. On the flyleaf of the family Bible one could read all the names — the regularly returning names — Douwe, Ate, Douwe, Ate. Of all those Wallingas there was besides himself only one still alive, Uncle Ids, owner and occupant of the farm called Metserd, near Holwerd.

Uncle Ids had never been understood fully. Douwe's mother told him what a queer fellow the old man had been. He refused to behave, and if the family had not intervened, he would have ruined his life by marrying a servant girl.

He was still a bachelor and lived with a housekeeper on the farm. He had an excellent place, as Douwe knew.

Yes, the Wallingas knew how to get their way; they were a strange lot, but never had any of them been a failure. Douwe also feared nothing. He took life lightly, and now everything would be right, for he would have a son!

If only his father could have seen that — a little Ate! His father's last words he would never forget, the words he had spoken when Douwe took over the management of the farm.

One day in early spring they had returned from the notary public, and they were sitting in the drawing room. Ate Douwes was not a man of many words, but he had said, "Douwe Ates, now the time has come to inherit the farm and you get it free from debts. In former days, boy, I do not know how long ago, there stood here the castle of the Wallingas. You have read more about that than I, but know that whatever they did, there were three things which stood above all else: their freedom, their pride and their honor."

That was all Ate had said, and Douwe had not expected more, but now these words came back to him. To stand above all others, to be free and to live like a king — that was for him the highest ideal. Sometimes he doubted that he would be strong and good like his father and his grandfather. To be sure, there were days when he felt like a king, especially the past summer, but after a season he became subject to a strange and powerful feeling — a feeling which he could not fathom but which mastered him completely.

At first he fought against it because he did not want to be swayed by another force, but that strong and peculiar power made him so weak that a mere trifle could trouble him.

One evening, after he had come through some bitter days of fighting this feeling, he had submitted to it again.

They were sitting peacefully together . . . Liesbeth and he.
She was sewing, the maid darning, Gelf sat snoozing and
Douwe was reading the newspaper.

The lamp threw a golden light upon the four, and there
was an atmosphere of calm and peace. As Douwe turned over
the second sheet of the paper, his glance fell upon a large
advertisement concerning the fall races in Leeuwarden, the provincial capital.

All summer the races had not occupied his thoughts. He
had merely kept Kol and Wardy in shape, but at none of the
races had the Douwe Ates' pair made their appearance. He
had not been interested; all his care and love he had devoted
to the management of the farm. But nobody knew what a
profound change had come over him during the past few
weeks, with what irrepressible feeling he had watched the
carriages that were on their way to the races.

No one knew it. Only Liesbeth felt some of his thoughts,
but she did not dare speak of them, for she was afraid to
stir up something unpleasant. Deep in her heart she expected
the outburst which might be delayed but was sure to come.
Now, noting a sudden movement of Douwe's body, she had
lifted her head. It was as if an icy wind had blown past
her face, and at once she had felt that the moment had arrived.
She had stopped her sewing and waited. Then these abrupt
words had shattered the silence: "Tomorrow I shall enter
Wardy for the races in Leeuwarden!"

Liesbeth had said nothing in reply and had been serious.
Gelf had been rudely awakened and thought, *There that
thunderous mess will start again,* but he had said nothing.

"Didn't you hear me?" Douwe had asked.

Then she had said softly, "Yes, but does that go so easily?
Would it not be better next spring?"

As if he had been expecting such a reply, he had retorted,
"Tomorrow I am going to Leeuwarden, and that settles it!"

He got up and went outside. It seemed to him as if he had
become another man. There was a strange whizzing sound in

his ears, and like a drunken man he stumbled to the gate of the meadow. There they had stood that night; there Liesbeth had told him about that great thing, but at the same time such a small bit of news. . . . And now, less than four months later, he had left her again. . . .

"Liesbeth," it was as if he heard himself saying these words. Then the feeling, coming as if from some foreign realm, overpowered him, engulfing him like a stream, sweeping him along to a place of darkness. With one jump he was over the gate, and he ran as fast as he could to the place where the horses were. Like a ghost he sought the animals, and he called, "Wardy, Wardy, come here!" He waited a few moments, and then Wardy came out of the darkness. . . . She turned and moved her moist nose along his arm. Suddenly, Douwe as if inspired by some unknown force, jumped on her back. It seemed as if Wardy also had been enchanted. She shot forward, jumped over the ditch, galloped through the clover field to the dam and ran up the gravel road. Douwe let the mare run where she would, but he guided her with his knees when she wanted to run on the gravel. He did not want to hear the loud noise of the horseshoes on the gravel. He wanted to hear only the snorting of Wardy. . . .

Racing through the night! It did not matter where they went. In the bend of the road, near the bridge in front of their homes, sat two workmen. When they heard the galloping horse approaching, they wanted to take a look at it, but before they could distinguish anything it had passed like a phantom, and they saw merely Douwe's faint outline. He seemed to be of one piece with the horse.

"I see it all," said one of them. "That is Douwe Ates. He has another fit."

Douwe Ates was indeed bewitched again!

He shouted with glee. *This is real life,* he thought. *How could I have done without it so long?*

He took the road to the northland, and there, with pastures and cultivated fields on either side of him, and above him the immeasurable sky, and around him the night, there Douwe Ates sang, sang disconnected portions of old songs, and he felt like one of his ancestors. He thundered through the night. So must his ancestors have lived; so they must have ridden on their fiery horses, like giants, like kings! So they must have fought against everybody and everything that did not want to submit to them. That was life!

Suddenly he heard the cry of a woman. Wardy sprang aside and wanted to rush forth again, but Douwe restrained her, shouting, "Ho there!" When the horse had stopped, the rider slid down and walked to the spot from which the sound had come. He heard someone say, "Well, what did I say, Auk? Do you see, the boer?" Then to Douwe, "we had gone up the road a spell, it was such nice weather. A short walk would do the wife a world of good. Then we heard the horse approaching, and the wife got afraid of course." Turning to her, he remarked, "Such funny jokes!"

Douwe looked at them — Keimpe, his new steady hand, who had come to the farm last May, and Auk, his young wife. They lived in the Sober Court. Douwe was not surprised that the woman had been frightened. She also expected a child.

Douwe observed that she did not have much use for him, and he said, "It is a bit lonesome for her down here, isn't it?" Keimpe again spoke for her: "Auk comes from a village, and this is our first year down here. That the boer can understand."

"Yes, yes," said Douwe. "Have courage, little woman. Perhaps next year you two will no longer be only two." At that moment he was reminded of the same words spoken before by Liesbeth.

He terminated the discussion, said briefly, "Good night," and left them. They saw him open the gate of the pasture, and then both driver and horse disappeared in the darkness.

While they were still outside Auk said nothing, but when they were back home she remarked, "What a queer person he is; I wish I had never come here." Keimpe shrugged his shoulders. "Can you change him? That man is riding on his own horse, and he has the right to do as he pleases."

"Well, I think he is awful. Who knows what we shall hear and see of him in the future? I don't like him at all."

So it went for a few more days on the Free Estate, and then one morning Douwe was waiting for Gelf who had harnessed Kol and Wardy to a wagon. When Gelf saw him standing there, with his legs spread out and his thumbs in the armholes of his vest, he could tell that there was something wrong.

"Who told you to use those horses?" he asked tersely, and Gelf answered, "Nobody, boer, but there they are. . . ." He had no chance to finish his sentence, as Douwe interrupted him with "Then take the horses away, and like lightning." His voice was not gentle.

"But which horses shall I take then?" asked Gelf. From the boer he heard not one more kind word. "That does not concern you. Loosen the harnesses, or I'll fix you!"

Gelf quickly took off the harnesses. He wanted to utter ugly words but was able to control himself.

Douwe had gone to the barn door, and there he turned and shouted, "Curry the horses, call Bouke, and get the buggy ready!" Then he went through the barn to the house.

"My clothes," he said to the maid, who was peeling potatoes.

Less than a quarter of an hour later, seized by an irresistible passion, he was speeding along the road to Brantgum.

In the yard stood Gelf. In the pasture Keimpe stopped his work for a moment, and both took charge of the buggy. Standing in front of the window in the living room, Liesbeth watched her husband until he was out of sight. In her heart a deep, stinging sorrow broke loose, because her love was not strong enough to keep him — not yet. . . . But within her was growing the new life, which someday, perhaps, would be able to make this man peaceful again.

As she sat there, deep in her thoughts, someone seized her arm. It was Jouk, the maid. "Come," she said. "Come, mistress. Do not stay there alone. . . ."

3

ON THE Free Estate there were days of unrest and turmoil.
Nobody could please Douwe, and deep in his heart he
was convinced that he had lost control of himself. That was
made clear when one day little Auke, the horse trainer, had
arrived at the Free Estate.

One night he had arrived from Leeuwarden. Liesbeth, who
had been sitting in the living room waiting for her husband,
had looked up with surprise when the little fellow entered the
room. When she had asked Douwe who he was her husband
had replied that it was the trainer for Wardy and that he
would stay one week.

That had made the situation no better, for the next morning as he was making Wardy run with the new carriage, he
had said to Douwe after the third round, "I don't want to
make you any false promises, boer. If she keeps on running
this way there will be no use of having her enter the races
in Leeuwarden."

"Why not?" Douwe had asked, and he had walked toward
Auke with a threatening air.

"Because the mare runs like a cow," was Auke's answer. "It would take me four weeks to correct all her faults. She does not start off the right way and she runs too irregularly."

Then Douwe had said, and his voice was as hard as iron, "I'll tell you one thing. One week from now Wardy will be in shape, and she will enter the races. Will you ride her, yes or no?"

Auke had reflected for a moment and then had replied, "I'll do my best. I must think of my family."

So that week had passed, and when the training had been finished it was plain that Auke had been in the right, for Wardy did not have a chance. Douwe was more confused than ever.

At the request of Liesbeth, Gelf had gone with Douwe to Leeuwarden, and late in the evening they were riding home, Douwe in a wretched condition as a result of great disappointment, Gelf filled with worry over the horses and the boer.

As they entered Hallum the place was crowded with wagons and buggies. Gelf tried to ride past them so that Douwe would not notice the commotion, but he did not succeed. From the inn came such a loud noise that the boer could not help hearing it. "Stop, Gelf," he shouted, "Stop!"

When he had gotten out of the buggy he had said, "Don't unhitch, but ride around a bit."

Gelf looked after him as with large steps he walked to the door of the inn, and he waited.

Douwe kicked the door open and stood on the threshold. He did not observe the guests. What struck him was the sudden and intense silence. How queer! A moment ago one could have heard the noise a hundred yards away, and now this sudden silence! Was that because of him? Had they been talking about him? Like a flame anger burned in him. Had these commonplace folk been babbling about him like old women?

He walked to the large table where fourteen men were sitting. In front of one of them, a boer from Marrum, he halted. For a moment he looked straight into the eyes of this man and said as calmly as possible, "Keep on talking, boer!"

"My good man," he answered, "I am not talking; I am listening."

"So, you are not talking? I can hear that. Nobody is talking any more as Douwe Ates enters the place!" His repressed anger was seeking an outlet. "Keep on talking." He shouted and struck the table with such force that the glasses tumbled and the boer from Marrum pushed his chair aside.

"Not one of you has to keep his mouth shut," he bellowed, and his eyes shot fire. "But the first who has something to say about Douwe Ates had better get ready for me!"

The innkeeper thought that the time had come for intervention. First he wiped the sweat from his face with his large red handkerchief, then he walked to Douwe and said affably, "Here I am, boer. I had said to the company that the boer of the Free Estate would not go home without first stopping at the inn of Jochem Draaier. What would you like, sir? I have an excellent ham; you would enjoy that. Yes, you had better take a seat in the special room. Should the maid get something ready for you?"

Don't try to get him out of here, Jochem, said the innkeeper to himself, *for he is in a condition to smash your whole bar.* In a loud voice he said, "And a pot of steaming coffee, that will suit you fine, boer! Hike, Hike, set his place ready! Come this way, boer, this way!"

Douwe followed Jochem, who with ingratiating kindness showed him the way to the guest room, and once more he wiped the sweat from his face. The farmers started talking again, the women also resumed their conversation, and the boer was in the special room.

"You must be careful and watch for the — " Jochem was trying to say, but as he turned toward Douwe the words stuck in his throat.

Douwe was standing with his back toward the wall. He did not hear nor see Jochem. He stood there, an angry snarl around his mouth, his fists clenched.

As he was about to ascend the short stairs he had detected
a few words. Someone had been laughing: "The Golden
Whip farmer." That voice he knew and that laugh he had
heard before.

Jochem, desperately afraid, wanted to seize Douwe's arm,
but the latter shoved him back so that he fell in the hall.
Douwe entered the room again; his glance was searching for
someone. His eyes were like knives, turning in all directions.
Chairs were pushed aside. Some of the women were frightened
and tried to get out of his way. But Douwe continued to
search, and his voice was ominous and sharp "Who says that?
Who says that?" He emphasized every word. Then his glance
rested upon a corner of the room and he shuddered.

Wilco Heerema! Wilco! The man who challenged him!
So it was he. . . . Douwe's eyes were like balls of fire. His
fine teeth sank into his lower lip. . . .

Jochem was terrified and tried once more to get the boer
out of the big room and into the guest room, but with one
move he shoved the innkeeper aside. Then he went directly
to Wilco.

The farmers were standing, the women started to leave,
and no one dared to say a word against the young boer with
his bony head and the curly hair that fell over his forehead.

Now he had reached Wilco and the farmers were sur-
rounding him. Was Heerema going to fight? Jochem ran to the
maid and whispered in her ear "Call the sheriff, but not until
I have raised my hand, you understand?" Suddenly they heard
the voice of Douwe again, loud and calm but full of contempt:
"So *you*, Wilco Heerema! So *you* could not keep still! *You*
wanted to doublecross me?" Then Douwe turned to the rest
of the audience. "Sit down, folks! You are not afraid, are
you? You don't expect me to fight that Wilco Heerema like
a common ragamuffin? Ha, ha, ha!" His laugh resounded
through the smoke-filled room. "Against that fellow?" He
tossed his head in order to increase the volume of his voice,
and he slapped his knees with his hands.

Wilco Heerema could not endure those words of contempt, and white with fury he answered, "If you want a scrap with me, Douwe, come along, but don't stand there laughing like an idiot. It is true, I said something about the Golden Whip farmer. If that is enough for a fight, come along then!"

Jochem was wondering whether this was the moment for calling the sheriff. Would it be a fight?

Then said Douwe, "Yes, that's what I said, and you know why I said it. And for that I'll give you a beating such as you have never had in your life. But not here, Wilco Heerema!"

"You don't dare," was all that Wilco was able to retort. But Douwe was laughing. "Don't talk like a child. Await your time. Did you think that I would act like a clown and fight you here?" He turned and went to the guest room, where Hike waited on him.

Half an hour later they saw him go out of his room. Without a word he left the inn. Gelf was ready. Douwe entered the buggy and said briefly, "Drive."

The servant took his seat next to Douwe, and they sped through Marrum, Ferwerd, Blija and Holwerd to Brantgum. Gelf was glad that they were almost home, and he drove as fast as possible. But occasionally he had to let the horses slow down a bit. The boer sat motionless in the dark evening. What was going through his mind? Gelf had never served such a boer, never. Sometimes one could get the boer to do anything for him, and sometimes he was a veritable demon. Gelf could not understand it. What ailed that man, anyway? An excellent farm, healthy cattle, a fine wife, one who was willing to accommodate everybody (didn't she give him a pair of warm socks last week?) — yes, the boer could be a satisfied and happy person. But that he was not, far from it. How could anybody cause misery to such a noble little wife, particularly at this time when she was expecting her first baby? Was that right? No, as the maid had observed yesterday, the boer liked her well enough, but he could not do otherwise. The Wallingas had always been a queer lot, and it would not be surprising if the child should be the same way.

Liesbeth was waiting in the living room; she did not dare to go to bed. If only she could make the time go faster. She knew her husband was expecting his son, but would things change after that? In her heart was the question *Have I ever been able to fathom Douwe, and shall I ever be able to do so?*

While Gelf let the horses run the last part of the way and Douwe sat in the corner of the buggy like a statue, Liesbeth prayed, "Dear Lord, grant me, in my humility, power and faith; let me never forget that Thy watchful eye takes care of all persons and things. Protect us in Thy goodness, and be with us in these dark, trying days!"

Suddenly she felt as if transported to the days of her childhood, when the old pastor in her little village told his people about the loving God, who never refused to listen to those who were in distress. She was by no means the first who needed God's care, for she was reminded of those stories from the Bible, Daniel in the lions' den, Jacob alone in a foreign land, Peter in jail and Paul fleeing for his life. Those stirring words of Jesus comforted her: "Come unto me, all ye that labour and are heavy laden, and I will give you rest."

But she was called back to reality when the barn door opened with a loud noise and Douwe called, "Lies, Liesbeth! where are you?"

She joined him. In the middle of the barn they met.

"Liesbeth," said Douwe "Liesbeth. . . . "

Strange, his voice was so soft, like that of a child, and at this moment it was clear to her that here was someone who had come to her for protection. As they were together in the living room she realized that he had had another fight with himself. He had returned to her, and she would receive him again in love. How long that would last she did not know, nor did she try to find out. He had come back, and he would have put his head in her lap if pride had not stopped him.

The boer of the Free Estate. . . .

As she lay there next to him in the old bed, long after he had fallen asleep, she was still awake . . . and she was wondering what was to come next.

4

OVER ALL Friesland hung the melancholy air of parting. Long, fine threads of mist were strung over fields and villages, and they had descended upon leaves and flowers. In the late sunlight the trees and shrubs were full of color. Dead leaves were falling into ditches and canals.

In the fields people worked hard to get the potatoes and beets out of the ground. In the potato field the men were busy pulling the potato plants out, and for every man with his fork there were two women who picked up the potatoes. Old Bouke also was there, although he had much else to do. He must prepare the storage place for the winter, and it had to be done with great exactness. It must be neither too wide nor too small, and the bottom must be as level as a threshing floor.

Tjeerd, Wiebren and Keimpe in turn carried the full sacks to the pile. They had observed that the harvest would be large.

The dead vines were sorted and piled. In the twilight they were to be burned. Then the smoke would spread over the

Frisian fields, and that would add to the melancholy. There
would be something like a sacrifice in it, a sacrifice that reminded one of death.

At this time of the year the old workmen gathered at street
corners in the villages, where they talked of the past. They
calculated how many of the sick would have a chance to live
through the winter. . . .

In this season the horses showed their power. Beets and
potatoes were hauled to the railroad station and the boats
in the canals, and after that the horses rendered valuable
service in the spreading of manure and the fall plowing. In
the morning they were taken out of the fields and then they
were hitched to the hay wagons and dirt carts. How strong
they were — stronger than at any other season! They pulled
the wagons loaded high with potatoes as if it were a small
matter, even though the wagon wheels were sunk deep in the
mud. They bent their proud necks taut and pulled. . . .

Slowly but surely they pulled the wagons out of the hole
where the manure pile used to be, and where the soft bottom
tried to clog the wheels. Together the horses were pulling, and
when one wagon was standing with another attached to it,
they immediately started to move. The driver did not need
to pay much attention to the horses. Unless something extraordinary occurred, no horse would run away in the autumn.

Douwe Ates was using the deep plow on the "tough
plot." It required twice as much care as other pieces. Four
horses were pulling the plow; the first two were leaders who
had served for seven years; the others were Kol and Wardy.
The little boy of Wiebren was guiding the horses. That morning he had arrived on the Free Estate wearing his first new
plow shoes and the snow-white plow pants with fourteen
buttons on each side.

Last evening he had bragged about his new job and had
told his friends in the village about his boer and the deep
plow. "You can follow the furrows with a thread, so straight
he can plow."

But they had laughed at him. "That boer of yours is good for nothing except racing with that crazy pair of horses!"

But Sierk had faith in his boer and he objected strongly to such adverse criticism. If they thought that Douwe could do nothing but race with the horses they did not know him at all, and they had better come over and watch him at work. And tomorrow they would start with the new plow. Sierk fetched it from the blacksmith who had made it himself, a magnificent work of art, wrought of Swedish steel. "There you are," they sneered. "What farmer would use such a hand-made thing? If you want to be up-to-date you use a Saxon."

Sierk did not pay much attention to the sneering of his friends, but when he was in the field with the boer he asked: "Why is a Saxon worth less than this plow?" Douwe looked at him and smiled. "Would you like to know that, boy?"

"Yes, boer."

"Very well, I shall try to explain. A Saxon is dead, boy, and this plow is alive. Look, in the factory where the Saxons are made everything is done with machinery. The iron is cast into molds, and the men who work there make the same little piece all the time. They run the machines, insert a screw here and there, next a bolt, and then they smear some green and red paint over it and the plow is ready.

"But this one! The carpenter saws the pole out of the tree; he turns and planes the arms and the handles. With his own hands he has shaped this thing; he has put his thoughts into it. The blacksmith does the same thing. You should see the rough piece of iron which the blacksmith uses for the plowshare. It is a square piece, and how often does he have to put it back into the fire! When the smith has made the form with his living hands he must harden, file and polish it. The same is done with the plow point, but that is made of pure steel. All the parts have been treated the same way. People who make such plows have put something of themselves into them, and for that reason they are called living plows. Do you understand?"

"Yes, boer," replied Sierk, and he tried to comprehend all this.

"Go ahead then again!" And the plow went once more through the deep earth. The four horses with taut muscles were walking to the east, those to the left in the plowed furrow, the others on the old ground. Next to the horse called Jonker walked Sierk, the reins over his shoulder, with Kol and Wardy behind him, and the plow followed — the plow which ripped open the earth and meticulously laid furrow after furrow against each other.

In this way the soil on the "tough plot" was turned. The farmer guided the plow with all his skill to keep the furrows straight and the land level. Around him flew the mews, swooping, then soaring to look for new prey. There was power in autumn plowing — the power of God, who made Mother Earth eternally willing to receive the seed which would bring forth a hundred, even a thousand fold.

Douwe Ates continued the work day after day. At dawn the workmen were on their way to the fields and late in the evening they returned home. From one field they turned to another, every day anew. . . . One evening after they had been plowing a remote piece where the mill indicated the borderline between the property of Douwe Ates and Wilco Heerema, the boer of the Free Estate heard in the darkness the voice of Wilco. By this time Sierk had hitched the horses to the cart and was waiting for the farmer.

"Where is the boer now?" asked the boy, and he walked to the spot where Douwe stood stiffly. Sierk waited again, but Douwe said in a rough voice that frightened Sierk, "Go to the place, you, with the horses!" Without daring to speak another word Sierk jumped on the cart and drove away.

When the cart had disappeared in the darkness and Douwe heard no noise except the striking of the horses' feet upon the soft ground, it seemed as if he had become another man. With a voice full of anger he shouted, "Wilco Heerema!" And again, "Wilco Heerema!" All was still, deathly still. Had

he fled? Was he so cowardly that he would run away like
a dog? "Wilco Heerema!" Douwe called again, and running
to the ditch, he jumped across it as he called fiercely, "Here
comes the Golden Whip boer!" Then came an answer, not
what he had expected, but he was pleased with the reply.

"Get off my land, you!" *Ah,* thought Douwe, *he hears me.
He is still here!* and like a hunter he sought his enemy as he
called continually, "Throw me off the land then, Wilco Heerema!" Douwe was out of breath from running. Now he was
going to show Heerema who of the two was master. . . . And
he waited, his teeth gritted, his fists clenched.

Gelf was in the yard when Sierk came with the horses.
"Where is the boer?" was the first thing he asked Sierk. As
he unhitched the horses he replied, "I don't know, Gelf. He
stayed there. Suddenly he began to act so queerly, turned
angry at me and sent me away."

Gelf reflected a moment and then, as if he had known it,
he said, "You were near the land of Heerema, weren't you?
Did you see or hear anybody there?"

"No, really not. . . . Yes, I did. I heard somebody call,
but by that time I was already near the tough plot."

"You heard somebody call; that's it! Get the horses, quick
to the land and home. But, no, hand them over to me. I'll
take them to the pasture. You can go." He paid no more
attention to the boy, led the horses to the pasture, took hold
of a big stick and ran in the direction from which Sierk had
come. When he was still a short distance from the "mill ditch"
he heard the noise of body blows and rough voices. It seemed
as if he were close to the men. The cold wind blew into
his shirt and he shivered. Should he go farther? Yes, he must.
There could be no doubt about that. His boer and Wilco
Heerema had begun to fight. There might be an accident.
Carefully he ran along the furrows to the ditch.

There he saw two dark figures. They could not be dis-
tinguished from each other, but from the noise he could tell
that he was not mistaken in his surmise. They were fighting

like beasts, beating with their fists, kicking with their feet, biting with their teeth. One moment they were rolling on the ground. The next they were up again, and Gelf felt that he should not intervene. This was like a fire that must burn out. He could do nothing but wait until this terrible fight had been finished.

Presently the decision came. Douwe lay on Wilco and beat him where he could. His anger seemed to redouble his strength. His fists belabored his adversary as if he were to grind him to pieces. From time to time Gelf heard Douwe make angry remarks. "That is for Hallum! That for the Whip farmer! That for the Golden Whip boer! That for the challenge!"

At last Wilco Heerema gave up and begged for mercy.

The coward! thought Gelf.

Douwe Ates stood, and panting, he said, "Now you will quit challenging the Whip boer!"

He let Wilco rise.

By that time Gelf had vanished.

For a moment the two men stood over against each other, panting and blowing, Wilco still the beaten one and inwardly afraid.

Douwe Ates felt his anger disappearing, and a quietness came over him. It was as if a hungry person had been satiated with his favorite food. His clothes were torn and the blood was running from his nose and mouth, but he felt satisfied.

To Wilco, who had been as badly torn as his enemy and was wiping the blood from his face, he said, "We have to have a talk."

Wilco was amazed. What did that crazy fellow want with him now? First he beat him half to death and then he wanted immediately to talk as if nothing had happened!

"Between us," remarked Wilco, "there will never be an occasion for talking, don't you think? It seems to me that this will do."

"We must have a talk," started Douwe again.

"You can . . ." *burst,* he wanted to say, but he controlled himself. *Douwe may start all over again,* he thought. Douwe Ates laughed. "You probably don't feel very well," he stated, "but the same here with me. If you want to know, I have nothing against you any more, and you must understand that after tonight we shall have no further occasion for grudges. You challenged me and I accepted the challenge, so that is the end of it. And to prove it to you I invite you and your wife to come over next Sunday after milking or after coffee. From that evening we shall be friends! That has always been my intention. What do you say to that?"

Wilco thought. If he followed his instinct he would seize his gun and shoot that conceited Douwe Ates like a dog. Friendship with such a fellow? But his reason won and he said, "I accept. Sunday evening you can expect us, my wife and me."

"Shall we shake hands on it?" asked Douwe, and offered his right hand.

Wilco waited a moment, turned and answered with suppressed anger, "My word will have to be enough. Till Sunday."

"That will do." And without another word Douwe ran to the ditch, jumped across and made for home. . . .

On the other side of the ditch went Wilco Heerema. In his ears resounded the invitation of Douwe Ates, but in his heart was a flame, a flame of hatred, a flame which would consume everything unless it be extinguished, which would destroy all that men would wish to build. . . .

Douwe Ates, happy as a child, told Liesbeth everything. He did not omit one detail, and he did not want his hands dressed. "I have to suffer something for it," he said to Liesbeth. "It is worth a lot to me that Wilco and I have become friends."

Jouk and Gelf had a different opinion, but they dared not say anything. . . .

5

THE LAST DAYS of her pregnancy, which were hard for Liesbeth, brought her closer to God. In her hour of need she turned to the precious words of Jesus recorded in the Gospels. She had come from an irreligious family, and attendance at church had been for her more a habit than a need. But recently she had undergone a profound change, as the day of her delivery drew nearer. Only in the Word of God could she find comfort. One text came to her many times, for it gave her an assurance of God's presence: "Blessed are the pure in heart: for they shall see God."

It was in these days as if some veil, some invisible cloak, rendered access to her difficult. Neither Douwe nor her parents, who came to call on her regularly every other week, could penetrate it. She acquiesced in everything, and that did not please Jouk, who was unable to fathom her mood.

When Douwe came home the evening of the fight she asked him no questions, and she had made no suggestions concerning the invitation. She merely looked at him and said, "You no doubt know what is best, Douwe."

They were sitting in the large drawing room of the Free Estate, Wilco Heerema and his wife, and Douwe Ates and his wife. The weather had been getting steadily worse; a strong northwest wind blew dark clouds across the sky, and now and then the rain pattered against the windows. But in the room the atmosphere was peaceful and pleasant. The stove heated even the remotest corners. After they had talked about the weather and the general news the conversation began to halt, but Douwe quickly ended the suspense. He rose and said, "Wilco Heerema and Mrs. Heerema, this is a strange evening for us. Everybody knew that there was something between Wilco and me. We were far from friendly to each other, until now. Often we had unpleasant encounters; usually we did not go beyond mere words, with the exception of one evening last week when we fought hard. I do not believe that I was the only one who received blows!"

"Indeed not," interrupted Wilco. "I can still feel them!"

"But now," continued Douwe, "after what has happened we decided that there should come to an end to this state of affairs. That's why I invited you both to our house, and I hope that this will be the beginning of a firm friendship between the families of Heerema and Wallinga."

"If we mean business," replied Wilco, "it is never too late, and I make no objection, though you must admit that I thought it a bit queer that after you had beaten me half to death you would make such a strange move."

"Don't think more about that," observed Douwe. "I can assure you that I mean what I say. And as far as my wife is concerned, she is mistress of the Free Estate and wishes to make a remark herself. You agree with me, don't you, Liesbeth?"

All three of them looked at Liesbeth, and each regarded her in a different light.

"Well, Lies?" urged Douwe, and then she said, "I know that Douwe will do nothing that is wrong. I mean, he wouldn't do something with a bad intention. For that reason I agree with him."

"That is well said," opined Douwe. "And what does Mrs. Heerema think of it all?"

"I? Fine and dandy, boy. I have never had anything against you people. On the contrary, I was always inclined to like you both."

A moment later Douwe said to Wilco, "Will you go with me to the barn a minute? The women will want to have a little chat and they won't miss us, will you, Lies?"

Wilco and Douwe went to the barn, and the two wives entered at once into a confidential discussion.

"Did Wilco tell you everything?" asked Liesbeth.

"Not quite. He came home last week with dirty, torn clothes, and covered with blood. He looked terrible. I almost died from fright. 'I had an argument with Douwe,' he remarked, 'but now everything is all right.' 'Well,' I said, 'It doesn't look as if you limited yourselves to words.' 'We fought,' he went on. But that was all I could get out of him. Not until day before yesterday did he mention your invitation. But now you must show me your clothes for the baby; I am interested."

"Come here," said Liesbeth. "I have them here in the cabinet." While she exhibited her treasures she told about the Wallingas, how each of them had been born in this room. "And now," she faltered, "there will be another one."

Piece by piece Liesbeth fingered all the clothes — shirts, dresses, sweaters and other tiny garments. Each had a history of its own. One was made during an evening when she was waiting for Douwe, another when Douwe was racing the horses on the way to Brantgum, and each stitch had meant a shudder for her as she pondered about that new life that was growing within her.

The golden light of the lamp fell on the two women, the clothes, the cabinet, the big Frisian clock and the exhibition case which protected the prizes won at the races. Five generations of Wallingas had put their imprint upon this drawing room.

In the barn the two farmers inspected the cows and then

they went to the horse stable. There were the workhorses and
Kol and Wardy, the racehorses. Here Wilco experienced another surprise of the first magnitude, for Douwe, after having
stroked each horse in succession, said, "I spoke about friendship,
Wilco," and then, putting his hands upon Kol and Wardy, he
continued, "and to prove my intention I am offering you one
of these two horses!"

Wilco was utterly amazed. First he stammered, "No, don't
do that! I couldn't accept one of these, you know. Those are
horses that have no equals, Douwe!"

"If you don't accept I'll know that you are not serious about
our friendship."

"Now really," continued Wilco, "let me choose one of the
others, Jonker, for example, or any other." But Douwe insisted, "One of these two, and no other!"

"Very well," replied Wilco. "Then let it be Kol."

"Agreed. After this the Frisian gelding Kol is yours. Soon
I'll show you his pedigree and tomorrow the servant will bring
you the horse."

Then, as if nothing remarkable had happened, the two men
continued their walk. They examined the famous bull "Marcus
Pel," whose many descendants may be found in America and
Argentina. They paused in front of the pigs, returned through
the barn and joined the women.

After their meal Douwe presented the pedigrees with great
pride and showed the prizes he had won in the races.

When they were seated again Douwe related in a matter-of-
fact manner: "I have just given Wilco the choice between Kol
and Wardy. He picked Kol and that horse is no longer ours."

"That? Oh, Douwe," and Liesbeth became animated, "how
nice of you!"

Frouk was surprised. "How could you accept that?" she
asked her husband.

"He had to," answered Douwe. "Friendship requires sacrifices, and when you give something it should be worth while.
Friendship is not to be looked upon as a dump where you can
cast away things you don't want any more."

"I shall remember, Douwe," said Wilco. "You can depend on that. And if you want to use him again he will be ready for you. To be sure, you can have the use of all my horses." He laughed as he talked, but still he was a bit confused. Frouk could not understand why this strange person could give away an expensive horse without asking anything in return. But Wilco and Douwe continued to talk in lively fashion; before they knew it the time was gone. Gelf had the buggy ready for the guests, and as he turned the reins over to Wilco the latter pressed a guilder into his hand. They drove through the gate, Douwe looking after them until they had vanished in the darkness.

Frouk was thinking about Liesbeth, what a dull person she was, and Wilco smiled blandly. What a fool that Douwe Ates had made of himself, giving away a horse that had cost him a small fortune, and of all persons to Wilco Heerema, his supposed friend! That was enough to make one laugh to pieces. His friend? A *friend!* Wilco found it difficult to suppress caustic remarks about Douwe's having had a brainstorm. Douwe should know how he hated him — had hated him since they were youths! His hatred had increased tremendously after that ride from Dokkum. And then that night at Hallum, where Douwe had spoken about him with the utmost contempt!

His hatred had become like a blaze.

"Queer that such a fellow cannot understand," thought Wilco on the way home. He could still feel the power of Douwe's fists. So much had happened to increase their hatred instead of their friendship.

The adjoining farms of the Wallinga and Heerema families were to be united by a bond of friendship — but only on condition that everything should go exactly as Douwe had imagined. When Wilco went to bed he was still laughing about the whole queer business.

On the Free Estate there was no laughter.

When the buggy had disappeared Liesbeth took Douwe's arm and so they walked together through the barn, where the cows were lying peacefully, chewing their cuds.

Liesbeth felt so rested now, and she could bear anything because of Douwe and for Douwe. It seemed as if a heavy burden had been taken from her shoulders. Only the debts on the farm prevented her from being supremely happy. Douwe's present had been a magnificent act. She realized how generous Douwe was, how superior to her in this respect. Wilco probably could not even fathom the extent of his friendship.

She was proud of Douwe and now she could look to the future with confidence. With him she was safe.

The next morning at ten o'clock the servants on the Heerema farm saw Gelf running up the yard riding Kol. They dropped their threshing flails, and when Gelf slid off the horse in front of the window of the barn where the men were threshing, Berend said, "What is Gelf doing here with that horse? That is Kol, of Douwe Ates!" Just then Wilco opened the door of the cow barn and Gelf, who had learned his lesson well, said to him, "The compliments of the boer, and here is your horse!"

" 'Your horse,' he said," whispered Berend. "Do you think they made some kind of deal?" Then they heard Wilco say to Gelf, "Fine, boy, we'll put him in the stable, and you must come inside, for the person who brings such a fine present deserves a fine lunch."

"A present!" Now they were completely befuddled, and during the threshing the three men kept on talking about the strange events that had occurred between these two farmers, who obviously had no use for each other. When Wilco and Gelf were in the living room, little red-cheeked Doutsen, the daughter of Wilco, came running to the barn. She raised her arms and said to the men, "What do you think, men? We have received a big horse, as big as a house, and it can run fast, and we don't have to pay anything for it, only a lunch for Gelf . . . ." Then she turned quickly and went back to the house. Auke was laughing so hard that he had to lean against the wall.

"If it is true that Douwe really gave Wilco that horse," remarked Auke, "then he will have to pay him threefold!"

"Our boer," continued Berend, "has something on Douwe, and he is taking advantage of him!"

They heard the barn door open again, and the threshing was resumed. But it was not the boer, only little Doutsen. She was on the way to her swing, which had been made out of a rope from the hay wagon and could go high. There she went, back and forth, singing an improvised song about the new horse:

> We have a very beautiful horse.
> It is standing now in the stable,
> With ribbons in the manes,
> In the clean, clean stable.
> His hair is black, his skin is black,
> And black are also his legs;
> A white star sits on his head,
> And therefore is he a Kol.

6

THE DULL, GRAY FIELDS were deserted and lay resting. Not until early in the spring would people return to start a new life. Dark and heavy, like slumbering giants, the potato heaps were scattered about, where the crop remained under a thick covering of mud. In the pastures the sheep were grazing, wandering from one piece to another, with the powerful ram near the flock, aware of his strength.

The men were now working in the barns, threshing day after day. Their wives were happy because now they no longer had to hang on the lines the old shirts, coats and pants which the men had been wearing in the fields until they came home thoroughly soaked.

Douwe Ates and Wilco Heerema went hunting each day. They had plenty of room and they enjoyed themselves in the open, where all plant life was dying. Douwe wanted to go largely because he was becoming bored on the farm, where things had become quiet. He needed action, but presently the nights became so long that he almost fell asleep with nature.

One day there was a heavy snow in the morning.

Old Bouke, who arrived on the farm every day at six, no matter what the weather, stood at five o'clock at the door of his little house in the village and looked with surprise at the snow. "That I had not expected," he said to his wife, as she was getting his sandwiches ready. "There will be a lot more," he added.

"Snow, yes," said she, "and I can't understand why you go in such weather to the farm, since the boer has told you repeatedly that you don't need to come."

"And I have said repeatedly that I'll go there walking as long as I can go. The wages that Douwe pays me I want to earn. But," and his voice sounded like the old Bouke of former days when he was so gay, "why do we spend our time talking in the early morning? Come, let me sweep the snow away in front of the house."

"What, in front of the house?" asked Foekje. "Your eyes must be getting weak, for otherwise you would have seen that the street has been cleaned quite a while ago."

"So, old lady, come here and I'll give you a good washing with the snow!"

Foekje had to laugh. That would have been a sight — Bouke throwing snowballs! All of Hantum would be standing on its head.

When Bouke had left she took up her daily work. She dusted and polished all the pieces of furniture in her little room, on whose walls hung the pictures of their children and grandchildren.

Bouke muttered as he reached the corner. "Dirty mess, three times a nuisance: when it comes, when it lies there and when it goes away. But a person has no control over such things." Carefully he walked through the village and then he took the road to the farm. It was no joke, that long walk, no, sir! "But I don't fail at the first blow," he remarked to encourage himself.

The boer would be there milking with the men, for he was

not to be stopped. No matter how early one came, there he was at work. How could he keep that up? And how could he manage to pay for everything? He must have money!

Bouke could not easily understand Douwe. His father had been so different — always the same calm, methodical person, not too kind nor too mean. One could always depend on him. At nine o'clock in the evening he was always through with the day's work. There had been no use to say that this or that task still remained undone. He would remark that one had had nearly eighteen hours in which to do it, and that was the end of the matter.

Yes, that was the way Ate had done things. Bouke nodded his head, although he was alone on the road. Douwe was so different. He was his employer and all that sort of thing, but when Bouke came home in the evening he would sometimes say to his wife that "our Douwe" was a queer fellow, and yet he liked him immensely. He had a wild nature, and one wondered where he had gotten that. It must be in the family. There was Douwe's queer uncle, Ids, at Holwerd. He had been a strange youth, and even now he could do strange things. Take that cow, for example. Douwe had been lodging there, and so he had heard about the incident and had told Bouke about it. That cow was sick and the veterinarian had advised him to kill it, but, oh, no!

Just then a queer little man had appeared from the wooded country to the southeast, a queer little man who made his living by helping the farmers with their cattle. He had asked for work and Ids had said that there was none. "But don't you do some doctoring with animals? Just come with me in the pasture and look at my cow, which according to the veterinarian has to be killed."

Well, the little man went with him, looked at the cow, touched it, examined its mouth and said, "That cow need not be killed. For five guilders I'll tell you what to do, and you won't have to pay me until it is cured." "Tell me then," said Ids. "She must have sea water splashed over her body each morning until she starts walking of her own accord."

Sea water. Could anything have been more ridiculous? But old Ids had replied, "If that helps, it shall be done!" And so each day for three weeks Ids Wallinga had gone to the North Sea with two horses pulling the sled with the cow on it. He had paid no attention to his critics, and in three weeks the cow was better.

Bouke had to laugh about that as he walked through the deep snow from Hantum to the Free Estate. Those men were to be admired for their strong wills! Farmers they were, heart and soul, people who felt for their work, Douwe included, although he sometimes did queer things.

It was cold this morning, and Bouke pulled his fur cap farther over his head. The snow bothered him, and he did not get on as fast as he would have liked.

As he plodded, his thoughts, partly spoken, were with his boers, especially Douwe. Lately that man had been a real boer, for, as Bouke knew, Douwe was spurred on by the knowledge that soon his son would be born. He muttered. "Can you imagine that, an unborn child? How is that possible!"

Once more Douwe had had a fling. It had not lasted long, but Bouke could not easily forget it, no, indeed, for he had imbibed heavily himself.

It had happened some time ago, but he recalled the circumstances as if the incident were an event of yesterday. The day had been busy on the farm; they were delivering potatoes, and grass had been cut; there was one more job to do; a wagon had to be used. Douwe had said nothing about this, and so Bouke had ordered Gelf to hitch Wardy to the cart. That had been done, but at that very moment Douwe had come running out of the house shouting, "Not that horse! I've got to go away myself!" Douwe had gone inside again and Gelf had unhitched Wardy. When Douwe had put on his good clothes and had driven away, Bouke said to Gelf, "Those proud, lazy snobs, it would be a good thing if they used their own muscles a little more!" Was that so bad? Apparently Douwe had heard his remark, for they saw him rise and shout, "Thunder and lightning!" He rushed back, and in front of the barn door he

pulled Wardy's reins so hard that she reared backward. The
workmen who were about to go to the field watched with
amazement. Douwe growled, "Come here!" And when they
did not run fast enough to please him he added, "Come here,
all of you, like lightning!" When they stood around him he
continued. "There is someone here who has said things about
me that are not complimentary. It may not be a usual custom,
but I'll give you this advice: say what you please, but look out
that I don't hear it, for the first whose words do not please me
will lose his pay at once, no matter who he is. There is only
one boss here, and that is Douwe Ates." Then he was gone.

Bouke had felt hurt, true enough, but he had said to the
men who had wanted to take his part, "He is right, folks, we
are his employees. Better go back to work!"

How well did Bouke remember all this now! But nobody
else knew what happened two days later, when he and Douwe
were busy in the cow barn. . . .

Bouke was sitting on the bench making brooms, with
Douwe next to him. Liesbeth had just brought the coffee but
she had said nothing. When she had left them and the door
had swung closed, Douwe had stood and with his back toward
Bouke had said, "Bouke, Bouke, she is quite right, but only God
knows what I have to stand."

That was the same Douwe, and that was why Bouke could
not get angry at him. As he continued with the cutting of the
twigs he remarked, "You are still young, Douwe. You are like
twigs. . . ."

Yes, thought Bouke, *on such a morning as this these things
come back to us. But I am glad that I am almost there, for it
is no joke, this walk in the snow. I'll see to it that the snow is
cleared away before the sun turns it into a mess. The frost is
not severe enough to harden the ground, though it might
change.* He looked at the sky, but he was unable to tell what
the weather would be.

*It may turn out to be very frosty after all. Very well, then,
I must pretty soon have a look at the sheep.* The old man was

cutting the day into a hundred thousand pieces: clear the yard; look at the sheep; go to the cow barn; make brooms, repair harnesses; wash tails.

No one told him what to do. Everybody let him go ahead as he pleased, but nothing escaped his attention. Who could better than he reprimand the old horse Jonker which always shoved the clean straw under his hind legs, so that nobody could remove the manure? Who could surpass him in telling the cattle about their bad manners when they lay in their own droppings? Who could tell better than he when a cow was to have a calf? No one of course! Good, there was the Free Estate!

Bouke went through the gate and along the road to the yard. At once he heard familiar sounds. The ducks in the canal, the hens and the rooster, the rolling of the wheels of the manure cart on the board and the clippity-clap of Gelf's wooden shoes as he guided it, the noise of the chains in the horse stables, the bellowing of a heifer — these had become a part of himself in the many years that he had been employed here. He had come here when a boy, when he had to jump to reach the pump, and now he was nearly seventy, sixty-eight to be exact. . . . But although he could not get around so fast as formerly he still had as much spirit as in the first years. He was ready to give his life and soul for the farmer. First came the boer, then the boer, and last, Bouke himself. . . .

"What a mess of snow, isn't it, Gelf?" he remarked, as Gelf came out of the barn with a wheelbarrow full of it.

"Well, of all things, so you are here. Haying is past, and you might just as well have stayed home."

Bouke did not vouchsafe an answer, and he went to the shed to get a shovel. As he was about to start working in the yard Douwe stood behind him and said, "Good morning, Bouke." Then as soon as Bouke had made a suitable reply, "Hey, Bouke, don't remove the snow, I have a reason for that."

"I have a reason for that," muttered Bouke. *Something*

funny again. What purpose can he have with such a mess of snow?

But Douwe Ates began to laugh and said, "Not one flake of snow may be taken off the yard, for listen, old boy, come with me in the warm stable, and I'll tell you." He took him to the bench and when they were sitting there next to each other he continued. "Do you remember, Bouke, what used to happen here on the Free Estate when there was a lot of snow?"

Bouke looked at him; for a moment there was a question in his old eyes, and then he laughed. "Sleigh," he said, and it seemed as if decades had fallen from his shoulders. His eyes sparkled and he remembered the scenes of the past.

"Your mother and you in the sleigh, and your father in the rear, yes, and once, no, more than once, you and I have ridden in it, do you remember? Riding in the sleigh. . . Yes, the black horse in front . . . everlastingly grand that was ...." Joyfully he looked at the boer. Then he heard Douwe say, "Just so, Bouke, and today the boer and his young wife will go in the sleigh . . . and . . ." *the son also,* he wanted to say, but he did not dare.

Bouke knew what he was thinking, and he said, "Boy, Douwe, would that still do?"

"Oh, sure," remarked Douwe. "My wife is young and strong!"

7

In the yard the sleigh was ready. Keimpe and Gelf got it from the attic and cleaned it thoroughly, and now it was awaiting its precious load, that beautiful sleigh, white with a swan's neck carved on it.

Gelf had gone with Wardy to the blacksmith to have the horseshoes fixed for slippery roads. Joukje had put the foot-stove in the sleigh, with two chunks of peat in it, aglow with heat. The red wool blankets and the hand-woven cover were lying picturesquely on the side of the sleigh.

Gelf came with Wardy from the village, and he and Keimpe hitched the horse to the sleigh. It looked as if Wardy knew what was wanted of her, for she stood proudly. The harness was covered with silver bells which chimed like little clocks with every movement of the horse, and the plumes on Wardy's head and back shone like gold.

Then came Douwe and Liesbeth. Douwe, with happiness in his face, went with big steps to Wardy and looked carefully at everything. Liesbeth stood quietly, admiring the sleigh, and she said, "How lovely that is!"

Jouk had come along, and she helped Liesbeth seat herself. She and Douwe put the covers over her as if she were a child, for they were concerned about her.

For a moment Douwe's hands touched those of Joukje, and as Douwe looked at her he read in her eyes the same anxiety as that in Bouke's eyes. He looked at them one by one, Bouke, Keimpe, Jouk, and he could tell that they were full of apprehension. As he put on his heavy coat which Keimpe had handed to him, sat in the rear on the little bench, his wooden shoes upon the steering pedals, and took the reins, he said, as if forced to talk, "The wife will return safe and sound, I'll guarantee that." Then to Gelf, who was holding Wardy in check, "Come along, boy, to the road."

So they moved slowly down their road to the gate, and the bells tinkled softly. "Let go, Gelf," called Douwe, and then they glided over the white expanse of Friesland, as if in a fairyland. It was as if Wardy knew who was in that sleigh, for she moved gracefully, her body seemingly standing still. On both sides of her nostrils a tiny cloud of warm breath rose, and she neighed merrily. Douwe looked at Liesbeth. "Are you seated comfortably?" he asked her. "Like a princess," she replied cheerfully. "How beautiful this is — perhaps too beautiful. I am so happy."

"So am I, girl," said Douwe.

"Perhaps, perhaps there is another," she whispered.

Wardy ran like a queen.

Liesbeth looked around. The whole white world was like a painting of peace and beauty. The big windmill seemed to be taller now. It dominated the whole landscape, including the house of the miller, the farm of Hiemstra and the canal. Beyond it was the hamlet called Hiaure, and still farther, old Dokkum. Directly in front of her, upon one of the ancient *terps,* she saw Hantum. First they passed the new dwelling of Jan the workman, built to resemble an old city house; then they moved along the high lane flanked by the tall elms which bordered the village.

The sunlight fell upon the fresh snow which had covered

the roofs, and everything sparkled as if the whole world were in festive garb.

At one corner stood a group of men. For a brief moment they moved aside, but presently their ranks closed again and they talked of Douwe and Liesbeth and the pleasant scene they made with that sleigh and black horse.

When they reached Ternaard they saw the dike, the golden hoop, now white, which girds the whole of Friesland. In front of the doctor's house Douwe paused. He saw the doctor approaching. "Of all people!" said the doctor, "Wallinga and his wife! I thought there was hurry, but now I see that we have time left."

Liesbeth and Douwe smiled, and Douwe asked, "Could we do harm?" "Harm?" repeated the doctor, as he gave Liesbeth his hand. "No, I guess not, but don't sit too long," and he raised his finger. "Where are you going?"

"By way of Holwerd, I thought," answered Douwe.

"Yes, that is all right, but then you must get out for awhile."

Liesbeth turned to Douwe and said, "Well, then we could pay Uncle Ids a visit." "Yes, we could," suggested Douwe.

"Agreed then," was the doctor's final remark.

Douwe thought that Uncle Ids would be surprised, for they were not in the habit of calling on him often. But then, what did it matter? He urged Wardy to go on.

At the Visbuurt they ascended the dike, and there they could see far and wide. To the north shone the dunes of the island of Ameland. So lovely was the picture that one would never be able to forget it. In the sharp winter air, with snow on the fields and the sky so blue, everything seems so near. One can feel the presence of God. Liesbeth hardly knew what to think, but she was happy and grateful. *Does my child experience any of this,* she mused, *this living picture that I draw into myself?* Unwittingly she said aloud, "I hope so." Immediately she felt Douwe's hand, and she heard him ask, "What do you hope, Liesbeth?"

"Did you hear that, Douwe? I was thinking about our child

and I asked myself if it would feel all that I felt as I was enjoying the lovely scenery." With a graceful gesture she indicated
the view.

"Girl," said Douwe, and he stroked her gently with his
strong hand, "that we cannot know, but we hope so. And soon,
when the child is with us, it will be our task to show it all these
things."

How much he loved Liesbeth now! At times her depression
had annoyed him, especially when he had one of his fits and he
had felt that everything must yield to his command. But this
morning he cherished a deep love for her. In this grandeur in
which Friesland lay before them and through which they were
gliding so majestically, hearing no sounds save those of the
horse's feet and the tinkling bells, Douwe felt at one with her.
An overpowering emotion seized him, and suddenly he thought
he would like to pray. . . .

Yes, even he could not always escape the conviction in his
soul that God, the Creator of Nature, was at all times near to
guide and direct sinful mankind. Douwe struggled against that
inner voice which so often tried to make him turn in thoughts of
repentance to his Father in heaven. As a rule he had his way,
and yet it was with a feeling of uneasiness that he emerged
from his imagined victory over his better self. Was there not
something back of nature? His mind could not comprehend a
universe so grand and beautiful without some sustaining force.
But, unlike his wife, he would not yield to the powers of God
and His Son, the blessed Saviour. Someday he would learn that
his false pride had led him to folly and injustice.

So they traveled together, firmly united. One of his hands
still lay on her shoulder, while the other held the reins. Liesbeth pressed her cheek against his arm.

When they reached Holwerd the situation changed, for
now the farmer must devote all his attention to the horse in
order to negotiate the curves. Both hands were needed for the
reins and his feet were occupied with the pedals. As they rode
through Holwerd and turned up the road to Waaxens, on

which the farm of Ids was situated, they attracted much attention from people who obviously enjoyed this unusual spectacle.
Here was a truly aristocratic sleigh with perfect appointments.
The glowing cheeks of the young couple were as magnificent
as the horse and the elegant contour of the sleigh.

Ids was standing in his yard to see from which direction
the wind would come when suddenly he heard the tinkling of
bells. He stared a minute or two and said, "I am a cabbage
if that is not Wardy." He ran to the house, knocked on the
window, and when the housekeeper, who had been darning
socks, looked up, he called, "Get tea ready, warm stove ready,
cut bread, there comes company!" Then he ran to the barn, took
Diemer the steward, who was threshing with the workmen, by
the arm and shouted, "Clean straw in the stable, oats in the
crib, hay in the manger, and to the yard!" He barely had time
to get to the gate and welcome Douwe and Liesbeth as they
drove in.

Hardly had they exchanged the customary "Good day"
when Ids remarked, "You must not come too often to Metserd
to look things over, for we have to keep something for ourselves. My, you were here only last year!"

Liesbeth and Douwe laughed, and Liesbeth admitted, "Yes,
Uncle is right. We should not stay away all the time."

"I am used to that, child; I am used to that. But never
mind, as long as you tell me now how you have been getting
along."

He guided Wardy up the yard and then let Douwe unhitch
the horse and lead it to the stable.

"I told the housekeeper to get things ready for you." He
laughed. "Come right inside."

Gepke the housekeeper, who had reluctantly gotten out of
bed at Id's order, took one last look at the living room, and
then she met the guests at the door. As she took Liesbeth by
the arm she thought, *"There you have another Wallinga trick
— taking out a woman who is so far along, driving with her
in a sleigh!"*

"Take my chair, Liesbeth," offered Ids, "and, Douwe, you here. You pour the tea, Gepke." But Gepke said, "You stay in your own chair and don't get so excited; Liesbeth will be glad to walk around a bit."

"I have nothing to say any more in my own house, Douwe. Do you hear that?"

Douwe laughed. He knew better than that, but Uncle acted as if it were not so. All his life he had been different from what people had expected. That he remained a bachelor was not without some good reason. Douwe was not sure what was behind the situation, but it had a history.

He was bound to get more surprises from Uncle Ids this very afternoon, for when, after tea, they had walked through the barn and had admired the fine animals, Ids said, "You must come with me to the front room, where I want to tell you something." Douwe followed him and while the servant hitched Wardy to the sleigh, Douwe sat in a big chair watching Uncle Ids walk through the room.

Douwe wondered what Uncle had on his mind. Did he want to talk about money matters? Suddenly the voice of Ids boomed through the room: "You idiot that you are!" Douwe jumped out of his chair, but Ids was undaunted. "I heard about that fight of yours last fall with Wilco Heerema, and I know of your foolish idea to invite him to your house and offer him your friendship."

"That is my affair," bellowed Douwe.

"Sure it is," continued Ids. "But you made a mistake: you cut your own throat!"

"How is that, Uncle?"

"Because you think that all people are like you, and that is not the case. You consider yourself a great friend of Wilco, but you will find out something just the opposite. That man hates you just as much as before. What do I say — just as much? Oh, no, much more than before. I have had occasion to make my acquaintance with that sort of person, young man. If your father had been alive still, this would not have happened, I can tell you that. You have gone hunting after a skunk, but his odor will not get the better of you."

Douwe was furious. That old fellow meddled in his affairs far too much.

"Uncle need not concern himself with my business," he asserted. "I'll take care of that myself."

"I have warned you," said Ids. "You go your own way now." Those were his last words.

On their way home Douwe thought a long time about their conversation. He was so quiet that Liesbeth was afraid. "Douwe," she asked, "what is the trouble? You are so quiet."

"Oh, nothing," answered Douwe. "Uncle Ids babbled about our friendship with the Heerema family, but I told him that I would take care of my own affairs. That is true, isn't it, wife?"

"Yes. That we can handle ourselves, Douwe."

Douwe thought and thought, and he could not find the reason for Uncle's warning. One could not notice anything about Wilco that justified such a conclusion. Formerly things were indeed different, but now Wilco showed no signs of hatred. He even helped with the management of the farm. On numerous occasions when Douwe had returned home in the evening he had found Wilco inquiring after Liesbeth. No, that was nonsense which Ids had suggested.

Liesbeth was quiet. All around was that beautiful expanse of white. The sun was setting, and it seemed as if it were sinking behind a wall of blue steel. It started to freeze again. The stars were beginning to shine. It was becoming cold. . . . In the twilight she shuddered, partly because of the cold, partly because of something that looked like danger lurking near her, but she could not tell from where it came.

When they had reached home she wanted to go to bed at once. In the stable Jouk said to Gelf, "They should not have done that!"

8

As THE WEATHER became more severe, and the frost knit all the villages together with a bond of ice, when young and old went out on skates, in a winter which forced all the work to be done inside, when young life grew in the barns among the cattle, Liesbeth reached the end of her waiting.

In one of those cold nights, when the sky was deep blue and the stars sparkled in the heavens, Gelf went to fetch the doctor.

It was two o'clock in the morning when Jouk threw the doors of the bed in the cow stable wide open and wakened him. It took a while to arouse him completely; as he looked at Jouk in her nightgown he could not grasp fully the meaning of all this. But when she said, "Get up, boy and fetch the doctor," he replied, "You can go, Jouk. I'll get up."

"Will you be sure to go ahead, Gelf?" she asked once more, but then she let him alone and continued with her work.

Gelf jumped out of his bed, put on his stockings, socks and trousers, let a stream of water from the pump run over his face, dried himself, put on his wooden shoes, then his shirt and

jacket, and ran to the barn. There he had everything ready for
his trip — cap, coat and skates. Near the canal he tied on his
skates. He had often rehearsed this very journey and had long
ago planned how he could reach his destination most quickly.

Well, here we go, he mused. He skated along the canal,
then walked across the highway with his skates still on, crossed
a dam, a short piece of ditch and finally arrived at the big
Mill Ditch, where the open spaces were before him. He raced
with the wind behind him.

So the hour had struck for the boer's wife. If only things
would go right! For a long time there had been a strange tension in the air on the farm, a tension which during the last few
days had become hard to bear. Now this would come to an
end. Gelf was glad for it, but also afraid. Thus far such
wondrous events had never taken place among human beings
whom he knew. When such a thing occurred in the barns,
when cows, pigs and sheep gave birth to their offspring, that
was part of his work, and he was used to that. But now this.

It was cold. He tried to warm his hands on his warm cap
and then in his pockets. He reached the Ternaard Canal, and
was alone on the wide road of ice. Jouk had said that he must
hurry, and that he would do, without a doubt. With his
shoulders bent forward, his head downward, his arms swaying,
he flew like a racer along the canal. He heard nothing, saw
nothing, merely skated as fast as he could. His hands were
clenched into fists. They were no longer cold; nor did he have
time to think about his message. He felt only the blood cours-
ing through his body and the scratching of his skates on the ice.

He entered the village. Two more bridges to go under and
then he would reach the doctor's house! As the boy came to a
halt he was highly excited and without taking off his skates
climbed the bank of the canal. Twice he pulled the night bell
as hard as he could. A window was opened and he saw the
head of a man. That was the doctor. "What does that clock
tolling mean, young man?"

"Could Doctor come at once?" he gasped. "Good," replied

the other, "but tell me first where." "To the wife of Douwe Ates," was all he could stammer. But he need not have said more.

"Wait a moment. I'll be right there." The window was closed again. Gelf stumbled back to the canal and not more than five minutes later the doctor was there also carrying his bag and skates.

"Hold this bag a minute, boy," he said, handing it to him. A moment later he skated with Gelf toward the Free Estate.

Now the great event was at hand!

Vrouw De Graaf, the competent midwife, was making preparations in the front room. The stove was burning as hard as possible. The warm light of the lamp shone on the old furnishings, the cabinet with the prizes, the wide oak table, now covered with a snow-white cloth, and the large bed. The doors stood open, and everything was in perfect readiness. Here many Wallingas had passed away, and here they had been born.

In the big chair sat Liesbeth. She looked very small and pale. One of her hands was lying on the side of the bed, and she seemed to be trying to pinch something that was disturbing her.

Douwe stood near her and held her other hand. He hardly knew what to do or leave undone, for everything seemed strange.

Liesbeth was feeling some pain. "Douwe," she gasped, and he, more frightened than she, called sharply, "Vrouw De Graaf!" The latter sauntered nonchalantly toward them and said, "Here I am, madam. Do you know what? Come along between us and walk up and down the room, just like a little child." But Liesbeth answered, "Oh, Douwe, I can't!" Her eyes were unusually large and she begged him to excuse her.

"Then let her sit down," remarked her husband. But the midwife laughed. She was the only one who kept her head, and with a deep voice she thundered, "Nothing of the sort, do you hear? What do you think, boer, from such a young, strong wife we don't want to hear baby talk."

"Keep your mouth shut," muttered Douwe. But she paid no attention to him, for she could tell that he was utterly confused. On such occasions she had heard even sharper words than these. "Come along," she said. "Oh, there is the doctor!"

"Good morning," greeted the doctor. "Are you sitting here waiting for the New Year to come? You are a bit late, for here we are way in the middle of January. Or is there something else? In that case I'll take off my coat. Gelf and I were running a match on the ice, and I must say that it was not so easy!"

Wouldn't I like to give that man a piece of my mind! thought Douwe. *Here we are confronted with a tremendous task and he acts as if.* . . . But then the doctor assumed management of the situation and Douwe saw that he could be efficient and serious.

When Vrouw De Graaf was about to take something off the table she whispered in his ear. "You had better go to the stable, boer. The great event has come." But Douwe paid no heed to her.

He refused to move. He wanted to sit in his own chair and wait for his child. Here his father and perhaps also his grandfather had sat waiting for their children. Here his father and mother had taught him to pray. But for years he had been too proud to communicate with his God. He, the strong and prosperous owner of the Free Estate, why should he have to think about such matters as eternal life and the soul? Children and old women might want to do that, but not Douwe Ates, the boer. It would have been wonderful if he could have been like God and help his wife in her hour of pain. Realizing that now he was face to face with the great problems of life — problems far beyond his own control — he suddenly felt the need of calling upon God, who in times of prosperity did not seem worthy of his attention. Frightened by the facts of life and death, he began to pray: "Lord, my God, hear me," and he seized the arm of the chair, and again. . . . The ticking of the clock was the only action that was proceeding smoothly.

How long he sat there in tension, filled with anxiety about

Liesbeth, he did not know, but suddenly he heard another noise in the room. . . . Douwe wanted to go to Liesbeth, but he did not dare. He rose halfway — tears were in his eyes. There it was, his child. . . . That was the voice of a child!

Like a drunken man he walked to the bed and looked at that small, living person. Then he bent over Liesbeth and kissed her forehead. He wanted to say something to those eyes that were so large, so wide, but he could not. . . .

The doctor beckoned him to the table, where he had washed himself, and said, drying his hands, "Well, boer, congratulations! It is a fine boy, and he is as healthy as a trooper." When Vrouw De Graaf also congratulated him and he looked at his boy as she was giving him a bath, he wanted desperately to go to Liesbeth.

"Not too long, Wallinga!" cautioned the doctor.

No, he would not do that. Just a moment they ought to be together — the three of them — Liesbeth, Douwe and Ate. Then he went to the other room, where Joukje, with cheeks as red as fire, was cutting bread and setting coffee. She jumped up and offered her felicitations; then she walked rapidly to the room. A moment ago, when the men were there, she had not dared to go.

The boer went to the stable. The long row of cows lay peaceful and quiet. Those in front were in the light of the candle lamp which Gelf had hung there. Slowly Douwe walked past the animals, and it seemed as if to each of them he announced the same news: "Tonight a boy was born — Ate Douwes Wallinga."

In the twilight he went farther. He did not see Gelf sitting on the bench in front of his bed. Now he was near the horses, the Belgian, Jonker, and Blacky and Wardy in the stanchions. He was eager to tell the animals one by one that there was a son now, but how was he to say that?

It was four o'clock, and the doctor stood ready to go. Then Keimpe rushed in, straight through the barn. He had been to Ternaard and had learned there that the doctor was at the boer's place. In this manner he had squandered an hour, which is a long time for one who is waiting sorrowfully.

"Doctor," he said, "the wife!"

"Well, I declare," replied the doctor, "this is going to be a good day for me. I'll go with you at once, Keimpe, my boy."

Keimpe trembled with excitement.

This night two children were born, one in a magnificent bedroom of the Free Estate, and named after his grandfather, Ate Douwes Wallinga; the other, a girl, in a small room of a poor workman's home, and named after her grandmother, Janke. Her name was not written in an expensive family Bible, her clothes were neither elegant nor numerous, but her blue eyes looked as clearly into the world as did those of Ate, and her parents loved her as much.

When the doctor arrived at eight o'clock from Keimpe's house at the Free Estate, he said to Douwe, "That is quite a coincidence; a couple, almost in one nest!"

"Yes," answered Douwe, "that is remarkable, and remember, Doctor, no bill to be sent to them. That is mine."

Liesbeth heard him, and she asked the doctor about all sorts of things, how the mother was, and if it was a pretty child.

"Yes, listen," said the doctor, "you must not get peeved at me, but your business is to go to sleep, and right away. Keimpe's wife you will see often enough, and as for that little doll, she is as lovely as a rose and as healthy as a fish. Now don't make any plans yet." And to Jouk, "Your mistress is so proud of her boy that she wants him to be united with Keimpe's daughter."

Keimpe's daughter and Ate Wallinga? That was too much of a joke for Joukje. Everybody should remain in his own class, for else there would be trouble. So thought Joukje while she cleaned the milk cans, and her thoughts wandered to that little child in the front room, little Ate. She hoped that this child might someday do what nothing else could do — bring Douwe and Liesbeth truly together.

Joukje never discussed the matter with anybody, but she

knew what was wrong. For a brief time it had looked as if they would be sweethearts again, but the situation deteriorated as soon as that fellow from the Heerema farm came regularly to call. She and Gelf had little respect for Heerema, for he visited the farm far too often, at first when Douwe was present and later when he was gone. No matter how friendly he seemed, he could not deceive Joukje. One should not suspect people of ulterior motives, but nobody could prohibit her from keeping watch over the affairs of the Free Estate.

Now everything would turn out for the best. The farmer had what he wanted, a strong boy, and his wife also, for she, too, longed for a child. What could now come between these two young people? She looked to the future with hope.

There came Keimpe. "Hello, Keimpe," she said, and joined him. The man was as gay as a child. "What a coincidence, wasn't it?" She congratulated him. "The madam a son and you a daughter. Isn't that a miracle?"

"Ah, girl, I cannot tell you how happy we are! I don't know how fast I got here last night from Ternaard. But now I must go home. The boer said I could have the day off." And there he went to his wife and little daughter. . . .

When he quietly entered the room his mother-in-law, who had arrived to help his wife with the child, was preparing lunch, and Keimpe, who could think of nothing except the two in that little bedroom, wanted to go past her.

Janke stopped him. "She sleeps, boy."

"Oh, is that so?" he replied in a crestfallen manner. "Well, then I had better peel potatoes, or what would you like to have me do?"

"First tell the neighbors, then drink coffee, then eat, and this afternoon register the child's birth," said the mother laughing. Register the child, yes, that was right. That, also, had to be done.

That afternoon two men, both on skates, went to Ternaard. One was Douwe Ates, the other Keimpe, his laborer. At Ternaard, in front of the inn, they took off their skates and left them at the inn. Then the three of them — there had to be a witness — went to the courthouse, where the official wrote: "On January 12 of this year was born: Ate Douwes, son of Liesbeth Winkel and Douwe Wallinga." And in the same volume, directly under the same date there was inscribed: "Janke, daughter of Aukje Kingma and Keimpe Feikema."

Keimpe did not go back with the boer. Douwe had given him a treat, pressed into his hands some paper money and said, "You can go home, Keimpe. I have to have a chat with the boers."

So it happened that Keimpe returned home alone, and happily he gave his wife the money. "Received from the boer, girl!" "Ten guilders!" She gasped joyfully. "Ten guilders!"

While Keimpe, cautious and anxious, held his daughter for a moment in his arms, Douwe sat in the inn at Ternaard, discussing his plans for the future. He was going to buy another race-horse to go with Wardy, but one that would go much faster. He would show what the family of Wallinga was worth, now that his son had arrived in grand shape. "Well, what do you say of that, men, my wife and that of the laborer both in the same night delivering a child, as if it had to be so! It doesn't happen every day that a Wallinga appears upon this earth."

"And takes his wife along!" shouted one of his pals. That made them all explode with laughter; it was a tremendous joke. They slapped each other on the shoulder and back, and their jests increased every minute, especially after Douwe had left them.

9

Days and days passed, and it was weeks since little Ate had made his appearance.

The festivities which followed his birth were extensive. As many as a hundred women had come to call. Even Uncle Ids had arrived, though he had made it a habit never to visit anybody. He always said that the whole world lay close enough to him. But one morning at ten o'clock he came, "like an old Batavian," as Gelf said. And he was full of admiration for little Ate.

They were sitting in the little room, but in the big room the stove was always heated, since at any moment more guests might arrive.

Ids and Douwe were in the drawing room. The old man had asked for privacy, for he had something on his mind.

"Every time I see you," objected Douwe, "we have to be alone. That does seem a bit queer."

"It is a lot more queer than necessary," said Ids. "I am not doing it because I am enjoying it, far be it from me. Last week you took a second mortgage loan on your farm?"

"Yes," replied Douwe, "but if you think that I should have gone to ask you first you are wrong."

"You can understand my feeling in the matter, Douwe. If you choose to disregard it at this particular time, now that you will have to be doubly careful, that is your privilege. But do not forget that you have a son who, when he is grown up, will be a living accusation against his father!"

"That is my affair," asserted Douwe.

"You stiffneck," burst out Ids. "Listen to some good advice. You could have gotten some money from me. Why did you have to go to the notary public?"

"How did you discover that?" asked Douwe, as if he had never thought of that possibility.

"I went to the notary public," said Ids, "or, rather, I had to go."

"To make your will?" Douwe asked merely to say something, not because he was interested personally.

"No," answered Ids, "I have given everything away. Someday I'll have to go, Douwe, but I want to tell you first what in my opinion will become of you."

"Go ahead, Uncle."

"If you do not pause and look around, if you do not take proper steps to save your farm, you will go down hill fast, and I'll live to see a Wallinga removed from his home. That I can guarantee!"

Douwe laughed aloud. "I thought you had better sense than that, to say that I would be forced to give up my farm, when I am in such a sound financial condition."

"I have heard about that," said Ids, "but you need not count on your friend," and in those two words, "your friend," a world of contempt was hidden.

"Wilco won't need to help me, but when I ask him he'll help me at once," argued Douwe.

That had happened long ago, and Douwe did not think of it any more. He was pleased with the way his life was arranged. Wilco often accompanied him on his trips to find his new horse. They went everywhere, but the horse could not be found.

The horse he wanted lived somewhere for him. He wanted it to suit his needs exactly, and no other would do. It did not matter how far they went, and Douwe was always a generous host.

Finally, in the spring, when love filled the air and Liesbeth was walking in the yard with little Ate, Douwe bought Prince, the choice of his heart. He was a brown stallion, the son of fast horses. They had been gone three days, and when they returned and Bouke let his thoughts wander freely, he saw what would happen next.

First he had tried to discuss the matter with the boer's wife, but she did not wish to check her husband. It looked as if she approved of his actions.

"The boer should know what is right," she had said. "He happens to like races, and he knows that everything is going fine here. If things should become too burdensome, Bouke. . . ."

"Oh, no, that isn't what I mean," he had replied. "I know what has to be done here, even though I am not the boer."

Slowly a dark cloud gathered above the Free Estate. What formerly had been whispered was now shouted from the house-tops: "All goes well with Prince, but with the farm all goes wrong." Then followed a dry summer, a summer of pleasure and fairs, of feasts and races, but also a summer of dead cattle, of dry ditches and of shriveled crops. Nights and days Douwe was gone, visiting every nook and corner of Friesland. It seemed as if he were in a dream from which he awoke only when he was racing with Prince.

When he was home with the horses, Prince and Wardy had to go each morning to make the rounds with the buggy. Douwe was completely immersed in this racing. It was his life. When on the race-tracks his horses defeated all the others, he felt himself far above all other things and people. Then he was glad that he had a son, for someday that son would assist him!

Wilco went with him less often. But that had also its good side. He had asked Wilco whenever he himself had to be absent more than one day to look after the farm a bit, and Wilco had promised him that he would do so. This had made Douwe feel more at ease. Wilco had wished it himself, and the unsuspecting Douwe had played into his hands. Joukje the maid, with her faithful eyes, who loved her mistress and would pass through the fire for her boer — she observed soon that something strange had happened to Liesbeth. Just what it was she could not tell, but she did not like it.

One year later she knew. Wilco did not come because of the cattle nor of the boer but because of Douwe's wife! It was a sin to say it, but it looked as if she enjoyed this. It happened often that Wilco remained to drink coffee, and still he would not leave. What did that mean? Would that terrible thing of which she had heard remotely but had never seen at work in her presence, would that be enacted here on the Free Estate? Would her mistress be a party to that, her gentle Liesbeth? But that was not possible! If one had a good husband and a darling son, she could not trifle with another, with a married man. . . . Jouk determined to keep her eyes open and to warn the boer if she saw something that was not proper. In that case Douwe Ates would show Wilco the door; then he would know that this man was not to be trusted.

And that dear, dear boy. Jouk must look at him again. She could go to the little boy but not to his father. That would do no good, for he had other things on his mind besides the farm. He was living only for his son and his horse. His boy, whom he often pressed to his bosom to show him how much he loved him. And that horse! With endless love and patience he had trained Prince for more than a year. There was not a muscle in the animal's body that Douwe did not know. He could tell in minute detail how high Prince threw his legs and how he started off. And there was something else that seemed remarkable. As soon as Prince had run a race he was put in his stable at the farm. Several farmers thought this action queer, but he paid no attention to them.

Although Douwe continued his ways as a lover of racing, he no longer was the rough person of former days. It seemed as if he would save his strength for the big leap, the quest for the Golden Whip of Friesland. More than ever this ambition grew in his heart. This coming autumn he must and he would win the Golden Whip! What did he care now about the farm and the crops? What did the whole world matter to him except that final race? His whole life was identified with that of his horse. He had become enamored of the magic in the Great Race.

There were, of course, those who warned him against his peculiar course of action. They pointed to his duties as boer, husband and father. He merely laughed at them. But his friend Wilco was his trusted companion. He was a man upon whom one could rely thoroughly. To him one could entrust everything. How he could appreciate Douwe's comments about Prince and the culmination of all events, the race for the Golden Whip! Gradually the day of that race drew nearer and nearer. . . . Three days ahead of time Gelf had gone with Prince in a railroad cattle car to Leeuwarden, and Douwe Ates, who was to follow him later, took leave of the little boy and the others.

They had drunk coffee, Liesbeth, Douwe and Wilco, while little Ate was playing on the floor.

Then Douwe had gotten up, walked toward Liesbeth and said in a trembling voice, "Well, Liesbeth, girl, the moment has struck. It is finished. Do you know that?"

"Yes," she replied calmly. "I know it."

Nothing else? thought Douwe. *Has she nothing else to say? Doesn't she feel what that means to me? But then, how can she be otherwise? She lives only for her home.* Aloud he said, "It won't make much of an impression on you if I win, will it?"

Liesbeth looked at him indifferently, and she said nothing. What was she to say? She could not very well. . . . That foolish man did not want anything else, did not see anything else except his horse! Only his horse? And what about little Ate Douwes, the boy who now sat high on his father's shoulders and went with him through the stable, still clean and empty, to the yard, where Wardy was waiting? They were talking together.

"Ate be good?"

"Daddy be good?"

"What does Daddy say then, boy? Do you remember?"

"To Leeuwarden, to race for the Golden Whip."

"To race for the Golden Whip. That's right, boy. When Ate is big he will go along, won't he?"

"Yes," said the little boy, and raising his hand above his head, he added, "Ate so big, Ate along."

Now they had reached the buggy and Douwe put the boy on the ground. Earnestly he extended his hand to his son and said, "Good-bye, Ate Douwes." The little boy, who responded readily to the play which for the father was most serious, answered, "Good-bye, Daddy. Good trip."

"Greetings to Mother," said Douwe, and then he went on his journey to Leeuwarden. He was filled with hope and all his thoughts were again on the race.

Little Ate walked through the barn again, stepping so firmly that the sound of his feet echoed against the wall. In the kitchen he saw Jouk, and he laughed. "Dad is gone," he said.

"Well, dear," remarked Jouk, "you'd better go to Mother and ask. . . ."

But the boy did not wish to follow her advice. He wanted to stay with Jouk. . . .

In the room the silence was profound after Douwe's departure.

Liesbeth had one of her moods again, which Wilco did not like. She realized once more that she was a sinner. It seemed as if God's eyes followed her into this room, as if she could hear His voice. "The wages of sin is death. . . ." When Wilco approached her she resisted him. "Don't do that, Wilco.

Not now." Wilco laughed. It annoyed him to be thwarted thus, but he knew how to overrule her objections. It was also an attractive task to win her as it were each time anew.

He was determined to win her. That desire was his great strength. His will power made him conquer in adversity. It was that will power which had rendered him calm when Douwe had proclaimed him a fool. It had made him stronger when Douwe had given him a thorough thrashing.

Wilco had sought an outlet for his hatred, and he had found it in Douwe's wife.

It had not been easy to make her bend to his will, but her reluctance had been what he wanted; it made his desire the greater and his conquest the more pleasant. At first only hatred for Douwe had spurred him to action, but later he was inflamed by what people called love. That supple creature with her soft eyes and her curly hair was indeed a treasure for a man of his type. His desire to possess her had overpowered him.

In this manner, under the mask of friendship for the family, he had found ready access to Liesbeth and her charms. She had need of someone who would show an interest in her little affairs and wants. She needed support in the days of financial difficulties which had been overlooked by Douwe but were obvious to everyone else. . . . And he whose duty it was to render her the assistance she so urgently required, he always went away with his horses and left her to bear her burdens in terrible solitude.

Was it a wonder that Wilco helped her, that he became her support on the Free Estate? Was it surprising that in those bad times of poor management and financial losses he took something that did not belong to him?

It had gone that way for more than a year.

Sometimes Liesbeth longed for death. She was unhappy, for it seemed as if everyone accused her. The people around her did not say anything, but in the eyes with which they looked at her she could read their thoughts, especially in

Jouk's eyes. The faithful maid still loved her deeply, and she could not play the part of a hypocrite. Constantly she did everything in her power to cause an estrangement between the guilty man and woman. When Wilco came to call and they sat in the big room together, one could count on it that Jouk had to wash the windows, or suddenly she felt obliged to rush into the room to fetch something. The worst of it was that she never said a word.

There were the blue eyes of her child. Liesbeth no longer dared to peer into them; that she could not do. When Wilco had succeeded in guiding her through one of her depressed moods she became cheerful again, and once more they were engrossed in their selfish pleasures, which loomed large before them. There were indeed moments enough when nobody saw them, when God was ignored. . . . If only one could remove God from one's thoughts!

Always when Wilco had left her she remembered suddenly that there was a God in the world who cares about all of us and for us. In the midst of worldly pleasures one would like to imagine that the Creator and Sustainer of all life has left our planet for a while, but the moment we have finished our short-lived misdemeanors we find it difficult to close our hearts to the truth. Liesbeth was no exception to this rule, and she sometimes wanted to end the evil relationship with one sudden stroke, to tell her husband, to confess all and then to obtain peace for her distracted soul. What sorrow and misery could she have prevented if she had but taken that one bold step!

The day of the Golden Whip had arrived.

The day of the Great Race! Who with a boer's blood in his veins wanted to remain at home on such a day? No matter how much one was attached to his farm or his business, no matter how he hesitated to take the long trip to Leeuwarden, the provincial capital, on that day of all days he would go there. That day of the Golden Whip could never be forgotten.

Before dawn all sorts of carriages went to the city. The

horses ran merrily along the crowded roads, and in the buggies one saw not only the boers and their wives but also their children and relatives.

This particular day was no exception. At nine o'clock long rows of carriages were in front of all the inns. Here and there among them one saw one of those newfangled conveyances on rubber wheels. These were somewhat lower and were streamlined.

At ten o'clock the streets leading to the new race-track on the Westersingel were too narrow to permit the crowds to hurry to their seats. But gradually the number of sightseers on the streets grew smaller and those seated or standing around the race-track became restless and eager. Row upon row of spectators were accommodated in the spacious arena of modern Friesland.

The sun was shining and the weather could not have been more pleasant. The sunlight gleamed on the pure gold and silver headgear of the wealthy women. Where else in all Europe could one find more resplendent displays of feminine ornaments than upon the Frisian beauties in Leeuwarden? And where else could one see more natural color upon the cheeks than that which provided the charming setting for the so-called "ear-irons" of Friesland's queens?

In the roomy stable numbered twelve stood Douwe and Gelf talking earnestly and somewhat excitedly. Prince was ready for the race. Days of intense training were behind them, days of training for both man and beast. The day before yesterday they had driven along the race-track, Gelf holding the reins and Douwe giving him directions. "Don't you ever pull the reins, Gelf, under any condition. He may not run fast. Just let him go as he pleases." That is exactly what Gelf had done, and Douwe had taken great care to watch Prince as he turned around a curve in the track.

"I will let him go around three times," said Douwe, "and during the first two times you are not to pay any attention to his speed, but the third course, that's different. Then he must run faster and faster, and you must tell me how he takes it."

Gelf had done his best, for confidence in his boer had inspired him to devoted assistance. Douwe had passed him twice, and he had paid little attention to the horse's speed. Even if he had been obliged to do so he could not have failed to be impressed by the combination of Prince and Douwe. It was truly a magnificent spectacle. During the third course Prince gave all he had, and now Gelf stood in the curve, watching to see if anything was wrong. But, no, he could observe no fault. The horse took the curve as only the best of race-horses could hope to do.

Calm and satisfied, the two men had sat the previous evening in the inn. There they had passed the last night before the great event. At last dawn and with it the crowds came to witness the thrilling display of horses and trainers.

First the bell rang for the opening ceremony. Fourteen horses made their appearance. It was a grand sight. There were almost as many colors as horses. Some were large, others small, some as black as coal, others as white as snow. As they stood there, eager to start, the spectators had already bestowed the prizes. Few of them had selected Number 12, the horse of Douwe Ates Wallinga. True, Prince had done good work, and he had won prizes of minor importance, but that would be all. Who was Wallinga but a stupid boer with a poor record? Some of the boers present had circulated the story of that sorry event at Hallum, when Wilco Heerema had referred sneeringly to Douwe as the "Golden Whip farmer." What could one expect of such a person?

The horses were off at last. The thousands of spectators were waiting with bated breath to see who would gain at the start. During the first two rounds Prince showed little promise of victory, and few cared to watch his progress. Then the better horses drew away from the group as a whole and it was becoming apparent which had the stamina to stay in the race until the end. A black and gray horse was taking the

lead, and a short distance behind was what? Douwe Ates with
Prince? Yes, indeed, to the surprise and consternation of many
who could not understand how this stupid person from Hantum
could perform such a feat. People looked once more at that
number, but they could not deny that it was Douwe Ates
Wallinga with Prince.

Oh, well, it won't last long, they thought. Soon that eager
horse must slacken his pace, for what else could happen?
But what the public did not yet know was well known to
Douwe and his faithful companion. Prince had by no means
begun to use his greatest power. That was still held in reserve.
Douwe still had to restrain him. *The supreme test has not
yet come,* thought Douwe correctly. Two horses gained on
Prince, and although they were unable to overtake him, they
did not let him get ahead again, not for a while. But during
the last four rounds the situation changed completely. Prince
charged ahead with such terrific drive that he surpassed all
the others. The tension among the spectators increased every
second. They now realized that Prince had a chance, but they
still did not realize that Douwe had absolute control of the
situation and kept complete surprise in reserve for the very
end. . . . Man and horse seemed one. There were still two
rounds left.

It was during these two rounds that Douwe Ates Wallinga
took advantage of his months of discipline and training. There
were still two horses ahead of him, and the drivers were certain that they could defeat Douwe. They were so sure of
themselves that they looked backward to see how the poor
fellow was getting along. But what did they see? They witnessed the concrete results of careful training, such as they
had not thought necessary for their own horses. But they would
not let this upstart prevent them from gaining ground. They
spurred their favorites to greater efforts, but in vain. It was
too late to find reserve powers; these had now been spent in a
lost cause. The gold-brown flame of Douwe surged onward
to the goal, and the spectators were hypnotized by that amazing

scene. What action! What speed! How was such a thing possible? The answer to that was well known to Douwe.

Now came the final round, and Prince had to take the outer curve, which caused him to fall momentarily a short distance behind. But that did not matter. At last one of the spectators fathomed the mystery, and he shouted with all his might, "Prince! Douwe Ates!" That was precisely what Prince needed — a word of encouragement and approval. Now he flew through the air like a veritable phantom, passed the two competitors and remained in the lead until he reached the goal. Douwe knew nothing, saw nothing. He had become one with his horse, and amidst the thunder of applause he negotiated the inside curve to receive the Golden Whip of Friesland.

Leeuwarden was for the moment too small and Douwe's heart too big. Naturally he did not come home that night, which was fortunate. In the afternoon of the next day he recovered from his excessive elation, and they loaded Prince in the cattle car for the journey home.

When he arrived at the Free Estate the first person to welcome him was the little boy, who asked him, "Dad win Golden Whip?"

"Yes, boy. Dad did win the Golden Whip."

He lifted the boy high on his shoulders, and so they entered their house together. Liesbeth and Wilco were sitting in the big room, but Jouk kept Douwe for a moment in the kitchen.

"Boer," she gasped. "Oh, boer. . . ."

"What is the matter, Jouk. Don't you feel well?" There was nothing wrong with her, but that which she had to relate was so terrible that she began: "The boer must not get peeved at me. I congratulate you on the winning of the Golden Whip, but it would have been better if you had never started with your racing. . . ."

That made Douwe angry. "Concern yourself with the milk cans and with your work in the house. You were not hired to manage the rest." Then he went to the drawing room. Those meddlesome females. Why couldn't they keep their mouths shut? What could she have had in mind? What except old woman's tales? Still enraged he entered the drawing room. In his big chair sat Wilco, and not far from him, though not too close, was Liesbeth. *How healthy and attractive she looks,* was Douwe's first thought, and he went toward her.

"Little wife," said Douwe, and to Wilco, "Wilco!" and to both, "Well, did I succeed or not?" Then he kissed Liesbeth and she returned the embrace, saying, "I am proud of you, Douwe. I really had not expected it."

Wilco laughed and added, "What we do not expect sometimes comes to pass. I congratulate you, Douwe!"

"Thank you," he replied, "and it seems to me that this evening we should celebrate. When you get home, Wilco, you must ask your wife to visit us."

"Yes, boy." Wilco laughed. "But, alas, there are in this world also other things besides making fun. Your wife and I have these last days passed through some difficult experiences. You had better sit down again, Douwe." Now he was another man altogether. "You have gone your own way for quite some time, and you have paid almost no attention to your own affairs. You have let your wife sit alone with all the troubles, and so it should not sound strange in your ears when I must inform you that the situation here on this farm is most unpleasant. The place is on the verge of bankruptcy."

"What is that?" he roared. "On the verge of bankruptcy? What is the trouble?"

Liesbeth laid her head on the table and began to cry. But that did not calm her. On the contrary, she became more disconsolate.

"What is the trouble?" His voice was raw, so that Liesbeth and Wilco became frightened. But what did Douwe care about that? He was far from complimented by these two people, who ignored his tremendous achievement and welcomed him with complaints. Was that fair to him? "What is wrong here?" he insisted again. "I want to know." He shook the table with his fist so that cups and saucers rattled.

Wilco replied, "Be calm, Douwe. You would not want to insinuate that we are at fault, would you? Liesbeth asked me to tell you that the second mortgage came due and could not be redeemed. I informed her that this was none of my business, but she had a different opinion."

"We need not hold back anything from our friends," remarked Douwe, who now became calmer. "May I see the letter, Liesbeth?"

"The letter has not come yet," she answered. "The notary public was here himself, yesterday afternoon."

Yesterday afternoon, Douwe reflected, *yesterday afternoon, just as I won the Golden Whip, they stole my place from me. That is extraordinary.* "And what did my lord the notary public want? Why did he come himself?"

Liesbeth looked at him in confusion. "That I don't know," she observed. "Tomorrow he was to send the official letter, and if you should not be able to redeem the loan he would be obliged to take proper action."

"Take proper action," he murmured. He rose, went to the cabinet where the prizes were exhibited, and placed the Golden Whip with the rest. Then he went to the door.

"Don't you want any tea or anything to eat?" asked Liesbeth. But Douwe merely gave her a wave of his hand, as if to say that he could not sit there at ease. He mumbled, "Jouk can cut the bread in the kitchen."

Jouk walked past the door where she had been listening. With a color like fire in her cheeks she slunk to the kitchen. She did not want to listen, and yet she had to have proof for her suppositions, even when the boer himself was there in the room.

Douwe was sitting in the kitchen with the little boy and Joukje. She had to talk, so eager was she to let him know what was in store for him. "You must forgive me, boer. That man in the drawing room, he was sitting here on this farm in your place."

But Douwe did not get angry, and he said, "Who of us shall say, Jouk, 'This is ours, and that is yours'? We don't

know that, you see?" Then aside to Ate, "And will Ate go
with me to the stable?"

"Yes," answered Ate. "Yes, Dad." And then the two went
to inspect the cows, the horses and the other animals. Nothing
was overlooked.

For Ate this was a feast, for Douwe a farewell, and this
walk was a pilgrimage.

As they walked through the cow stable Douwe called their
names . . . Pietje II . . . Marijke . . . he named them all.
Now and then Ate looked at his father and he called the
names after him. They had reached the calves and the sheep,
and they began to count. Ate counted one, two, three, eight,
ten and then again. It was a pleasant game for him. Next
they went to survey the fields. The little boy enjoyed himself
immensely. It was pleasant to walk this way with his big
father, as if he were his equal. Through the little door they
entered the barn. They paused a moment, for the transition
from the light to twilight was too quick for their eyes. Douwe
looked around the huge barn, at the immense heaps of hay.
As he stood upon the floor of the threshing room he succumbed
to a feeling of frustration. He turned his head, moved his
arm as if to stop the impending doom and whispered, "Here
the notary public will sit when the farm will be sold."

He saw the people in the barn, in the cow stable, in his
living room, in the fields, and he heard them laugh about
that proud Wallinga family and about his household affairs.
He would have to be content with a much smaller place and
a few cows perhaps. . . . And then suddenly he felt a small
warm hand in his own, and he looked into two eyes that
were seeking his.

It was as if they were asking him a question, perhaps far in
the future, of another Ate, and loudly he answered it. "No,
boy, this farm will remain ours and for you. We will not let
it be sold."

That man who had advanced the sum of eight thousand
guilders would not find Douwe unprepared for the blow. With

one swoop he put Ate on his shoulder, and so they entered the house. He paused in the kitchen, where he deposited the little boy and said, "Be very quiet here, boy." Then he walked into the front room, and in a voice full of apprehension he said, "Wilco, you know how things are with us now. There is a first mortgage and a second mortgage; there are in addition some interest and debts. We have plenty of property to cover these loans, but since that person started things rolling by asking for his interest he may cause my downfall by demanding the whole sum of eight thousand guilders. Can you and will you help me, Wilco?"

He walked to the window and added as he looked over the fields, "The interest is up to you." Although he refused to admit it, he waited with tension for Wilco's answer, and when it came he was happy.

"To tell you the truth, Liesbeth and I have discussed this matter. Tomorrow you will have the money."

"Thank you, Wilco. I knew that I could depend on you." Douwe left the room at once and returned to his little boy, who was still waiting for his powerful father.

In the room sat a boer, Wilco Heerema, and next to him a boer's wife, young and beautiful. The boer laughed aloud. He must have an outlet for his exuberance. The hot blood coursed through his veins. At last he had achieved the victory for which he had waited so long. The interest on his loan was beside him. It lay in the lovely eyes of Liesbeth. He could ask for money and thus cause the downfall of the entire family, and he must explain to Liesbeth what it would mean to her husband that he would be saved by Wilco Heerema.

What would become of Douwe if he could not have money for his drinking, his bragging and his racing? Douwe loved only his son and his Golden Whip. He had obtained both, and now Liesbeth must tell Wilco how much she meant to that spendthrift! "Look here," he continued, as he pointed to the cultivated fields and the pasture lands. Liesbeth went to the window. There walked Douwe Ates and his son Ate. . . .

He walked with firm steps, his head erect, and little Ate had difficulty keeping up with him. Neither of them showed any interest in the farm nor those who were at this moment looking at them.

Liesbeth turned from the window, and Wilco laughed. Douwe Ates talked to his boy: "We shall see how things go, boy, but you may rest assured that Uncle Wilco is our best friend. Upon him we can rely." Then he saw that the boy could not keep pace with him. Smilingly he put him on his shoulder again and said, "Come here, little chap. Dad will carry you."

They went. And their friend talked about the interest. . . .

PART TWO

10

LIKE A STATELY castle lay the Free Estate in Friesland. The
tall elms around the moat seemed to reach for heaven.
The huge branches were thick where they left the trunks,
but became steadily thinner until they ended in fine, broad
wreaths which swayed in the wind. It was spring again, and
in the highest branches lived a colony of rooks which were
busy at this season, when the contest for suitable wives and
places for nests caused heated arguments. In the midst of these
trees stood the farmhouse, large and heavy, with strong
foundations.

The orchard was in bloom, fragrant and colorful.

At the side of the barn and in the rear of the yard all was
peaceful. The large, wide doors were standing open, and in
the threshing house one could detect that peculiar atmosphere
of emptiness, that longing for treasures from the fields. Here
one saw nothing but quiet and rest. The throbbing life was
no longer here, but outside!

In the fertile fields and the pasture there was much hard

work going on, and one could hear the pleasant voices of singing workmen and the happy grunting of satisfied animals. The cattle were grazing in the pasture. They were the pride of the master, those sturdy black and white Frisian cows. In another plot were the sheep. To the right one saw workmen in various positions, some crawling, others erect or bending forward. Their duty was to prepare the soil for an abundant harvest.

Life and growth were everywhere. While the plants were caressed by the wind, the weeders proceeded carefully through the rows, their tools in readiness for the tasks of separating the crops from the weeds. In the light green flax walked Sierk, his brother Jetse, and Gelbrich. Each wore an old glove with which he pulled the weeds out of the field for the last time. After this they were going to let grow what would grow, for the flax would be strong enough to subdue all intruders.

Far to the rear, and on the other side of the road clicked the mowing machine through the luxuriant grass. Two of the horses were pulling it and Gelf sat on top. He had shed his shirt and vest and his sleeves were rolled up. He sang with the rhythm of the machine, and occasionally he called Bouke, who walked along the rows of cut grass and here and there laid aside the heavy bunches with his haying fork. Day after day the scene was enlivened by the labor of man and beast, as the season advanced and made way for the changes brought by summer.

All of this was a revelation to Ate Douwes, who was now six. Every day he discovered something new and impressive. He did not recall when first he started this thrilling adventure, but he did know that the most startling experience of all was the finding of two deep, blue lakes in his mother's eyes. They were almost without bottom, so immense was their depth. Sometimes he saw there a picture of himself. And what treasures had he not found on the floor! There were also a great many things he had to remember. He was not permitted to do more than sit and look at the box with clothes in it, but

Mother and Jouke had the right to open it at any time and take things out or put others into it. The fire in the stove was fascinating, too fascinating to leave alone, for he must not touch it. The cat he could stroke, but he must not pull its tail. He was not allowed to take the peat out of the foot-stove, though Mother and Jouke always did it as a matter of fact. When they put something into it, no matter what, it was all right, but when he put something into the stove, even a piece of crust from the cheese he had been eating, they said it smelled bad and he got a spanking. He could lean or sit against a wall, but it was not wise to fall against it, for that hurt, and then he started to cry. Ate had to crawl into a cold bed, while Gelf, who was much bigger, could go into his warm bed in the stable, at least when the cows were there. So it had been for years, and still the end had not come. Gradually he had classified the adults around him, and he weighed them on a scale of his own making, understood only by himself.

Joukje, for example, was the maid who had much to say about the cleaning of the milk cans, about washing and about the cutting of bread, and he could sit quietly at her side. She never would do or say anything to shock or surprise one. . . . Joukje was always there, and she always had some time left for Ate when he was tired and wanted to sit on her lap. For that reason he loved Jouk best.

Next came Mother. He always had to be careful with her. At one time she caressed and kissed him, but the next she might be angry with him, or she would pay no attention to him at all, just when he was eager to have a companion. There were days when she was delighted with him and would tell him wonderful stories, and then there would come another day when she was cross and despondent, particularly when Uncle Wilco was there. He did not like that man, even if he brought him candy or cake.

Then there was Dad . . . his all . . . Dad, of whom he was so fond, and of whom he was also so proud. . . . Dad,

who was such a giant! And when Jouk of an evening related
one of her wondrous tales, with giants and dwarfs in it,
with fairies and ghosts, Ate always thought of Dad as *the*
giant who helped, who fought, who stood for righteousness.

Yet with Dad he also had to be careful, in spite of the
fact that he cared so much for him. One could tell by looking
at him in the morning how to respond, either to seize his hand
and walk along with him, or to say nothing and not walk
in front of him.

Aunt Frouk, that was Doutsen's mother and the wife
of Uncle Wilco. He liked her rather well, and Doutsen also.
She sang and composed verses, which they sang together in
the barn, where they played.

Ah, there were so many people, and always more came,
workmen and men and women who were hired to weed.

Old Bouke walked crooked and bent far forward, but one
must not say a word about that, far from it, for else he would
become angry. Ate had asked him if he had lost anything,
since he always walked with his head bent. But something
terrible had burst loose the next moment, something which
frightened Ate. Worse than the old man's cross words was
the beating the boy had received for his question. He could
still feel the tender spot where Dad had struck him.

Gelf was his teacher, with whom he felt more at ease
than with anyone else, excluding of course, Joukje. Gelf would
never go anywhere with a wagon or a loose horse without first
having called for Ate. Gelf taught him to ride horseback, to
steer, to milk the sheep, to drive the cattle, to prepare food
and bring water for the pigs and to hunt for eggs. That Gelf
— well, he was a useful person!

There was Keimpe also, and yet Keimpe was different.
And Grandfather and Grandmother from Tjummarum had
been a disappointment to Ate. He had stayed with them a few
days, but they had not turned out so well as he had expected.
No, he reflected, *they were not so nice as I had thought!* He
shook his head, just as he had seen Bouke do. He was sitting

on a wooden pail, in the pleasant spring sunshine, thinking about all these things.

No, I am not going back there. Grandmother has a headache every day, Grandfather complains about everything, and I get my clothes wet. Well, what could one expect when nobody attended to his needs? Those people should have been like Joukje. *No, I will not go back.*

He was angry now, and he beat his little fist against the side of the chicken coop, so that one of the hens became frightened and flew to the rooster.

Ates mused further. One could not always have his own way. In the coming week there would be a tremendous change in his life. He was going to school. For that he would have to "go through the ditch," as Uncle Ids would say. Uncle Ids, yes, he was a nice man. Ate would not mind staying with him. Uncle Ids, with his bushy hair and his big hands, no, of that man one need not be afraid. But now it would no longer be possible to visit his farm, for school would prevent such pleasures. Suddenly he said, "But what will happen here on our farm, I do not know. Dad is nearly always gone. It would be much better if . . . yes . . ." But how was he to know what was best? He looked around, over the yard, along the road. And there he made his latest discovery, Janke Keimpe, the girl from the workmen's quarters. She was standing at the end of the lane with a woman, but Ate was not interested in the woman. He had eyes only for her little girl. *I'll have to go there,* he decided.

He rose, put his hands in his pockets and walked to meet the girl who was now coming up the lane. When she was near he said, "This is our yard." He waited to see if she would deny that, but instead she turned and said,"This is Mother."

Ate did not know if it was necessary or not, but he looked at the woman and answered, "My mother is inside."

"And my mother is here," remarked Janke. She had assumed an earnest air and was standing still. Then her mother began to laugh at both children. She looked keenly at Ate and asked, "You are Ate, aren't you?"

Big people can ask the dumbest questions, thought Ate. He did not even want to answer. *Who else could I be?* he mused. If the woman did not even understand that, she must be stupid. But he liked the little girl, and he observed her curly hair, her dress, everything about her. As he was about to take her along to Jouk and Mother, a clock began to strike.

"Listen," he observed, and he laughed happily. "The clocks are singing. That is Hiaure; that is but a small clock, do you hear? *Ting, ting, tang, tang.*"

Janke listened and Auk listened. The workmen were leaving the fields. "Listen," said Ate, "There you have Foudgum; that one is still bigger — *tim, tim, tam, bim, tim* . . . but the old tower of Hantum, that is still bigger — *bim, bam, bim, bam.*"

"And when is Ate going to school?" asked Janke's mother.

"Next week," answered Ate. "You too?" he asked Janke.

"Yes, I too, don't I, Mother?"

"Yes, you too," said her mother, "so you are going at the same time. How could it be otherwise?" But at that moment Janke ran up the yard and Ate heard how she called, "Father." Then he saw how Keimpe seized her. *So it is the daughter of the workman from the Soberhoek,* thought Ate.

Ate did not know much about the Soberhoek, except that Keimpe lived there, and also another family whose children sometimes came here to work for his father. That Keimpe had a daughter he knew, for Keimpe had often talked about her.

He felt at ease with Keimpe, and as he came closer he asked, "Is that she now, Keimpe?"

"Yes, that is she, and does she suit you?" Keimpe did not laugh when he made that remark, and so Ate did not laugh as he said, "Yes, we'll go to school together."

"Funny," remarked Keimpe, "so then she will become your maid." Auk started to laugh at that jesting husband of hers, but Ate did not laugh. He looked upward where Janke sat on a throne, like a princess. He was thinking hard and became quiet, but because they were waiting for a reply he said, and one could not tell that he was sorry, "I do not think so, for Jouk is our maid." Then suddenly he was gone, running after Gelf, whom he spotted not far away.

When Keimpe, Auk and Janke went home, man and wife were discussing the boy, and Janke was listening.

"Last week I had to laugh so, Auk," started Keimpe. "Old Bouke's eyes are beginning to draw water so often. The poor fellow should stay at home, but he is too conceited for that. Well, Bouke and I were standing in the yard, and Gelf and Ate were coming from the field. And just at that moment the boy began to sing, as loud as he could, 'Roll, roll, water eyes,'* Bouke became angry and tried to hit Ate, but he got away. Then he blamed Gelf for it, since he must have told the boy how to change that line of the poem." The three were greatly amused.

In the kitchen Ate was sitting on the bench. In front of him on the table were tea, rye bread with bacon and a currant bun; but he did not eat so eagerly as usual. Mother had to urge him, and whenever he had an opportunity he looked out of the window in the direction of the Soberhoek. He listened sharply when Jouk talked about Janke and her mother at the Soberhoek. They often mentioned him without their asking him anything. For example, Mother said, "Janke is much shorter, and you would guess that Ate is a year older rather than that they are the same age." And Jouk observed, "But that girl is no simpleton, I can tell you. When after a while they are both going to school. . . ." Then Ate interrupted like an adult and said, "We have talked about that already, Joukje. We are going to school together, next week." Then he went away again, back to his old place on the wooden pail, and he resumed his meditation. There he sat in the golden sunlight, surrounded by the smell of manure and decaying animal life, but also of growing things.

High in the heavens the clouds sailed by, wondrous, curious

---

* In the Frisian it should have read, "Roll, roll, water waves," but the boy did not remember the exact words.

ships and animals. One could make anything out of them, and every moment they assumed other shapes. They turned, whirled, tumbled, shoved, but always they united again and followed the course set for them.

In the afternoon Jouk joined Ate again and asked him a multitude of questions, while he in turn asked her all that he could think of: why they must go to school, why they were brought by the stork in the same night and why Keimpe always tipped his cap when he met Ate's father and never when he talked to any of the workmen.

There was much he could not understand as yet, for he was still so young. Jouk told him that he would have plenty of time to discover the meaning of it all, and deep in her heart she feared for that time when certain great mysteries would have to be revealed to him.

When at seven o'clock she put him to bed and told him one of her Bible stories, she paused suddenly and began to think deeply. Ate looked at her and said, "Go ahead, Joukje," and Joukje, a bit confused, began to sing:

> Little ship under the care of Jesus,
> With the flag of a cross high at the mast,
> Take as ark of redemption
> All who are in need of Thee.

And when she began to sing about the miller's daughter, Ate was asleep and was aware of nothing.

11

EACH DAY the children went to school at Hantum. They came from all directions, over mud roads, across church yards, through pasture lands and along the gravel road. Among them was Doutsen Heerema, one of the older children. Some of the former classmates had not returned, but new ones had been added, among them Ate and Janke.

Every morning at eight o'clock Ate was ready with his new lunch box, in which were sandwiches, a pencil and sponge. The first time he went to school Jouk had to take him, but that was no longer necessary. He soon made friends with some of the children who went his way. He paid no attention to Doutsen, who wanted to take charge of him. He went his own way, and he adjusted himself to the novel habits and regulations, the worst of which was that of sitting still twice for two whole hours. Imagine that, two hours! He who at home had at his disposal a barn, a stable and some twenty acres of land had to sit still in a small room that measured five by eight meters! Equally hard was the fact that he could not talk when he simply had to do so, for example, when he wanted to ask the teacher why that boy in the big picture, the boy with the hoop in his hand, had his mouth wide open and two sausages at his side. That was a veritable punishment for Ate. And why did the teacher talk a language that differed so radically from that of the children?* Hers sounded so queer, so queer. One morning she held a picture in front of him and asked him what kind of animal was on the picture. He had answered in Frisian, "That is a ram." "All wrong," the teacher had replied. She had turned to the window, pointed to a ram and said, "That is a ram." She was talking to him in a foreign language. Was that fair to Ate? But was he perplexed? Oh, no, he laughed, pointed to the picture and told the teacher, "That is an English ram with horns, and that kind we do not have here!"

At first there were more misunderstandings, but gradually they disappeared.

On the very first day he had seen Janke, and when the next morning he saw her again he had asked her, "Is not your mother here?" She had come along the North Road, and he had left the group of boys with whom he was playing. She had replied, "No," and from that day they had always walked together to Hantum. Soon it seemed to Ate as if he had been going to school for years.

The group of children gradually became smaller and smaller. At the North Road three of them went in another direction, then two more at the double home built for workmen, and so there remained Doutsen and he, Doutsen, big, and he, small, and always ahead.

When they walked together at the end of the day's walk, they discussed the affairs of their respective farms, and they bragged about their fathers' cattle, land and horses. Ate always had the last word, for he said, "And your dad has never won a Golden Whip!" Then they were silent for a few moments until Ate opened the gate of the lane, took the lunch

* There is a great difference between the provincial Frisian language, spoken in the rural districts of Friesland, and the Dutch taught in the schools.

box off his shoulder and shouted, "So long, Douts." As, his cheeks red, he ran home, he panted like a dog. Then he took off his good clothes, put on his old trousers and his blue shirt and ate as fast as he could, that he might go to the fields as soon as possible. The farm and the work took first place in his heart, and if he could help with the milking or some other work, he was content. After the first school year he changed. Now he became a child, a real child. The old little man he had become through his association with adults on the farm disappeared to make room for a new Ate.

He came home later after school, and he sang, played and fought with the other boys. He cared less for the cows, pigs and sheep, and often the maid had to fetch him from the village.

One evening he wandered to the Soberhoek and played with Janke until it became dark. Keimpe took him home at eight o'clock.

"What on earth have you been doing?" was his father's remark. He replied, "Playing at the Soberhoek with Janke." "But that is not the proper thing to do. You must come home right after school, and you shall not go to the Soberhoek. Stay here or go to Doutsen instead."

Ate did not reply, for what was the use of antagonizing a man so big and strong as dad, and what was the sense of starting a fight against him? Ate would surely lose.

Doutsen. It was always Doutsen. "What Dad can find in that girl is a mystery, isn't it, Gelf?"

They were sitting together, the three of them, Gelf, Jouk and Ate. Dad and Mother had gone to the Heerema farm to drink tea, and Ate had asked this question to see what his friends would say.

Gelf laughed and remarked, "Your father probably would like to see you and Doutsen . . ." But further he dared not go. That was partly because Jouk interrupted him: "We may not talk about that, Gelf."

"Why not?" asked Gelf. "Let me tell you that as long as

we discuss only that problem we could do little harm, compared with some other things, for example." But just at that
moment, when the discussion turned to subjects that concerned
Ate, the clock struck eight mean strokes, and it was bedtime for
him.

When Jouk put him to bed he wanted to find out more
about the Heerema family, but he did not get far. "Joukje,
why are Dad and Uncle Wilco such good friends now?" The
reply he received was far from illuminating: "Yes, boy, that I
would like to know myself."

"But why, then, Joukje? I don't understand it at all." And
she was so eager to tell the little boy something about that
which had caused her intense pain and which hung like a dark
cloud over the Free Estate, but what could she say? When big
people did not dare to say a word, how could one talk to a
little boy?

"Will you fall asleep soon, Ate?"

"Yes, Jouk," he replied, "but I wish so much that you
would tell me something."

"Tell you something? What would it be?"

"About Moeike of Wierum," he whispered. And she wondered why he thought about that subject, but since she owed
him something she told the tale that had been told so many
times before.

"Long, long ago there lived in Wierum a woman who was
as stingy as she was false. Her name was Willemke, and her
husband, like all the men of Wierum, made his living by fishing. He went away each time with the fishing fleet of Wierum,
and did not return for days and days, not even weeks sometimes.

"Willemke sold the fish, carrying two baskets on a yoke to
the old city of Dokkum, and she earned much money. But she
could not endure the fact that others earned still more than
she. It almost made her cry when other women had sold their
fish long before she did, and to the ladies of Dokkum she
began to say that the fish of her competitors was spoiled.
Because she could talk so fluently and flattered those ladies so
cleverly they believed her story, and in a short time she sold

hers to them. It happened sometimes that she was on the way home when the others were still busy trying to sell their fish. But still she was not satisfied, and she hoped that many storms would come and drown some of the men who were away fishing. Each time when another man was drowned she would visit the bereaved widow, and when she was home again she would say to herself, 'Well, who will it be next?'

"One stormy night when the waves reached the very top of the dike, the women of the village were afraid, and they walked along the dike, worrying about their husbands and the boys. Willemke was with them and moaned as loudly as the rest of them. But she was not worrying about her own husband, for he was a clever man and had no doubt landed safely in some port.

"It was the custom for the women and the old men to watch the sea and when the water had fallen far enough to render the approach to land safe, they lit kegs with oil. There were ten of them and each was ten meters from the others. This night Willemke was one of the ten who had to watch at the dike. To her had been assigned the keg farthest removed from town. Now the wicked plan occurred to her to light her keg while the water was still too high, and whoever would answer her call was bound to perish as his boat was ground to pieces at the top of the dike. There she stood and waited . . . .

"Who would it be? She hoped that the fisherman would not wait too long, for else the others would discover her aim. She listened again, and there indeed came the familiar noise of an approaching boat. She heard in the darkness the vessel heading straight for the dike . . . .

"She laughed wickedly . . . There it is! She must move aside, for it was coming in her direction. Then something moved past her over the dike. She heard a crash, a shriek. Then nothing . . . Willemke lay unconscious . . . In the light of the oil lamp she had been able to read *W L 17*. That was the boat of her own husband, who with his two sons, Knelis and Hoite, had sailed on this very smack. They were on their way home, and now all three of them died there on that spot.

"For years Willemke wandered along the dike and visited

that same place of tragedy, until she became insane. One morning she was found upon the dike, dead.

"And every night when there is a storm, Willemke is there again with the oil lamp and she searches for her husband and her two sons. . . ."

Jouk paused a while after the story had been told. It seemed queer that at this particular time the boy had asked for this tale. She did not understand why she was so affected by the tragedy of Willemke. After all, none of these events actually took place, and what had they to do with her mistress? Or was the story intended for all sinners, and should one change the details to fit each person in particular? That thought worried Jouk. She took a quick look at Ate, but he was fast asleep. She went to the kitchen, where she could no longer find Gelf.

Liesbeth. Wierumer Moeike. What a resemblance! She longed to help her, but who could do that? Liesbeth . . . .

Liesbeth was with her husband at the home of the Heeremas. She was listening to her husband, who said, while he looked at each one in turn, "Why don't we fasten our bonds of unison still more firmly?" He laughed broadly, and he looked at Wilco, who asked, "But how is that to be done, Douwe? I don't see how that is to be done, do you, Liesbeth, and you, Frouk?"

Neither of them made a reply, and then Douwe continued: "Look here, you have an only child, a daughter, and we have but one child, a son; both are splendid children. And so I ask you why we could not intend to make the way for their union in marriage some day." Wilco jumped up, went to Douwe and said, "That proposition is worth a handclasp, fellow! I agree with you."

Liesbeth looked up from her knitting to both of these men. She was quiet, but her heart was full of misery.

Frouk said the proper thing: "Now listen here, your intentions may be good, but you cannot treat children like cattle and sell them!"

"Nonsense," replied Wilco, "it all depends on how we

regard this matter. If you with your big mouth want to prevent this, that will be a pity."

"The women must go ahead and tell what their opinion is, for or against," cautioned Douwe. "And you, Liesbeth?"

"I don't know, Douwe, I . . . I don't think that we have the right to make a decision, do you? Let us wait a few years. Ate is only eight now . . . ."

Douwe was angry. "So you with your *May not, May not.*"

But Frouk added, "Liesbeth is right."

"If Douwe and I are agreed," said Wilco, but then Frouk jumped up and interrupted: "If Douwe and I are agreed, what ails you anyhow? Once again, they are not a pair of old cows or horses!"

"Remember who is boer here," threatened Wilco, but Frouk did not keep still.

"You are boer here, true enough, but I am mother. You can sell your cattle, horses, land, everything, but my child, that does not go so easily, do you hear? It looks as if Liesbeth does not care much what becomes of her child, but I do!"

"That is enough," shouted Wilco. "You need not offend anybody here. What will you do next? Nobody will touch your child. But we have discussed this matter before, Douwe and I. As I said before, I am strongly in favor of it."

Soon it was time to break up the meeting. On the way home it seemed to Liesbeth as if she had lost all control over her feelings. This night marked the beginning of her penance. She knew that she had earned a tremendous punishment.

Even if there were no God in the world nor such a thing as one's soul, she knew that retribution followed all evil deeds. One could not run away from guilt, as the Apostle Paul had said; "The wages of sin is death." He had warned also that our sins will surely be called to our attention. How could Liesbeth overlook the evil she had wrought and the injustice she had done to her husband, even though he had not done his duty to her at all times? She remembered the familiar saying, "Two evils cannot make a thing good." No matter how much her husband had neglected her in the past, her faithless manner of living could never make up for that.

Was her sin perhaps so great that she did not even have the right to fight for her child? How privileged Frouk was when compared with herself! She could still hear those significant words, "I am mother here." Liesbeth had lost that right. Perhaps she would never recover it. Douwe, seated next to her, looked gay and cheerful. He laughed a bit and said, "That Frouk has a big mouth when she really gets started." When he received no answer, which was not unusual, he continued. "Yet I like her way of doing things. She says what she means, and she does not mince matters."

"Stop this, Douwe," begged Liesbeth. But he continued and why should he not do so?

As soon as they had come home Liesbeth rushed to her boy. She could not restrain herself. She bent over him and kissed him gently. "Mother will stay with you, Ate," she whispered.

Did Ate understand that? Or was there some magic wand that made Ate open his eyes? "Mother," he said, "I dreamed about Wierumer Moeike." And he laughed. But Liesbeth did not laugh. She also knew about Wierumer Moeike.

12

Six years passed. Ate grew taller and taller. Presently he was through school at Hantum.

It had been difficult to make him discontinue his studies at school. Two vitally interested persons had begged that he go higher. The old teacher was the first. Many times he had come to talk with Dad about his project. Mother also had favored that plan. She could think of nothing more pleasing to her than Ate's becoming a minister of the Gospel. Perhaps that might have helped her forget her great sin.

But Ate had received no support from his father. "My boy," he said, "shall become what I am — a boer. That is as noble and grand as all your learning." And Ate had agreed with him.

"It probably has not occurred to you," continued Douwe, "that we have only one boy, and that the Free Estate will fall into the hands of others if he does not become a boer."

The teacher could talk as fluently as any preacher, but he failed to impress Douwe. He could only make him promise to let the boy attend the agricultural school in the city.

"Now we both have our way, teacher," he had said. "I get my boer and your pupil will not grow up a wild barbarian."

Liesbeth had heard the whole conversation, but she had said nothing. *And what about me?* she had thought. Perhaps that might still be taken care of. But, no, it was too late. She could no longer make amends in time.

Ate became a boer. He loved his work so well that he forgot his former companions in the village, and he thought no more about Doutsen and Janke. He regarded everything from the standpoint of his supreme interest: the farm.

All week long he labored as hard as the poorest of workmen; nothing was too troublesome or too difficult for him. He grew and became a young man powerful in mind and body. His thoughts were directed not only to the management of the farm but also to the many problems that he wanted to solve and could not without further study. He was particularly interested in the Bible. Hours and hours he spent reading both the Old and the New Testaments, creation to the end of the present dispensation, as revealed in the last book of the Bible. How profound, for example, were those majestic words in the opening verses of Genesis 1: "In the beginning God created the heaven and the earth. And the earth was without form, and void . . . And the Spirit of God moved upon the face of the waters." Equally illuminating were those remarks in the second chapter of Genesis: "These are the generations of the heavens and of the earth when they were created, in the day that the Lord God made the earth and the heavens. And every plant of the field before it was in the earth, and every herb of the field before it grew."

Ate could not forget the stories from the Bible, the thrilling accounts in the Old Testament and the strange but wonderful sayings in the New. He remembered the remarks of his teacher, who had quoted often from learned works written in many countries. He had given Ate an insight into the Scriptures. Moreover, he had lent some of his books to the boy. What many scholars had failed to accomplish had been

414

achieved by the teacher at Hantum and the young boer on the Free Estate.

The Bible had been important in Ate's life. His mother took him to church and he liked to go, not because of the sermons, but because there he could meditate on life, what it was and what it meant.

For a long time Ate had been puzzled by the pastor. His mother and Jouk had told him of sin and how to obtain forgiveness for it, but the minister never spoke of that. One Sunday while the boy watched the shadows of the birds as they swooped and rose and swooped again, he sought an explanation for this disturbing lack. *The pastor never speaks of sin, nor does he pray for forgiveness. Mother always prayed for that. He speaks only to please these fat and sleepy people who do not want to be disturbed. They want to save themselves, and the minister is trying to make them believe that they can. They do not want to hear that they have sinned. They want to hear only pleasant words. The pastor is afraid* . . . Suddenly Ate heard a sonorous "Amen" and it was time to go.

Through the week he pondered the problem. *Sin — the pastor is afraid to speak of it,* Ate concluded, and the next Sunday as he sat in church he was sure that the conclusion was right.

How weary he was of those flowery phrases and long words, spiritual sedatives with which the pastor eased the hearts of the rich and arrogant. *'The wages of sin is death' is what Mother used to read from the Bible,* he mused. "All have sinned, and come short of the glory of God . . . For God so loved the world, that he gave his only begotten Son, that whosoever believeth in him should not perish, but have everlasting life." His mother had taught him these verses, and many nights as he had recited them to her she had been close to tears. Ate remembered the story of the publican and his words "God be merciful to me a sinner," and suddenly he felt as if he had known the publican for a long time. *John the Baptist preached of sin,* thought Ate as he remembered his mother's description of the wilderness prophet. *'Behold the Lamb of God, which taketh away the sin of the world,'* is what John the Baptist said, but the pastor is afraid to say that. *I wonder — perhaps he does not believe in Christ as the Son of God and the Saviour of sinful men* . . .

So he mused as the swift hours passed. He was sad that Sunday as he went home. He had come hungry, and hungry he had gone.

The pastor was not the only one in the Old Reformed Church who had lost the faith of the fathers, and there was a good reason why many had left the church to start a secession. When King William I, about the year 1830, had tried to check the movement for reform, a number of devout clergymen had begun what was later called the *Afscheiding,* or Secession. Further persecution impelled some of them to go to the United States.

Ate's relatives had remained in the old church, but he had found some friends who had explained to him the nature of the Secession. In Ferwerd, Holwerd, Hantum and Dokkum there were hundreds of sincere Christians who had returned to the standards of the orthodox believers, who had accepted Christ as their Saviour and Redeemer. They felt exactly as Ate did when at times they had to listen to a sermon that did not touch their inner lives or that did not draw its inspiration from the Bible as the Word of God.

In spite of these empty sermons delivered by the pastor, Ate had had unforgettable experiences in church. He remembered one in particular. It had begun when the carriage was left at the inn. They had walked along the lane of elms. The bells were tolling, and one was almost forced to walk in step with their rhythm.

In front of the door had stood the young people, and as in the Middle Ages, so thought Ate, when the people stood in two rows and their lord walked between them, so the people had moved to let them through. Then they had walked over the old tombstones to the Wallinga pew, which was beautifully carved and stood over against the pulpit. Who could tell how many Wallingas had been buried in this building? Ate could not describe that feeling of peace and strength which had come to him when he heard the stately music of the organ. During that entire Sunday morning he had been in a dream.

Once it happened that a sunbeam had come through the window, and passing the bench of the elders and a group of women, it had rested upon his mother's head. That light had been so beautiful that Ate had wanted to come to her and put his head in her lap, but of course that could not be done, and so he had merely pressed her hand. He had not even looked at her but she had understood his love, and she had stroked his hand.

In his school years Ate never had much time for his mother, but now that he was at home more and was getting older, he saw her more often and thought much about her. She was changing, was becoming more beautiful. He did not know how to describe that change. He remembered vaguely how gay she had been when she returned home with his father from some festival. She would laugh and joke with him and Dad. That she never did any more. Mother was changing, but Dad remained the same. Dad was still the boer, a man of horse racing, and in that also Ate rejoiced. He had a horse of his own now.

One afternoon they walked through the fields and the pastures, the pleasant sun was high and the cattle were chewing contentedly. Douwe explained to Ate his love for horses.

"I'll teach you to ride horses, boy," he said. "I'll transmit my power and knowledge to you. But you must first learn to know each horse. You will see that horses are much purer than people. They are the great heroes of life, the creators of the great races. Whatever you may read in the history of the earliest ages onward until today you will find mention of the horse, which always gives its strength, always, always. But people often scold them, for they do not understand their sacrifices. Think of that, boy — wherever you may be, no matter how far you have been dragged through the mud, as long as

you retain the friendship of a horse you will not be alone.
They have so much to tell us, boy. We can learn so much from
them. I know that now, after many years, and you must also
learn that. Come!"

Together they reached the pasture, where Wardy walked
with her daughter, Hisk, a tall colt, nervous, with eyes like
those of Wardy.

Like a child, a small child, big Douwe talked to the colt,
and slowly, dancing around him in shorter and shorter circles,
Hisk finally came to him, almost touching him. Ate thought,
How much that man must love horses! Then Douwe remarked
suddenly, "That colt is yours from now on. Hisk, the daughter
of Wardy, is your horse!"

That had been something tremendous for Ate. Hisk his
own horse! Who could have imagined that? He already had
so many things, a new bicycle, a gold watch, two cows, but
those possessions meant little when compared with that horse!
Now he would be able to tend to that colt himself, and under
the supervision of his father he would learn to ride it, and
then to make it race. In that also he wanted to imitate and
follow his father. He also wanted to go to the horse races. He
even wanted more than that, he, Ate Douwes!

As he had grown older, many thoughts had crowded his
mind. He realized that there was something wrong, that the
friendship between the Heeremas and the Wallingas was not
wise and good. Whenever Jouk and Gelf discussed Heerema,
who was supposedly their friend, they did not say pleasing
things about him. How was it possible for his father to like
that man so much?

Gradually Ate learned that this and similar questions would
require time for a suitable answer. It was his task to find the
proper solution. He must fight and persevere. Who had said
that? Ah, Uncle Ids, who had quoted that great thinker of
Friesland, Waling Dijkstra of Holwerd. That was a man after
his heart! Not a bit afraid. He had seen this man for the first

time when he was staying with Uncle Ids, and one afternoon as they were going to Holwerd with the mud cart, they had met him.

He had looked a bit gruff as he came walking down the street. Uncle had called him and said, "Good day, Dijkstra. What are you doing here? I thought you wanted to go and live in the province of Holland." Dijkstra had replied, "Yes, Ids, but slumber was going too, and it died first." Then he pointed to Ate and said, "What kind of stuff have you there on that sled?"

"That," Ids had answered, "is the son of Berend Oost-lander. I'll take him to the saddle-maker, who will cut him into belts."

"Belts," Dijkstra had mumbled, and he had looked so sadly at Ate that the boy did not know whether to laugh or to cry. "Belts. That's what I have to work with. That concerns me deeply. Belts? No, sir . . . ." And he had walked farther shaking his head. "It is a shame."

Uncle looked ill pleased, as if he did not know what to do next, and he had shouted, "But then what, Dijkstra?"

Dijkstra had replied, "Take him a few houses farther to Piet Bakker, and let him turn the boy into a cake, and we shall eat him some evening when I come over for a talk."

In that strange manner they had parted, and Ate would never forget what Uncle Ids had said next: "Gid-up, old horse! That man, boy, has done more for the future of Friesland than all the others put together. But they let him peddle little books in his old age. It goes with him as with so many other great thinkers: you must first be dead!"

Ate wanted to ask his father at supper time how things were coming along on the Free Estate, but unfortunately he did not get an opportunity.

During the meal Douwe said to him, "You must as you go to night school call for me at the carpenter."

"All right," answered Ate, "and what shall I tell him?"

"Ask him if he can come over to take a look. The roof of the barn has begun to leak, and the wall of the stable is getting wobbly. . . ."

"But we can't have carpenters on the place now, can we, Dad?"

"No, boy, but I wanted to know how much it would cost, and if it should be too much then next spring we'll take the whole barn down."

"The whole place? But then," said Liesbeth, "where are we going to get all that money?"

Ate looked at his mother, and he thought deeply about her question, which cast further unwelcome light upon the present state of affairs. Ate thought that his father had plenty of money, but he was troubled by his mother's question and the answer given by his father: "That is my affair. Ate, you know your message?"

"Yes, Dad" said Ate, and he went to the front room to change his clothes.

That evening in the village Ate was talking with the boys of the night school, and he told them nonchalantly that his father was going to do some thorough repairing. "If necessary," he boasted, "the whole place will be torn down to make room for a new one." But the situation on the Free Estate was made clear to him, and he received an answer to the profound question he had pondered often. Unwelcome and unexpected though it be, still he would find it a useful revelation. One of the boys named Klaas, the son of Tjerk Ages, said sneeringly, "Your father has as much to say about the Free Estate as my father!" In the tone he used there was perhaps more contempt than he had intended, but it seemed to Ate as if someone had lashed his face with a whip. He turned white, as he walked to Klaas he said, "What do you mean by that?" They could see how angry he was.

Klaas did not want to argue, and he remarked, "You ask Heerema!"

That was all he was able to say, for the moment Ate heard that hateful name he struck Klaas' face so hard that the blood spurted from his nose and mouth. He kept on striking, and Klaas struck back. Though Klaas was stronger than Ate, the latter was so furious that he seemed to have superhuman strength. He bit and kicked with all his might, thinking about Heerema but belaboring another.

The boys fought like lions until the blacksmith, who was about to take away the newspaper, separated them.

Ate remained behind. He was ashamed of himself, for he had punished an innocent person. The blows intended for Heerema had fallen upon a boy who had nothing to do with the sad state of affairs on the Free Estate. That man, Wilco Heerema, he could not touch. Why did he have to be Dad's friend? So that was the secret. Heerema was the real owner of the Free Estate!

Ate suddenly observed that the blood was running out of his own nose and mouth, and at the same time he saw a girl standing there, Janke, bashful but eager to help him. She asked softly, "Ate, does it hurt?"

"No," he replied, "not at all," but she came closer and looked anxiously at his bleeding features.

"Your face is all cut open," she declared. "You had better go with me to the school pump." And there in that cold winter evening Janke washed his face with the tip of her apron.

After the lessons at school, during which Ate had learned nothing whatever about the Dutch language nor about algebra, Janke and Ate walked home together.

She did not know why she was suddenly so happy, although Ate did not utter a word. "Does it still hurt?" she asked him again, but Ate did not bother to reply. He shook his head merely to show that it did not hurt any more, but he felt a stinging pain which was not caused by wounds of the flesh. Now he knew why he always had refused to give Heerema his hand. He had always known the truth, known it from the beginning.

They had reached the North Road, and Janke said, "Ate!"

He replied, "Janke," but did not even look at her, for how could he with all that anguish in his heart? But poor

Janke, who did not know his profound secret, determined never to help him again, no matter how much he might have to suffer, that conceited pup!

As soon as Ate reached home he asked his mother and Jouk where Dad was. "In the living room," said Liesbeth, and without saying a word he went to that room.

Douwe was in the big chair, which seemed to have been built especially for him.

"Dad!" and then he dared not go farther.

Douwe looked at him and saw that he was concerned about something of importance. He got up and took a few steps in his son's direction. "Did you want to ask something?" Now he was going to say it at last. He had pondered and rehearsed it so often, and yet he did not know how to start. Then suddenly he blurted out the question: "Why does Heerema have more authority here than Dad?"

Douwe's face was white, and for a moment it seemed as if he were going to seize Ate and give him a whipping, but then he turned away from him, and with heavy steps he walked up and down the room. The boy watched him go from the door to the cabinet, from the cabinet to the closet, and back, and then again. . . . Then Douwe confronted him with these words: "You have nothing as yet to do with this affair, but I want to tell you something. Wilco Heerema has loaned money to Dad, a whole lot of money, that is true, and if he were my enemy he could have the whole place sold, but that he does not wish to do. And as for the rest, that you will hear some other time. Now you had better go to bed."

"Good night, Dad," said Ate, and then Douwe observed how badly cut his face was; he lifted his son's head and asked, "How did you get that?"

Ate squirmed and halted, but he did not succeed in evading that simple question. So he finally confessed. "I had a fight."

"Boy," said Douwe, "was it about that?"

"Yes," responded Ate nodding, as he was no longer able to speak.

"My fine fellow," said Douwe. "My big, strong fellow!"

13

THE SECOND HALF of November was dark and still, and for days a dull, gray mist hung over Friesland. The fields were lying without life, waiting for another season. Finally the weather changed; the wind turned east and it started to freeze.

The boys, Ate, Tjerk and Wieger, went often to the canal to see if the ice was thick enough for skating. They were ready to skate to Dokkum, although the ice was not yet trustworthy.

None of the boys had said a word about the matter at home, and it was assumed that they had gone to the places where shallow water covered meadows and pastures, where they could do little harm to themselves.

When at ten o'clock they tied their skates on at the bank of the canal the weather was lovely. Ate had a strong rope tied around his waist, Wieger carried a long pole, and Tjerk a hook. Wieger tied the other end of the rope around his waist, and Tjerk was last. Now they were prepared for the worst, and they started for the old town of Dokkum.

Often they became a bit too bold and with long strokes they moved merrily ahead, sometimes five yards from each other. There were many places where the wind kept the water from freezing, and there a treacherously thin coat of ice covered the water underneath.

Ate was in front, because he was the lightest, and with his skates crosswise he took a step wherever the strength of the ice required testing. Wieger held the pole in readiness and kept an eye on Ate, to whom he was tied. When Ate had taken about ten steps on a weak spot and nothing discouraging had happened, they moved ahead again until they reached the unsafe areas, some of which were under the bridges, where they walked on land.

The journey required three hours, but at last they reached their goal, and they had accomplished their heroic deed. This entitled them to an age-old honor: their names would be placed on the log and they would receive free treats at the inn.

They went to the inn called "Altena," where they took off their skates, and Klaas, the old waiter, asked, "Where did you boys come from?"

"From Hantum," they replied.

"From Hantum all the way over the ice?"

"Yes, except under the bridges, where the ice was not safe."

"Come with me," said Klaas.

There they went, their skates over their shoulders, behind Klaas, who told everybody about the amazing feat of the boys, who thus far had been the first to venture that risky trip to Dokkum. The innkeeper came to meet them, and when they had confirmed the report that Klaas gave him, he invited the boys to seat themselves around the big, round table, where each drank a large cup of hot chocolate. Then the innkeeper placed a chair in the middle of the room and took a piece of chalk. He was ready to write their names on the log. "What is your name?" he asked.

"Tjerk Riemersma," answered Tjerk, and the innkeeper wrote his name upon the huge beam on the ceiling.

"Now you," to Wieger.

"Wieger Blanksma."

"Wieger Blanksma," murmured the innkeeper. "Yes, now the last one."

"Ate Douwes Wallinga," answered Ate, and the innkeeper wrote that also. As he reached the name "Wallinga" he bent over the arm of the chair and asked, "Are you the son of Douwe Ates of the Free Estate?" and he continued to write.

"Yes," answered Ate proudly. "That is my dad. Do you happen to know him?"

The old man wrote steadily, and the boys watched intently. Their names were there at last! And now they read: "On the 22nd of November came the following on skates from Hantum as the first of the season: Tjerk Riemersma, Wieger Blanksma and Ate Douwes Wallinga. The innkeeper of the 'Altena,' Sikke Dijkstra."

"And now," remarked the old man, turning to Ate, "let us have a word about your father. You asked me if I knew him? Well, I should say I do, that I can assure you. Very well indeed!" He took a seat, made himself thoroughly comfortable and said, "Your father, boy, is the greatest expert on horses in Friesland, and he not only knows them in the minutest detail but he knows also how to ride them! I shall not soon forget that day. It was the time of the annual fair, when your father with Kol and Wardy won the race here in Dokkum on the street called Broadway. Late that evening, I should say, rather, that night, they entered my inn. I don't know how it started, but I heard a tremendous noise, talking and shouting, and I saw a man stand and shout at your father, 'Yes, with you sitting on a tilbury or sulky, then you are the big shot, but I don't call that riding.' Then your father jumped up and replied, 'I'll show you something. You and I shall race on horseback, from here to the mill of Banga and back again, do you accept?' "

" 'I offer a silver plate' said I to your father, but I had misunderstood his intentions; he refused to accept a thing from me."

" 'I present a gold coin,' said your father. 'Do you accept,

Herke?' 'Yes,' he responded, 'what else had you expected?' "

"And then they started the commotion. They all went outside and pressed close around your father and Herke. Herke had taken off his coat, shirt and outer pants, but your father had taken off only his coat."

The innkeeper was laughing. He was enjoying the scene all over again. "Klaas went ahead to warn all those who might still be on the streets that night, and he called, 'Move to the side, to the side! Two mad farmers on two crazy horses. It is a matter of life or death!' "

"The old blacksmith counted, 'One, two, three.' There they were off." He rose when he repeated the counting and remained standing in the middle of the room. "Well, boys," he continued, "I have seen many horses racing in my life, but never anything like your father that night on Kol's back. A ghost he was, a ghost! He was back already and sat here feasting again before Herke returned with his wretched horse. What applause your father got that night!"

The old innkeeper remained seated as the boys left for some sightseeing. He mumbled, "So that was the son of Douwe Ates Wallinga!" When the boys returned each received a heap of potatoes mashed in "farmer's cabbage." After their repast they thanked the kind innkeeper once more and returned to Hantum the same way they had come. They were proud of their achievement and hoped that this would be the beginning of an old-fashioned winter.

And that is exactly what it was. The frosty weather continued for many days. They continually went skating, and they visited every place they could think of, for they had plenty of time and money in their pockets.

One afternoon Ate skated with Doutsen Heerema. How they had started he did not recall, but there they were. Close behind him, her white hand in his, she flew with him over the ice, and everybody who saw them concluded that they made a fine couple. Doutsen was a bit older, but they were the same size. It was rather late when Ate took her home. A bit clumsy and bashful he was, and peeved at himself for being unable to find the proper words. This was all the more remarkable, since on the ice they had discussed with great gusto a wealth of topics. He examined her features when she was not noticing it, and he concluded that she was pretty.

Doutsen looked at Ate the same way, and yet they both knew what they had been doing, and suddenly they began to laugh. That ended the tension, and now they walked together. . . . Only the moon saw them, just as it was peeping at them from behind the big tower. But soon it sent for a cloud and hid itself neatly.

Ate kissed Doutsen, and it seemed to him that a strange sinlike impulse made him do it again. Arm in arm they walked along the lane that led to the farm home of the Heerema family. They were powerfully attracted to each other, and their young love was like a feast.

Wilco and his wife were sitting in the kitchen when Doutsen and Ate arrived at the barn. Wilco heard the movement of the door and listened as he stopped reading the newspaper. "My daughter," he remarked, "has a beau. I am curious to know if this one is another or the same chap she had yesterday."

"Why would it be another," said Frouk, "or do you really believe that she can pick and choose?"

"She has many admirers on the ice," laughed Wilco, "and she can get any boy she wants. She is indeed a favorite with the young swains."

"Yes, with those who are interested in her for only one day."

Then the door opened, and Doutsen put her head around it. She laughed with much amusement, for she had heard of the parental negotiations, and she asked, "Who do you think is here this time? I bet you could not guess."

"I suppose another one again," said Wilco. "Tell us, dear."

"Ate Douwes Wallinga," she stated with glee, and she came with Ate into the kitchen.

Wilco jumped from his seat and walked to him. "Good for you," he exclaimed. "I am glad about that." He made a gesture to shake hands with Ate.

Suddenly Ate knew that he must under no circumstances accept that handshake. At the same time he felt that he should not offend the father of his friend.

Did Frouk see that? Could she feel that? Ate did not know, but suddenly she had put herself between the two, put Wilco's hand down and said, "Yes, it is fine, man, and you sit down, boy."

Ate seated himself, and the next moment Doutsen had returned from the hall, so that he did not have time to think. She was exceptionally busy and bewitched him, so that he was in no position to reflect upon anything except the fact that he liked the girl immensely. When an hour later they were standing in the stable and she put her arm around his neck, Ate asked, "Tomorrow again?"

"Surely," she replied at once. "I'll be glad to go. . . ." And cautiously, as if he were afraid to break something, he kissed her and departed. How long it took to walk the distance between the two estates he did not know, but like an enchanted person he arrived home, barely aware of his surroundings.

His mother was reading the Book that in these dark times was her only consolation — the Bible — and her husband was busy with his work. The coffee was bubbling on the light, and Ate's meal was ready.

"Good evening," he said. That was all, but his parents looked attentively at him.

"What is on your mind?" asked his mother, and Douwe said, "What has happened?" But he also chose to wait and see what the boy would reveal.

Ate could not keep still, and he said as he began to eat, "I have been skating with Doutsen, tomorrow we'll go again."

"With Doutsen?" Douwe jumped excitedly from his chair and slapped him on his shoulders. "With Doutsen Heerema? Well, boy, that suits me."

His father's behavior reminded him forcibly of Wilco's reaction. Both men showed the same feelings. Why? Then Ate looked at his mother and wondered what her reaction would be. Would she also . . . but he received a terrific shock when he looked at her eyes. There was a strange light of fear and terror in them. She raised her hands as if in defense against some imminent danger, and the gesture frightened Ate. He jumped from his chair and went to her, saying, "Mother, what is the matter? Mother, calm yourself. . . ." He looked fearfully at his father, who stood there with a stony glare in his eyes, as if her action did not concern him at all. "Cheer up, Mother," Ate continued. "Mother. . . ." He was almost weeping, and in his confusion he called for Jouk, who was in the kitchen.

Jouk entered the room and took a handkerchief and eau de cologne from a closet. Douwe left. Jouk quickly administered the perfume to Liesbeth's temples and held the bottle under her nose, while Ate looked pensively at the door through which his father had just left the room. Soon after his mother had gone to bed Ate went outside to find his father, who was waiting for him in the stable.

"Dad," asked Ate softly, "does Mother often have these attacks?" He waited anxiously for the answer. Douwe took a deep breath before he answered. "Yes, but I am of the opinion, boy, that it is not so serious as it may seem." *It is plenty serious,* thought Ate, and he asked if they should fetch the doctor.

"The doctor? No, boy, I know exactly how each case develops. Mother worries too much." Looking straight into Ate's eyes, he continued. "There is something strange about her. . . . She has a tremendous dislike for the friendship between our two families, and now that you are keeping company with Doutsen, she feels as if cold water has been dashed all over her."

"I don't understand that," observed Ate. "It is not so long ago that her attitude toward Wilco was very different, and I can well remember, though I was very small, that Heerema was here nearly all the time, and she had a lot of fun with him."

"I can't understand it either," answered Douwe. Then there was a long silence, as both men, father and son, sat thinking deeply about a mystery that as yet had not been revealed to them. A long time afterward Douwe said, "She reads too much in the Bible, and sometimes I fear that this is going to affect her mind adversely. But, Ate, you can safely go ahead with your romance. Everything will turn out all right with you two young people. The three of us, Wilco, his wife and I, are much pleased with you."

Those words encouraged Ate, and that night he dreamed about his girl, Doutsen Heerema.

But in the bedroom of Douwe and Liesbeth the situation was tragic. Liesbeth could not sleep.

In this way that terrible evil in her life had returned with a vengeance. She had hoped and believed that it might gradually fade after she had confessed her guilt before God, but she had been mistaken. That man who had flirted with her and had sought to make her forget both Douwe and Ate, besides everything that was good and beautiful in her life, for whom she had sacrificed five, six good years of her youth, in order supposedly to help her own husband, that Wilco was a thief, a beast who knew that he stole something from Douwe, and that had been his chief aim.

She had wanted to tell Douwe, but she did not have the courage, because of herself and because of cowardice regarding her son. Now her son was to be married to his daughter, and then they would have control over everything on the Free Estate. But that should not be permitted to happen. If only she had the power to act. "Dear Lord," she prayed, "I am not worthy that I should call upon Thee, but protect my son, Lord. Let him not be punished for my sin." So she prayed silently for a long time.

14

Liesbeth continued to suffer in solitude. At the request of Jouk and Ate the doctor had been called, and he had given her a thorough examination. To her mother, who had been fetched by Douwe, he had said, "She had been excited too much over something." But to Douwe he remarked, as he stopped him in the stable, "Your wife is affected adversely by a mental illness. She is worrying about something that seems very serious to her. Unless she gets relief from that strain she will be in a hopeless condition. My medicine, Wallinga, can do her no good. The trouble is far deeper than physical."

Then my surmise was correct, thought Douwe. *Religion has her in its power.* He tried to think of something that might turn her attention to other subjects. He was eager now to aid her, but Liesbeth remained the same, one day a little worse, the next day a little better, but always quiet and despondent.

Throughout that winter Ate and Doutsen were much in each other's presence. Ate was puzzled about his behavior, for he feared that he had become too passionate, as if he had entered another world. Not even the serious condition of his mother could restrain his affection for Doutsen. When he looked into her glowing eyes, full of fire and animation, he yielded fully to the desire to love her. At the mere thought of her attractive features he was thrilled with pleasure. Both he and Doutsen were seeking fulfillment of their inner wants, and they found it in those cold evenings when, arm in arm, they skated with long strokes over the ice. They spent quiet evenings in the drawing room of the Heerema estate, telling each other of their love, unending and never fully satiated.

It was like a grand feast, like a series of festivities, from which one could not disengage one's self. . . . Until spring came. . . .

Spring did not arrive at once; Winter fought bravely for mastery, but in the end he had to quit and, exhausted, leave the scene. At last the earth was freed from the clutches of frost and snow.

The water in the drainage and irrigation ditches was set in motion again, and the windmills started to turn the water from one ditch to another. The doors were opened for the pigs and the horses, and often the wind turned southwest. As the rays of the sun became ever warmer there was great unrest over all of Friesland; it could no longer be resisted. Sometimes the workmen sat half frozen in front of the stove, and yet less than an hour later they would be in the fields to see what should be done first and what last.

Outside the men began with the same task that had been the last in the autumn: they took the manure to the fields and spread it over the ground. Women and older workmen had to work in the barn. Seed potatoes were sorted and set aside for the potato patch.

The doors of the stables remained open, to let the fresh air come in. The animals were no longer satisfied to stand tied to their stalls. Shovels and forks were fetched, the wagon was greased, and all was ready. The horses, four of them, were prepared for the task of hauling the manure. Gelf took two of the horses, and Ate had Wardy and Jonker. Both men were extremely careful, for at this time of year the horses were full of mischief. At the slightest noise they were ready to run away.

Day after day the loaded wagons were driven to the bare fields. Little heaps of natural fertilizer were deposited as the wagon moved ahead, and later some of the workmen would distribute the manure evenly over the fields.

In the barn the seed potatoes had been cleaned and put in a warm place to sprout. The seed beans were sorted again over the screen, to see which of them must be thrown away. When the time for seeding came, all must be ready.

All the people on the Free Estate were busy, with the exception of one, old Bouke, who did not survive the winter. About ten weeks ago he had passed away, but otherwise everything was the same.

The call to work resounded over all the fields and orchards of Friesland.

The people in the rural districts who lived close to nature, were the first to feel the touch of spring.

That was true also of Ate and of Janke, the daughter of Keimpe and Auk, who had arrived to work in the fields. One morning when they were about to put the seed beans into the ground, and Ate had placed the necessary tools on the cart, Janke came with Beth, the daughter of the day laborer, also from the Soberhoek. As they entered the yard, Beth began to smile, and Ate, whether he wanted to or not, had to look at her.

She resembled a slender young bird, and Ate experienced a strange feeling of pleasure when he looked at her. It seemed almost like a betrayal of Doutsen. He would like to look at Beth all the time, merely look and say nothing. *That is queer of me,* he thought.

"Do you feel like it, girls?" he asked, and Beth, who was far from bashful, remarked, "Like what?" and again she laughed.

"To go out riding with me," said Ate. "The carriage is ready for you. Come along."

She gave Janke a gentle push and observed, "He would much rather go riding with Doutsen." But Janke did not laugh, for what was that to her?

That proud Ate Douwes, she thought. When he was in trouble, as he was that evening after his fight with Klaas, when she flew to the pump to wash his bloody face, she was good enough for him and he was willing to walk with her after night class, but after that he had never bothered to associate with her.

And all those days she worked in the fields she refused to talk to Ate. Beth, however accosted everybody — including Ate — freely. But then, that was her privilege. Janke remained quiet, and the men and Beth sometimes tried to involve her in a joke or two, but she would not participate in the jesting. "I am what I am, and what are you going to do about it?" She continued to ask that until Beth reprimanded her.

"You are quiet, but I know very well that you are not always that way," said Beth. "You know how to talk when you feel like it, as you did this winter when you were skating with Tjerk."

Ate was discing near the place where the girls were working, and he heard every word they had said. He could not understand why suddenly he felt irritable. He spoke rudely to his horses, which was most unusual: "Gid-up, you old lazy-bones!" They all looked at him in amazement, including Janke, though she only for a brief moment, and immediately the girl bent over her work again, and nobody saw how red her cheeks had become.

Beth turned toward Ate and laughed. She was bold and liked excitement. "Ate, boy, your horse is getting older and you have a girl now. Don't forget that!"

"Keep still, girl," scolded Keimpe when he saw how Ate was offended by her remark. But Beth tried to justify her action by adding, "What of it, Keimpe. You know that it is all true."

After Ate had left the field they continued to talk about him for a quarter of an hour, but Janke did not participate in the conversation. Still she did not forget Ate's shouting, and she did not know what the outcome would be.

Ate in turn was wondering why he became so angry, but he did not have time to worry about it, for when he arrived on the yard his father was waiting for him. He said, "Now we must let Hisk go outside. Don't you think so, boy?"

That suggestion chased all unpleasant thoughts from his mind, and he replied, "Sure enough, Dad. I'll be happy to do it." When he approached the stall in which Hisk was tied, the colt began to dance merrily as if to ask why she must stay alone.

Ate took the colt out of the stable and examined her black skin. She was in high spirits, and Ate had great difficulty in keeping her under control. She would not stand still for a minute; first her front legs were raised up in the air, next her hind legs, and then she jumped on all four feet to the side. Ate and his father laughed at that silly, young horse. Finally she had the bridle in her mouth and danced up the road. Douwe remained some distance to the rear, while Ate walked next to her, and in this manner Hisk gradually became used to bridle and rein.

"This afternoon," suggested Douwe, "you should let her run around you with the long rein; it seems to me that the horse is now able to stand that much from you."

When at two o'clock the workers returned to their tasks, Ate was busy with his colt. He stood still while Hisk ran in wide circles around him, exactly as his father had recommended.

"Look!" said Beth to Janke. "That's the way Doutsen Heerema pulls Ate around." "Oh, you with your talk," answered Janke, "what do I care about that fellow anyway?" But she felt the hot color on her cheeks again, and she was ashamed of herself. Would Beth notice her red face?

But Beth was too busy for such scrutiny; she had other things on her mind, and laughingly she asked Ate, "Are you playing at the game of soldiering, Ate?" "Yes," responded

Ate. "I'll soon be finished with Hisk. Would you like to have the bridle in your mouth?"

"Thank you politely, but I do not need a bridle. Janke, on the other hand, could use it to advantage, for she talks far too much." She enjoyed her joke immensely, and pushed Janke in his direction, saying, "Here, take her." But Janke pulled herself loose and walked into the field, followed by Beth, who was still laughing about her embarrassment.

Ate watched them and his pleasure was gone.

At four o'clock he and Keimpe and Gelf went to feed the cattle in the muggy barn, and here also there was an intense longing for the air outside. The cattle would not remain here long.

When he was milking the cows he suddenly began to wonder again about his mother's condition, and he questioned himself concerning the nature of her trouble. Nobody understood her case, not even the doctor and Dad, with the result that everything was suffering somewhat from the mystery of it all. This evening Doutsen and her parents were coming for a visit, but there would be little fun in it under the present circumstances. Douwe had asked Liesbeth if she objected to the visit, but she had said, "Let them come. I am this way regardless."

But Ate knew that she did not relish the prospect of their coming, and he tried to discover the cause of her discomfiture. This was hard to bear, and he must find a way to solve the mystery. Otherwise the situation would get out of hand. Liesbeth did not dare to discuss it, and yet she was opposed to his friendship with Doutsen. Then suddenly he remembered Jouk!

Jouk. If there was anybody who would know about this matter, it would be Jouk. He had known her from the time when he had started to distinguish people. Jouk, who always had been his support and solace, who helped him, led him, took care of him. . . . As soon as he finished milking he went to the kitchen where Jouk was setting coffee and cutting bread. Ate sat in front of her and said in a strange voice, "Jouk, I want to ask you something."

Jouk, with the knife in one hand and the bread in the other, looked at him, and then she felt too weak to walk farther. So she put down the knife and the bread and asked him, "What is the matter, Ate?"

He had to swallow first, but then he began in a firm voice, though not loudly, "Just what is there between the Heeremas and the Wallingas? You must know that, Jouk. You know it; you can know it. I am almost eighteen now, and you can safely tell me."

Jouk remained standing and thought deeply. She could not, she ought not to tell the poor boy what was wrong, and yet she had to satisfy his curiosity. So she said, "Well, I'll tell you. Your dad, when you were still very small, got into serious financial difficulties, and the day that he won the Golden Whip he had to raise a large sum of money within three days or else he would lose the Free Estate through a forced sale. At that moment Heerema advanced the necessary funds, and for that reason your dad has such a high opinion of him."

"That is easily understood," observed Ate, "but then how do you explain Mother's sad condition? She does not like him at all, at least not any more, and she objects to my going with Doutsen. Do you remember that evening when she felt so sad the minute I told her about my skating with Doutsen?"

Jouk became deathly afraid. The boy looked at her so keenly and searchingly that she did not know what to say or do next. "Ate," she stammered, "your mother is ill, we do not know how seriously, but let us not talk about that, don't you think?" Ate shook his head and went to the little room in which his mother lay.

He entered the room as softly as possible, but Liesbeth heard him and waited. . . .

"Mother," said the boy, and he saw how thin she was and how sunken her eyes were . . . those wide, wide eyes.

"My boy," answered Liesbeth, and she removed her right hand from under the blankets and held it out to him. Then she wanted to raise herself into a sitting position.

"No, Mother, stay down," he said. "I am going to sit here for a while at your side. He placed a chair near the bed, seated himself and stroked her cheek awkwardly.

Liesbeth looked at him. *Just like Dad,* she thought. *The same eyes, white forehead, even wrinkles, those blond curls which dance loosely on his forehead, that strong, broad chest, a Wallinga through and through. . . . And yet he is my own boy. He must have something from me within himself; I can see it in his eyes, and I can feel it in his hands.*

Then said Ate, and it came to her like an unexpected storm, "How much do we owe Wilco Heerema?"

"How much do we owe him? Oh, dear." Suddenly she was overcome with woe and anguish, and it was hard for her to breathe. She wanted to sit up again. "Owe him . . . owe him. . . ."

"Better stay quiet, Mother." He tried to calm her, and he was sorry that he had asked her that question. But soon he heard her talking, and he listened intently.

She was lying quietly again among the pillows, but Ate saw in her eyes that she was beside herself with grief. She was utterly confused but determined to make him listen to the whole truth.

"I must say it, Ate. I cannot die until I have told you. I have sinned so greatly, boy, so terribly. . . ."

Then she began her tale of marital infidelity, and confessed every detail — her love for his strong father, her delight at first in accompanying him to festivities, the loss of income as a result of his extravagance and then the estrangement, when Douwe became too much attached to his horses, his races, under the influence of his overwhelming ambition to win the Golden Whip of Friesland. She told Ate how she had been left alone on the Free Estate with the cares and worries, which grew day by day. Then followed the friendship with Wilco. . . . How difficult it was for her to continue at this point, but she had to go on, for her boy must know the whole truth. She explained how Wilco took advantage of her with his affable personality, offering help and advice, not to mention love. Douwe was constantly in a bad humor; Wilco on the other hand was always pleasant, calm, sympathetic. . . . Then she became his willing tool and accomplice in a nefarious undertaking, the nature of which she did not immediately comprehend. Finally, the threatened foreclosure sale . . . .

Ate remained seated at her side, listening with bated breath, saying nothing. . . . "When the Free Estate was about to be sold, because the second mortgage loan could not be paid on time. . . . I knew that this would be a mortal blow for Dad. Then he came, boy, and told me that he could help us keep our home and farm, that I would be able to save it for us all . . . . for Dad and also for you, Ate. Then . . . . the worst happened." As Liesbeth recalled those terrible days of illicit love she felt the punishment like fierce blows of a whip.

"If only I had been able to feel some affection for him, real love, I might perhaps be in a position to account for my actions. But, boy, it was then that I realized how great my sin was. I began to feel a strong aversion for him. I utterly detested him. He, Wilco, is Dad's enemy. Listen, Ate, I am guilty to death, but he is your dad's enemy!"

She paused for a few minutes, remembering those ghastly days and nights when she had aided Wilco's scheme. Then she continued. "I did not dare to say it, Ate. Your father was always for me the strong, heroic Douwe, who knew no injustice, no dishonesty . . . but I . . . all those years I have prayed to God that I might be removed from the scene of my guilt. I can no longer look you and Dad in the face. Do you understand, Ate?" Then she sank into the pillows.

Ate sat quietly. He was chilled to the tips of his fingers. He swallowed as if he could not breathe any more, and he watched as she lay there weeping. At last the riddle had been solved.

Slowly he rose, moved the chair aside and walked to the door. On the threshold he stood still and turned around.

Liesbeth looked with a dreadful fear at him, her boy, who

perhaps would never want to be with her again. She lifted her emaciated white hands, and in her eyes there was such sorrow that it seemed to Ate as if something within him had been torn to pieces. With a few long steps he was at her side again, threw both of his arms around her neck and whispered, "Poor, dear Mother. I love you just as much as before, and Dad will also when he knows this."

Then he left the room.

15

THE FARTHER Ate walked the clearer it became to him that there were things in life that had to be borne, as they could neither be removed nor escaped. One had to face certain facts with courage and resolution. Sometimes it was even desirable to meet and deal with them before they were per-mitted to become too formidable. Overwhelmed by the tale told by his mother, Ate walked and walked, from one field into another, trying to cope with the present situation. He could not run away from it, for wherever he went that great tragedy of his parents accompanied him. Everything drove him forward to the one supreme aim: the search for the truth.

This evening the Heeremas were coming to visit them, and Doutsen, his girl, would be sitting in the big room with her mother and Wilco Heerema.

Did he regret that Doutsen was involved in the tragedy? Well, how did that concern her? Because of his mother, his father and himself he could no longer wait; he had to face the issue, and it made no difference at all that Doutsen was

Heerema's daughter. He had to perform his duty, and if Doutsen could not stand that, it was her own affair. Suddenly he stood still and thought, *But won't I feel sorry about that? Doesn't Doutsen mean more to me than that, or am I but little affected by her relation to Wilco?* It must be that Doutsen was of comparatively little importance to him; otherwise he would be concerned about the possible loss of her affection. He was amazed at himself, for during the past winter he had been violently attached to her, though afterward he had cared less for her. That was true, but he had never stopped to analyze his feelings. During the winter, with the skating and long, pleasant evenings, they had been in love with each other. He had embraced her fondly and whispered the most endearing words into her ears, but later his life had become again what one might consider normal. His visits to Doutsen became more a habit than the result of a burning desire. "Just as everything else becomes a habit," he said. With firm steps he walked back to his home.

Once I fought for Dad; now I shall fight for Mother. But, no, refrain from using such high-spirited language. Stop it. He walked erect, without looking at anything in particular, until he entered the kitchen. He could hear the voices of Dad, of Wilco, of Frouk and also the warm voice of Doutsen. Then Jouk came to the kitchen. She was laughing heartily, and seeing Ate, she said, "Why are you sitting here, Ate? They are all here. I had to laugh at Heerema, for he can tell such funny jokes, can't he?" Then she saw in the light of the lamp the disconsolate features of Ate.

"Ate," she observed, "what is the trouble this time?" And she became frightened when he replied, "There is nothing, nothing, except that you all, and you, too, have lied to me. That means you, too, for only two hours ago you told me that there was nothing between the Heeremas and the Wallingas except a financial obligation. That was a lie; there were far more serious things than that!"

Jouk turned pale, but she did not dare to turn. She continued to look at him.

"Yes," she admitted, "there was more, Ate, but that happened a long time ago, many years, boy, and for that reason you need not pay any attention to it any more. Better come along."

"You don't understand it, Jouk," he argued, and he walked through the hall into the drawing room. The closer he came the louder the voices sounded. Just as he opened the door he heard Wilco and Dad bragging about a certain adventure of theirs. That did not increase his respect for Heerema, and he remained standing upon the threshold. Douwe and the women looked at him, and Doutsen suddenly became uneasy.

"Good evening," said Ate, and Douwe saw the contempt in his eyes.

"If you wish to say 'Good evening' in such a voice you had better keep your mouth shut," he remarked. He was aware of Ate's dislike for Wilco, but would he never change his attitude?

At that moment Wilco looked at Douwe and said, "Let him talk; the young folks probably had a quarrel, and that will soon be over with. Don't you think so, boy?"

"There are things that can never be made good any more," Ate answered. "Those are suffered too long."

"Well, Doutsen, girl," laughed Wilco, "you have annoyed him terribly it seems."

"If that were true, I would not be here," observed Doutsen, and she laughed as hard as her father.

Frouk and Douwe did not laugh. Frouk felt that there was something serious behind Ate's remark, and Douwe knew that voice well. Slowly he rose and said, "Ate Douwes, make yourself clear, and tell us plainly whom you have in mind."

"It is Wilco Heerema!" Like the striking of a clock those words resounded in the room. Douwe continued "Say what you have on your mind, and don't beat around the bush. Explain the whole matter."

"We had better go outside, Dad," replied Ate. "I don't want to hurt anybody who has had nothing to do with this affair."

"Dad, and all of you, it is well known to you that Mother is ill, but nobody seems to understand the nature of her illness.

I also did not realize what ailed her until this evening. Now I know what it is. One day you told me that Mother was worrying about something, that she was too much engrossed in religious matters. But you did not guess very well, and I shall explain to you all what I happen to have discovered. That man," and he pointed to Wilco, "he knows why Mother is in her present condition."

"You scoundrel," exclaimed Wilco, and he took a step in Ate's direction. But Douwe restrained him and said, "Wait a minute." But Wilco continued angrily. "You are going too far." "That is also my opinion," admitted Douwe, "but be patient for a few moments more." He turned to Ate and said coldly and slowly, "So my son has the nerve to come here and tell old women's tales?"

Ate was still standing erect at the door and looked at the two men. The thought occurred to him that he might sow dissension between his father and himself. But he did not and could not stop. He took two steps ahead into the room, looked questioningly at Doutsen and Frouk and said plainly, "All my life I have disliked Heerema. But I never knew the reason for it. Last year I thought I had found that reason when I learned that Heerema had loaned money to Dad."

"Now look here, you meddlesome fool," snarled Douwe, "you know it all now, and why shouldn't you know it?"

"Yes, Dad," continued Ate, "but I know it now for the first time. I know how much interest was paid on that loan. And if Dad knows it also, then . . . ."

"Douwe," shouted Wilco as he got up, "Douwe, let that boy of yours keep his mouth shut. Did we ever talk about interest; did we ever have a quarrel over it? Douwe!"

"Ate, keep still, I tell you." Heavy and threatening was Douwe's voice. "I cannot keep still, Dad," he said softly. "I cannot . . . ."

His thoughts were confused now, for he was concerned about his mother. But he must tell the whole truth for her sake. "There lies someone in that little room who has kept still because of Dad and because of me, and that is why she is lying there. I am not going to keep still!" How difficult it was for Ate to find the right words! He could hardly keep his eyes steady, but in a clear voice as sharp as steel he said, "That man, Wilco Heerema, demanded Mother as interest on his loan to Dad!"

Like a thunderbolt those words struck, and the silence which ensued was full of suspense. What would happen next? For one brief moment there was silence. Then two men sprang at Ate: Douwe and Wilco. Douwe was ahead, and like a tall tower, a giant, he stood.

Frouk rushed to Wilco, but he moved her aside.

"You and the girls must leave the room," Douwe panted. But she, as shocked as her husband, remarked with severity, "And you in the meantime will pounce upon the boy? Douwe," she begged, "don't hurt him, but let him go outside."

Douwe's voice thundered through the room. "Here justice shall be established. I am not going to let my son offend anybody in my house." Turning to Ate, he asked, "Do you know what you are saying?"

"Yes," he answered, "and I am ready to die for it!"

When Douwe heard those words something snapped inside of him. Suddenly he did not know what he was doing. A terrific wave of anger deprived him of his reason and kept possession of his body until the diabolical deed had been accomplished. He took two steps, pushed his strong fist through the glass door of his beloved cabinet, seized the Golden Whip and . . . .

The Golden Whip flashed through the room as Douwe lifted it high above his head and struck Ate's cheek with terrific force . . . .

Doutsen shrieked and covered her face with both hands.

Frouk wanted to go to Douwe, but Wilco held her back, saying, "You keep still." "Let me go," she begged him. But again he said, "You keep still. This is none of our business."

The Golden Whip danced and flashed. Doutsen rushed

crying out of the room, and Frouk shouted, "So that is none of our business when someone is being beaten to death?"

The Golden Whip scourged Ate's face, and he bled.

Douwe slowly raised the whip high in the air, set one foot forward and struck again, and again, and again . . . .

Silently Ate awaited the blows. He said not one word, nor did he wish to raise a hand in his defense as long as that scoundrel was in the room. The warm blood flowed down his cheeks. His right eye was completely closed, but he merely gritted his teeth.

You go ahead, Dad, he thought. *You go ahead.*

Douwe wielded the Golden Whip with such power that it broke in pieces. But still he was not satisfied, and coming closer to the boy, he struck him with the lower portion of the whip. It was no longer only anger that impelled him to such insane action but also sorrow. At every blow it seemed to him that he was getting two himself.

He lost all sense of sight and hearing, and he did not notice that Wilco and his wife finally left the room. He saw Ate, and so it went for a long time, with no human power to stop him.

Gradually Ate became weaker and weaker; first he held himself stiffly erect, but he could do that no longer. A black mist rose before his eyes. He became senseless, turned halfway around, saw the floor rising to meet him and fell like a block of wood on it.

Douwe stopped. His eyes were a terrible sight. His right hand still held the whip aloft, but he did not strike.

At first he looked around like a person bewitched. Presently he saw his son lying on the floor, and then someone else at the door. Who was that? An avenging angel, perhaps? No, it was only Liesbeth, his wife, in her nightgown.

There she stood with her eyes looking straight into his own. A volume of accusation was written in those wide, silent eyes, and yet they were not silent. Then she looked at her boy and said, "You have beaten the wrong person, Douwe. The boy wanted to help you." Then she knelt beside Ate, saying, "Dear, strong boy. Mother could not come sooner, and she was not permitted to intervene. Oh, what should I do first?" She tried to put his head in her lap. Douwe stood at her side.

Then Jouk rushed into the room with a jug of water. She looked with great anxiety at Liesbeth and said to her, "You must go to bed. Oh, dear, why did I have to be away on an errand? Here boer take your wife to bed!"

Suddenly Jouk blurted out these biting words: "At least if your hands are not lame. To beat up a fine chap like Ate, murderer that you are! Yes, even if you should chase me off the farm I must say that you are both murderers, that other man also who sneaked away with his wife! Oh, if only I could have been here before!" She spoke softly to Douwe. "Come, man, take your wife back to bed, and then we must help Ate."

Douwe raised Liesbeth from the floor and put her to bed. After that, still seemingly out of his senses, he and Jouk put Ate in the big bed. Then he went back to Liesbeth's bed and sat beside it without saying a word, but he could feel her eyes upon him.

Jouk washed Ate's face with her rough hands, as gently as she could, and gradually removed the clotted blood. Then she dressed the wounds with cloths of her own making. Next she turned her attention to Liesbeth, in spite of Douwe's presence. He left as soon as she arrived, and Jouk took care of Liesbeth as if her mistress were a little child.

In the middle of the night Ate regained consciousness. At first he could recall nothing. His head throbbed as if a hundred nails were being driven into it, but before long he remembered it all, piece by piece. *Dad was too much in a hurry,* he thought, *and he will probably be sorry about it. I must tell him.*

Softly he slid down the bed, stood still a while, because he grew dizzy, and, spying the water jug, he immersed his head in the cold water. Then he felt much better, and slowly he walked to the door and then into the hall.

He spent a few brief moments in front of his mother's little room, and then he must move on again, in accordance with a well-conceived plan. He walked through the cow stable to the rear.

Suddenly in imagination he saw a scene from the dear past. He saw his father walking with a little boy, hand in hand, along the row of cows, or was it in a field? He did not recall, but wherever it was, he must forget it and think only of the present, when he must say farewell. Should he go to his horse? Oh, no, that would be childish, he decided. He opened the barn door and went outside. He walked down the lane and took the road that led to Brantgum. He did not care where he was going, but he must take leave of the place.

Not far away was the Heerema farm. There people were also still awake.

When the three had come home that evening, Wilco had said, "After this evening we are through with those people. Not one of us is to go back there. Do you understand?" Frouk did not hesitate long in answering him: "Is that so? Are we through so suddenly? Let me tell you something: you are afraid of that boy. I don't know what he meant exactly, but if he told the truth, if you did that to Liesbeth, then he should not have had that beating, but you, mean person that you are!"

When Wilco was about to make a feeble reply, she continued, "Don't try to talk yourself out of it or start a big line of fine talk, for then I'll ask Ate and Liesbeth just what happened, you mean rascal!"

After that Wilco was quiet, but he said to Doutsen, "Ate is not to come here again, child!"

Doutsen continued to think about Ate's courageous, strong face, and in her mother's presence she cried a long time about him. Wilco had been to bed a long time when Frouk and Doutsen were still talking together. The mother said, "Such is life, child. I dare not ask just what happened, so afraid I am of the truth. I wish we had as much courage as Ate Wallinga." Doutsen did not know what to say to her mother. She was sorry for Ate and ashamed of her father. She could feel that Ate would disappear from her life.

At the fork where three roads came together stood Ate. The night was dark and cold, but he felt nothing. He looked back at the Free Estate lying amidst the tall and stately elms, and then he turned away and continued his journey. It hurt him again to think about the future of the Free Estate. He felt as he had when he first went to school, when he had asked himself, *What will become of the Free Estate tomorrow?* As he proceeded slowly he heard someone calling and he waited.

Out of the darkness came Jouk, panting. "Ate," she said, "Ate, don't go away!"

The boy looked at her and realized how fond he was of her, the good maid, the dear maid, Jouk. He put his hand on her shoulder and said, "Joukje, do you have to walk that way on the road?" He looked at her nightgown and laughed.

"Come, boy, I am so afraid. Come with me." But Ate, fully aware of his love for the farm and its inhabitants, felt he must renounce his heart's desires, his affection for Jouk, who had been so good to him.

"No, Jouk," he replied, "I do not care to return home. But don't be afraid. I'll go to Uncle Ids. That seems to me the best way. Tell the folks that tomorrow, will you, please?"

"Is that really true?" she asked him.

"That is true, Jouk. You go back and take care of Mother. But I need not ask that of you." Then he turned and with long steps took the road to Brantgum. Jouk watched him as long as she could, and then, shaking her head, she returned home.

16

RED-HEADED Ids Wallinga, proprietor of the estate called Metserd, which was a medium-sized farm extremely well managed, was throwing beets to his cows with lean Iepe and the stout workman who was regularly employed there. They said little, for it was still too early, and Ids did not approve of much conversation. But Iepe had just remarked, "There is already quite a hole in the pile of beets, boer," and Ids had replied, "That is a good thing, for the whole herd is going to leave for the pasture before the end of this week."

For a long time they worked silently in the muggy stable, where the air had become almost unbearable. *The floor is so slippery that these wooden shoes are treacherous,* thought Ids. Just then he almost slipped, as he came carrying a basket of beets on his hip. He was barely able to get hold of the pump.

Iepe was unable to keep from laughing, and Ids became furious.

"You skinny broom handle," he shouted. "You will laugh when I lie on my back in the coffin." And Iepe, who knew how to use his tongue, and who knew his boer, replied in turn, "I'll think about it, boer," and he continued quietly with his work.

Ids was sitting on the bench and waiting for the pails and the milk cans. When they had been brought he stood and, with the milk pail in one hand and the stool in the other, was about to go to one of the cows when he heard someone at the door of the stable. "Who is there this early in the day?" he shouted. "The day has not even begun, and there we have another peeper."

Slowly the door was opened, and he saw in the light of the lamp that it was Ate.

What can he want? he thought, and suddenly he had an idea — an idea which made him afraid of something. He pulled his leg back, put down the pail, dropped the stool and went to meet Ate, who slowly, very slowly, walked toward him, so slowly, in fact, that it seemed as if he lacked the power of locomotion. The old man noticed that, and at the same time he observed in the twilight the disfigured face of Ate.

On his cheeks were gaping wounds and long, red stripes; his right eye was almost entirely closed. A wave of pity engulfed the kind, old uncle.

He took hold of Ate's arm, and without saying a word he took him to his house. To the housekeeper, who was busy with the breakfast and lifted up her hands in astonishment, Ids said, "Don't babble. Pour tea and give the boy a sandwich. As soon as he has eaten that you must let him go to bed." With these words he turned and went back to his milking. But he did not make as rapid progress as usual.

Frequently he looked at the barn door, and then it seemed as if the boy were entering again, the boy who had been so cruelly beaten.

That satanic family, he thought, but, no, he must not say that, for he was a member of it himself. But something serious had happened, as anyone could tell. He would soon learn from Ate what had taken place.

After the milking, as the four were sitting in the kitchen,

the boer acted as if nothing remarkable had occurred. He did not even inquire after the boy, which did not please Gepke, the housekeeper. No one remarked about his face.

Ids had little time for work that morning. He rose, removed the crumbs from his lap and said, "Iep, you must go this morning with the wheelbarrow to the pasture back of the big trees. Take along a shovel, some wire, a few fence posts and the nail box, to look over the fences. Tomorrow or the next day the cows will have to go there. The others still have their own work to do."

When the men had left the kitchen Ids said to Gepke, "My other clothes; white handkerchief; I must go." Then he went to the room where Ate lay in bed.

Ids thought that he must be careful in opening the door, lest he awaken Ate. But when he looked around the door he saw that Ate was already awake.

He approached the bed and asked, "Have recovered a little, boy?"

"Yes," answered Ate. "I'll soon get up. Uncle had better say what I should do."

He is a bit too much in a hurry, thought Ids. "There is but one thing to do, Ate," he said. "The old horse before the buggy and we together to the Free Estate." Anxiously he awaited Ate's answer.

Then Ate said, and Ids knew that he was serious, "I am not going back to Hantum. I want to stay here if Uncle does not mind."

The old man took a few steps through the room and paused a moment, whereupon Ate started to wonder what his uncle would think of his plan. It was not easy to tell as yet, for he had his back turned to the bed.

Suddenly the old man turned, stood close to Ate's bed, looked straight into Ate's eyes and asked, "Has anything happened of which you should be ashamed?" "Not at all," replied Ate. "Who beat you?" No answer was forthcoming.

"Who beat you, stiffhead?" This time Ids was almost angry because of his pride in the boy. But again he would not reply. "Then I know who it was," concluded Ids, and he left the room. But at the door he stopped once more and said, "If you don't want to leave the bed for a while yet, you may stay there. I am going to Hantum, and you may go with Iepe to the pasture to repair fences. Take along posts, hammer and shovel."

"Which horses shall we take, boer?" asked Iepe a few minutes later when he and the boy were ready to go out with their tools. "I can't spare the horses; you must either carry the tools on your backs or use a wheelbarrow. And don't look so puzzled and downcast Iepe."

"That isn't the way I am looking just now," answered Iepe.

"Well, then you will do it later. You have no more questions? Then I conclude the meeting, and the president goes into the house to change his clothes."

Ate went with Iepe to the yard, and before long they took their tools in a wheelbarrow to the pasture. *This is quite a different situation from that of yesterday and of the day before,* thought Ate. But then, what did he care? It was honest work, and it helped him take his mind off unpleasant subjects.

Ids used the black horse. Ate and Iepe could see the buggy through the trees, and they could see Ids' red, wild beard. He had raised his whip as a warning.

The horses and driver disappeared and Ate thought, *Let him go.*

Uncle Ids drove as fast as he could, and the moment the buggy entered the yard of the Free Estate, Ids got out and called Keimpe, who was loading manure. "Will you take care of the old horse, Keimpe? I'll tie him at the ring, but he might get loose. You can never tell."

"Fine, but shouldn't I unhitch him?"

"If I had wanted you to do that I would have asked you." Id's beard bobbed up and down as he talked. Keimpe could not help laughing as Ate's queer uncle entered the stable.

With heavy steps Ids walked along the row of cows, opened the door of the kitchen and entered. There he found Douwe and Jouk. "Here I am," said Ids.

"I see that, Uncle," answered Douwe. "Are you going to stay for a meal?"

"Eat with you, man? I wouldn't be able to swallow one morsel of food before I find out what has happened here, and what you people have done to that boy."

"Is Ate at Metserd?" asked Jouk.

"Yes," said Ids, and with a snapping noise his mouth closed.

But Douwe still refused to talk. He was sitting there, looking indifferently around the kitchen as if the whole matter did not concern him. His silence made the old uncle the more angry. He went to Douwe, stood in front of him and said to Jouk, "Let me talk to this boer alone, girl," but he became frightened when she remarked with much feeling, "No boer, I stay here. All right, look at me as if I am crazy, for I do not want to witness again what happened here last evening. What do you think?"

"Well, you stiffhead," he said, though he was glad, "you funny stiffhead."

"Yes, I don't care what you think of me. I know this: you people are Wallingas, and when there is something wrong and ready to break you will go ahead and fix it so that it can never be mended again."

"Jouk." Douwe started to speak, but she refused to wait for him.

"Yes, Jouk — Jouk, who last evening was away just long enough to enable a father to beat his own son half to death with a whip as if he were a wild beast. You big idiots! Now there are again two Wallingas together, and I don't want another scene like that. I have grown old on this farm, and I hope to remain here, but I would rather have the boer chase me away than that such dreadful things should occur again." She had become excited as she recollected the insane actions of her employer.

Uncle Ids had been calmed considerably by her report.

"Joukje, you worry too much, and you can safely let us alone. We shall not resort to beating with whips. I can guarantee that."

"Very well," she replied. "Then I'll go to the milk cans." So she went to the ditch to clean the milk cans.

Faithful maid, thought Ids, and he said, "Now you and I, boy. Are you ready now to tell me what happened yesterday?" And as Douwe remained silent the old boer thundered, "You fool that you are, shall I ask your wife about this?"

These words seemed to rouse Douwe, for he said, "She knows nothing about it." As if he had needed just such a beginning for his confession, he spoke rapidly. "Ate had the nerve to offend one of my friends in my own house. It went hard against hard. He did not want to keep still, and neither could I. One word led to another, and I let go of myself. How it all went I do not recall. I took the whip, the Golden Whip, and I beat him as hard as I could."

"And that 'friend' was Heerema, I suppose?"

"Yes."

"Well, dear nephew, you beat the wrong person. I shall go to see Liesbeth, and then I'll drive back to Metserd, where your son is and where he can stay as long as he likes."

"He is not yet of age, and I can have him taken back," replied Douwe, but could surmise what Uncle Ids would say about that.

"That is true, you can, and so you had better summon the whole police force of our district, if it has to be hard against hard."

Then Ids went to Liesbeth, and she was glad to see him. As he looked at her he said, "Liesbeth dear, what a sight you are! Yes, but not ill; so lively; so young."

Liesbeth asked, "Is Ate with you?"

"Sure enough, and don't worry a bit about him, girl. Don't worry about him." He thought, *You dear little sick woman, the future looks dark for you.* But he gave her his hand and said, "So now I am going away again. You get better quickly, and don't laugh at your old uncle!"

He took his leave promptly, and as he entered the yard he was impressed by Douwe's behavior. The boer was loading manure. He had taken off his shirt and vest and had rolled up his sleeves. There he stood. The big fork with four teeth went back and forth from the manure pile to the wagon. Douwe picked up enormous chunks at a time; his muscles bulged and large wrinkles appeared in his face. He did not look up as Ids drove away, but he continued to labor, harder and harder, so that his back hurt and the sweat had no time to dry.

Keimpe, next to him, did his best to keep up with his employer, but he soon discovered that this was impossible, for Douwe was working too fast for him. Keimpe did not understand the sudden change in Douwe, but there was something wrong. That was clear. No sane person would want to ruin his body in such a way. Years ago, when Keimpe had been on the Free Estate but a short time, the boer had gone hunting or drinking when he had one of his fits, but it seemed that with the passing years he had changed his habits. Keimpe liked to work here now.

During the first years his wife, Auk, had wanted him to leave, but gradually she had withdrawn her objections to the place and the neighborhood. *Strange,* thought Keimpe, *that you think of all those things without any apparent reason for it.* He continued to work as hard as he could.

"Take it easy, Keimpe," advised Douwe, "and pay no attention to me."

"That is all very well," replied Keimpe, "but the boer is at work as if it is a matter of life or death, and I want to do my share of it." "Well, Keimpe," observed the boer, "it is indeed a matter of life for me, for else it will get the better of me."

That is all they said to each other during all that hard work.

That evening when Douwe was washing himself Jouk said to him, "Uncle Ids asked me if I would tell you that your wife needs some attention. She lies in her little room far too much alone, and the man is right about that. I can be in only one place at a time."

Douwe gave her no answer, but after the meal was over he went to the Soberhoek, to Keimpe and Auk.

He went directly to the table said "Good evening" and without looking at the chair which Auk had placed for him he remarked, "Janke must not go to the field tomorrow morning with the other people, but she must come to our house. My wife has been lying in bed a long time now and Jouk cannot take proper care of her any more. You understand the situation, don't you? She naturally takes her meals at our place, and in the evening she goes home. If it should become necessary to stay overnight I'll let you know."

At first no one said a word. Auk answered with her eyes, and Keimpe scratched his head. He still did not know what to say. The boer had walked into the room without knocking at the door and issued an order. It was true of course that the girl was employed by him, and it was largely a matter for the boer to decide whether she was to be transferred from one task to another. One could not make serious objection to Douwe's behavior. Nevertheless, even poor folk were human beings, not cattle, and they treasured a few kind words.

"What do you think of it, Janke?" Douwe looked at her, and his look indicated that he expected an affirmative answer. "Would you like to do it?"

Janke blushed again, but she was able to make a suitable reply. "Yes, boer; but I have never served as a maid."

"Oh, that will be taken care of, for I know what kind of mother you have. So I expect you tomorrow morning, but you won't have to come before seven. You won't have much to do. Ate is gone; he went to Holwerd to stay."

"Ate away to Holwerd?" She had spoken without thinking.

Why should she have shown so much concern about that boy?
She was deeply ashamed.

Douwe said in a commanding voice, "Till tomorrow,
Janke." Then he left, accompanied by Keimpe, who showed
him the way in the darkness. When Janke's father had come
back into the living room, he was in a pensive mood and said,
"There is something the matter with the boer, but I don't know
what it is. He is ill or he is worrying about something serious.
Well, girl, there is your order: from the fields to the farmhouse. You won't have much work to do."

"I don't know about that, Keimpe," said Auk. "There is a
sick person to take care of." "What sick person?" grumbled
Keimpe. He went away to take off his clothes for the night,
and he said as he left, "I have been loading manure today with
the boer, and it was plain to see that he had something on his
mind that tormented him. Something of great importance must
have happened yesterday. In the evening the Heeremas were
there on a visit, all three of them. Before that, during the
milking, Ate was in a state of agitation, and this morning he
was gone. Now Douwe says that Ate is staying in Holwerd,
no doubt with Ids, for they have no other relatives there. And
this morning at nine o'clock Ids was there already, with a head
like a bull and steps like those of the big Belgian horse. There
has been enough going on to write a whole book about it now.
I must first have a good night's sleep. Janke may be able to
find out tomorrow just what happened. Good night!" This
time Keimpe was behind the doors of the bed which was con-
structed like a closet with doors that opened into the living
room.

Janke and her mother spent a long time that evening
getting the girl's clothes ready. A person could not wear the
same clothes while serving in a home that she wore while
working in the field. They mended and examined even those
clothes which she would not need immediately.

The next morning at six-thirty she was ready to report for
work with Jouk.

"At first she must take it easy," Liesbeth had said to Jouk, but that advice had not been necessary, for Jouk understood perfectly what had to be done when new help was initiated. After a few days it seemed as if Janke had been there for a long, long time, and Liesbeth and Jouk were greatly pleased with her. Nothing was too difficult or too hard for Janke.

Douwe acted in those days as if he were struck dumb. He spoke only of work. Load manure and spread it, plow, disc — it did not matter what kind of work it was. As long as he was occupied he could forget his great sorrow.

But it was not easy to forget such a tremendous burden as that which hung heavily upon his mind. At unexpected times the pale face of Ate would rise up before him — a face with accusing eyes. He could not flee from it no matter what he did or where he went. His sorrow increased each time, and so did his self-contempt. He tried to understand why Ate had treated him with such lack of respect.

He still could not fathom the whole mystery, but soon, when the cows were in the pasture, he would learn more about it. Then he would go to Wilco Heerema to obtain further information. Wilco must not imagine that he beat his own son merely for the fun of it. Those were heavy blows — even for him.

17

At this time of year the doors of the Frisian farms were standing open, and people and cattle could no longer be kept inside the buildings. They seemed to obey a powerful force, and everybody wanted to go outside, into the fields.

The boers in some respects resembled commanders of armies; from early morning until late at night they were in a state of tension; they issued commands, watched everything and controlled all operations. When the great day arrived and every animal was freed, all must be ready.

The auspicious moment had arrived!

A wide board was laid over the trench behind the cattle, and fresh straw was put on top of that. Then, one by one, the animals were set free and went bellowing awkwardly through the stable door.

Having arrived in the open air, they stood still for a few moments, blinded by the mighty, broad light which surrounded them, but it lasted only for a short time. Then they rushed forward, their heads close to the ground, their tails in the air.

The workmen, brandishing sticks and twigs, tried in vain to check the eager cattle, but the animals were not to be kept in check with body blows. The men could only run with them as fast as they could. Through the gate they ran, turned, manipulated a long rope and let the animals go where they pleased, far into the green pastures. First they ran to the end of the field, making queer movements with their legs to show their happiness. Occasionally they halted suddenly, frightened by a mere blade of straw. Presently another group of animals made their appearance, and there they came — two, four, eight, catching up with each other, ready to run through the pasture again.

When the calves came the festivities were complete.

The older cattle had been there before, and they were familiar with the gates, the ditches, the grass and the flowers; they knew that the land was intended for grazing, that a ditch was similar to a pail of drinking water and that gates were closed when they were to stay in a certain pasture.

But the calves! They had been put into the quarters reserved for them in the barn, where hay had been stacked. There they spent many long days in twilight, between the straw and the hay. All they knew about the world of men was that a few times each day a certain person came with water, buttermilk and mash, which they were permitted to devour, and they spent much of their time licking each other.

But now they had been brought to that large open space and that bright shining light which they saw in front of them. It seemed to them that they had to go through that light, but, no, there was no end to it! They were completely surrounded by it when once they entered it. The sunshine was a great novelty to them; it gave them a strangely pleasant feeling.

When they were in the pasture, they stood still to assimilate what they suddenly saw around them, and they made many queer gestures, until a little bull ran ahead with full speed.

The others saw him go, and then suddenly they wanted to follow. There they ran with their tails high in the air. When they reached the ditch they discovered that they must stop, but they were unable to come to a perfect halt, and their hind legs were folded under their bellies. Then they saw in the water the reflections of the other calves. How amusing!

Next came the horses, who immediately took possession of the entire pasture by running majestically over the land, royal creatures, proudly throwing their front legs forward and upward. Often they cast up big pieces of dirt. Their heads were erect, their tails spread like fans.

The people who witnessed this spectacle would never forget it. The farmers, their wives, the workmen and the visitors — all were deeply impressed, and they realized fully that this was a part of their own lives.

In the meantime the cow stable lay completely neglected. The straw was piled in little heaps; the drinking water was in dirty receptacles; everything was slimy and slippery. A pale light slipped through the small windows, now that the warm breath of the cows no longer formed a curtain. Thus the situation remained until the workmen came to clean the barn.

When the maid had hung the curtains the boer took a walk through the stable, and soon the place was transformed into a storage room for bicycles, a play pen for children and a sleeping room for the men who helped with the haying.

So it went on the Free Estate, and so it went everywhere else in Friesland.

Janke had been waiting on Liesbeth for a long time, and she was well liked by all who knew her.

One morning the doctor came, and he was highly pleased with the appearance of the young maid. "Well," he said, "a new one. That suits me fine. Who are you, child?"

"Janke, Doctor, of the Soberhoek." Her cheeks assumed their habitual color. Why did the doctor look so attentively at her? But then she heard him say to Jouk, "Janke! But, Jouk, that is the girl who was born the same night as Ate!" "Yes," replied Jouk, "she is the same age as Ate. She seems a bit too young, but she is a great help to me."

"Young enough, you say. What you should have said is that you are too old. That goes for you, too. Formerly you could sing like a lark, and now you look all dried up. I suppose you are no longer keeping company?"

"Oh, well," answered Jouk, and she did not wish to continue in this vein, but the doctor would not change the subject. When Douwe entered the room the doctor asked him, "Does the girl ever sing any more, boer?" Then she could not help saying, "You lose your desire to sing in this place."

"If you are dissatisfied, Jouk," remarked Douwe, but she interrupted him. "You know very well, boer, that it is not my doing that causes things to run down hill here."

Douwe and the doctor went into the yard, and Douwe asked him, "How is the situation now, Doctor?"

"I don't know, boer," he replied. "It looks bad to me. My medicine does not do her any good. If we should want to try something else, we must . . . ."

"Perhaps I do not know what should be done, but I believe that it may be too cold for her here. She should be taken south for a few months, to Brabant or south of Amsterdam, where she would be in the care of capable physicians. But you must first make the necessary arrangements, do you understand, Wallinga?" Then he left, and Douwe did not hesitate a moment before going to Liesbeth.

Her room had been properly cleaned and rearranged. Liesbeth lay in the warm rays of the sun, and she was looking at a bouquet of flowers in a vase on the table next to her bed.

Douwe took light steps to her bedside, thinking that she must have fallen asleep. But she had heard him. "Liesbeth," he said, and she replied, "Douwe." There was silence until Douwe moved his chair closer to her.

They both looked at the fields. The orchard was in full bloom, and far away in the pasture grazed the contented cows. The black and white cows were shining in the sunlight. Still farther away were the workmen in the fields, and on the horizon stood the tall tower of Ternaard.

"It is getting beautiful outside, Liesbeth," he observed, without looking at her.

"Yes, Douwe," she answered. "It is getting beautiful."

"Wouldn't you like to go out?" he asked, but she shook her head.

"To walk together in the garden, that would be very nice. You certainly have no intention of spending the whole summer in bed, do you?" He laughed when he said that, but his laughter was brief for she remarked, "No boy, that is not my plan; I am going to leave. But we must first have a talk, you and I."

"Yes, that is fine," agreed Douwe. "That's what I would like." He turned to her and continued. "Liesbeth, what has happened in the past is now behind us. I would like to see you as you used to be — cheerful, gay, hopeful. It is true that I have made things unpleasant for you at times, and the recent developments have cost me much sorrow. But if we, you and I, started all over again, and — how shall I say it? — if you were a bit more lively, just as you once were . . . It is not so long ago that Gelf was married, and we went together to the festivities, do you remember? And how happy the young people were that we could help them with the money for two cows, weren't they? Then you were cheerful, Liesbeth."

"Are you willing to listen to me, Douwe?"

"Yes, indeed, and why not?"

And so, while Douwe sat close to her she confessed once more her guilt, the great and terrible secret that for so many years had tormented her. At first when she recounted the story of their early years of married bliss, Douwe smiled happily in retrospect. But when she moved to another period in their lives and he heard of the years when he left her at home days and nights in succession, something snapped inside of him and called for a hearing. She told of her loneliness, his drinking and racing, the financial burdens that fell upon her shoulders and all those trifles that had accumulated into an unbearable partnership for her — not as an accusation but as a revelation, sharp and piercing, though spoken in a soft and tender voice, spoken in love and deliberation. At times Douwe placed his hand on hers, as if to ask forgiveness, but he did not hold it there long.

Then she arrived at the point where her confession became painful for herself and most difficult to narrate. That was the most sorrowful part of her life, that sin committed because of him and for his sake, a sin he had sown himself, her husband whom she defended as much as she could while she acted as if her guilt were greater than his.

Douwe was calm. He did not reveal the thoughts that coursed through his mind. For Liesbeth this confession was a deliverance from the bonds that had fettered her so long.

At last her voice was silent. They sat quietly — they who had ruined their lives through their fateful silence. Suddenly Liesbeth's voice was heard once more, and she mentioned something that concerned Douwe only. "Ate had wanted to tell you that night; I know that now. That fine, strong boy, he wanted the truth to be made known, and that would have been a good thing . . . ." She could say no more.

Douwe sat still for several minutes, and he did not know what to do next. Liesbeth waited.

Then suddenly he rose and said, "My wife . . . Liesbeth, you have lived in the deepest of misery, and even in that you have performed your human duty. Your sin does not fall upon yours but my shoulders. I can see that! In your own goodness you were as unable as I was to distinguish good from evil, but I should have known better, for I had been warned two or three times . . . ." He bowed his head in shame and anguish. "Stay quiet, Liesbeth, and be at rest. Douwe Ates is not going to leave you again. But one thing more. The doctor said that you should go south; he thought that you would improve faster there. What do you think of that?"

Liesbeth did not answer him. He asked again, "Liesbeth, come now, what do you think of that plan?"

He lowered his head still more, and he knew that she was crying.

"Liesbeth," he said, and he did not know himself how tenderly and softly he spoke to her. "Liesbeth darling." Then he felt her arms around his neck, and she pulled his head closer to her. In the midst of her crying he heard her say, "Now everything is getting so different, so light, so free. You have no idea how relieved I feel. Yes, boy, I want to go to another place, to get better for you, for our boy . . . . Do you remember those days when we were expecting him?" Her voice was nearly a whisper.

"Yes, I know . . . ."

"You longed for him even more than I did, I believe. Oh, Douwe, you talked so often about him."

"And I am so fond of him still, and perhaps for that reason I beat him half to death." He expressed a thought that was seeking utterance, for he did not want Liesbeth to hear that, even though the thought might tear him to pieces. His boy, who had known everything about his mother, had stood there like a king, and not a word of reproach had he spoken.

Liesbeth talked again. "Soon he will come home again. It is true that he is enjoying himself at Uncle Ids' place, but home is home, and he should soon be helping you, shouldn't he?"

"Yes," answered Douwe, "and you too. You must get better, and then we shall try to make amends, and regardless of how old we are, we will start anew, girl! And you must sleep now, and I'll go to the field . . . ."

Cautiously he released her, and as he left the little room she watched him. A great happiness filled her heart. As Jouk walked near the door she heard Liesbeth singing these well-known lines:

> I will render thanks to Thee, O God,
> And praise Thee in my evening song.

Jouk walked on without pausing. She did not like that kind of singing. The voice was so oppressive, so weak and false. No, Jouk was far from satisfied.

What Jouk did not seem to understand was that Liesbeth had at last made amends to her husband for having been unfaithful to him in the past. She had confessed her sin, as the

Apostle James had exhorted his followers to do. Now a great burden had been removed from her shoulders, and in her happiness she thanked God for having given her the courage to tell Douwe all. Her physical weakness was of no account when compared with the guilt of an unrepentant sinner. She was confident that God had heard her prayer for forgiveness, and she could now depart from this life in peace.

Douwe was riding his bicycle. He sat stiffly and tried to control himself, but his hands pressed the bar almost to pieces. In that state of mind he went to the Heerema farm.

Wilco was standing in the yard and was about to go to the field. He became frightened when he saw Douwe, but he remained standing and Douwe approached him.

Be firm, be firm, Douwe cautioned himself. How was he to overcome that terrible desire to forget everything, to throw himself at his adversary, to fight, to kill, in one swift flame of hatred? But he would try to suppress that evil desire.

He had reached Wilco, and he said, "I wanted to make a settlement with you tomorrow, Wilco Heerema!"

That remark overwhelmed Wilco. *Doesn't Douwe know anything yet?* he thought. He would be glad of that, and he answered, "There is no hurry, Douwe, boy, for I don't need that money." But Douwe saw the situation.

"When I talk of making a settlement I mean something more than paying money, Heerema, for I don't want to have anything to do with you any more. You know what I mean. Will you come to our place tomorrow evening or do you want me to come here?"

"You had better come here," suggested Wilco. "I will take care that everything is ready."

"Agreed," said Douwe, and, he turning his bicycle around, prepared to leave. As he approached the little bridge he saw Doutsen standing there, and she asked him, "How is Ate Wallinga?" Douwe could tell readily how concerned she was.

"Fine, girl," he replied. "Tomorrow evening I'll be back and then I'll tell you all about him."

That afternoon Douwe drove through Hantum with Wardy in front of the buggy, and next to him was a little box.

He drove fast, so that mothers pulled their little children out of his way and reprimanded him for his disregard of human life. But Douwe heard nothing of this; he must have money to be free from indebtedness to Wilco — free from everything.

Now he knew what a slave he had been all these years, — he, Douwe Ates Wallinga.

When he arrived in Dokkum and had allowed his horse to be unhitched at the Aalsumer Gate, he went directly to the street named Broadway, where lived a merchant called Tjalling.

As they sat at the table in Tjalling's room, Douwe opened the little box and pulled out a large number of documents, nothing but papers.

Tjalling looked at them with deep interest and said, "The pedigree of Wardy!" "And of Prince," added Douwe. "Look, these are of Hisk — that is my son's horse — and I have to keep that one. But Wardy and Prince and the colt of Wardy I want to sell. And also the horse I have just bought." "To sell, you say? Are you willing to sell them? Yes, I know that Wardy is getting older, but as a breeding horse she is worth a great deal, and Prince and that colt and that new horse?"

"Yes," replied Douwe. "Do you want to buy them or not?" Less than half an hour later Douwe was back at the Aalsumer Gate with a large sum of money in his brief case. Tjalling had the bill of sale: "To deliver in four days the horses Wardy, Hisk II, Prince and Ulke, in good condition . . ." It was signed by Douwe and Tjalling.

Soon Douwe was going along the road to Hantum, with Wardy in front of his buggy for the last time, but for the first time he had a feeling of liberty.

18

DOUWE did not regret greatly that he had to sell his horses, but when he thought of the cause of the transaction, of the man to whom he owed the money, there was bitterness in his heart.

The previous evening he had told Liesbeth about the sale of the horses, and she was of the opinion that his sacrifice was too great, as she told him frankly. But he put his hand on her mouth and said, "My sacrifice is far less than yours, girl." That is all they said about the matter.

Now he was with his horses for the last time. They were in the pasture, and Douwe talked to them. Old Wardy, the famous Frisian mare, who had served him so many years, and who had won so many prizes for him, the heroine of so many village festivals, the faithful companion . . . . He communed with her the longest, and it seemed as if she felt what was going to happen.

"My black girl," said Douwe, "you were my life. When as a two year-old colt you arrived on the Free Estate we did not yet know how things would turn out, but the next year you went with me to Tjummarum, to get the wife. Then began the festivities of the boer who was no real boer. I spent more time with you than with my wife, Wardy, and that has caused me much sorrow."

Then he went to Prince, the winner of the Golden Whip, but after that he did not go back to the horses again that day.

Liesbeth knew about his agreement with Heerema, and she was afraid of this evening. She did not know what would happen, but she knew Douwe, and she longed to go with him and help him suppress his bad temper.

When Douwe sat at her side in the twilight she wanted to discuss the matter with him. But he brushed her fears away with a laugh. "Don't imagine a lot of trouble when it is not necessary, for I am not going to start a quarrel. He, Heerema, will be paid this evening, and that is all."

"But what about Doutsen and her mother, Douwe? Do you know the situation between Ate and Doutsen? If they love each other won't this separation hurt them?"

"There is nothing we can do about it, Liesbeth. But if they are fond of each other they will suffer from the forthcoming events. We can't help that. Well, that will also turn out all right in the end."

Douwe talked lightly, superficially, as if the conference with Wilco would be a simple affair, but his emotions were assailing him like a tremendous storm, and this time he was fully determined to control the evil force. His struggle would be intense, and he did not dare tell Liesbeth about that. She must remain quiet.

That evening he walked to the Heerema farm. During the entire meal Jouk, with her faithful eyes, had been watching him keenly, but she had said nothing. She knew well, however, where he had to go. Calm and thoroughly prepared, he arrived in the cold evening air at the Heerema place. He did not open the front door but pulled the porcelain knob and waited. He heard someone approaching — Doutsen. She opened the door, invited him to enter the hall and asked him at once about Ate, for she could no longer suppress her desire to learn something about his condition. "Wallinga, how is Ate?"

"Fine, girl. Fine." But, alas, that was not what Doutsen wished to hear. She wanted to know how their love could be salvaged, but how could one ask that? A person could not make public her affection.

"Dad is expecting you," she said, and she took him to the large drawing room, which was the same size as that on the Free Estate, but it had been furnished elaborately in the latest style. Sitting in one of the chairs was like reclining on the softest of beds.

Wilco was seated in one of these chairs. He was wearing his best clothes and looked dignified indeed.

Douwe thought, *What a cheap show he is making, for he knows that his display of elegance will do him little good when he receives the mental thrashing he so richly deserves.* Then Wilco remarked, "Good. There you are. Act as you have always acted." But Douwe made no reply; he remained standing at the table, opposite Wilco.

"Have you gotten the papers ready for me?"

"Oh, sure, but sit down first." Wilco was becoming confused, for Douwe was standing there as if . . . . Yes, Wilco was afraid of him. He knew him well, this Douwe! He realized that a man of steel stood across the table from him; that man of steel would yield to nothing. He understood fully that this man who would give away all he had, who had a heart like that of a child, full of pity and compassion, who would sacrifice himself to help another — that same man, now that he knew everything, was hard and strong, and a cool pride had replaced his former tenderness. Wilco was afraid of the ghost which he himself had conjured up on this fateful night.

Douwe did not answer the invitation. He remained where he was and asked again, "The papers?"

Wilco arose and searched in the drawer of a modernistic buffet for the papers, and these he placed on the table in front of Douwe. He looked carelessly at them for a brief moment, took his billfold out of his pocket and counted the money for Wilco in bills of one thousand, one hundred and fifty. He gave him some silver money also. "There," he remarked. "You count again."

"What a queer business you are making of this!" Wilco laughed, but he was trembling with fear, and he counted the money carefully.

"In order," he said, " and shall I give you a receipt?"

"Yes," replied Douwe sharply, and Wilco wrote the receipt with shaking fingers. He knew that Douwe was watching him.

When Douwe had taken the papers concerning the second mortgage loan and the receipt for his money he tore them forthwith into small pieces, and it seemed to him as if with each piece a part of the debt, the guilt of Liesbeth, no, the crime committed against Liesbeth, was canceled.

"But, Wallinga, don't destroy those papers: they are the proof that you paid your mortgage loan."

"That is true," said Douwe, "but I trust you, Wilco." Putting the fragments into his pockets, he continued, "Now that is finished. Much obliged to you for your help. The interest was a bit high, but that cannot be helped, and among friends one must not be too particular. I am sorry that it took such a long time, but that was not my fault."

At that moment Doutsen entered the room with a tray upon which she presented tea to Dad and Douwe. She looked fearfully at the two men, and said briefly, "Here is the tea." Then she left again.

Douwe laughed heartily and observed, "You are getting to be important people, aren't you, Wilco?"

"Well, the women want it that way, and what harm is there in it?"

"No, and it gives a person a restful feeling. Does your wife realize now that we are most intimate friends?"

"Douwe," said Wilco suddenly, "you are continually talking, but couldn't you allow me five minutes in which to defend myself? It is true that I have acted wickedly. I have behaved badly with Liesbeth, that I admit, but that happened almost fifteen years ago, and how were the circumstances? For days in a row you were gone, and you showed no interest at all in the management of the farm. I went there to help and keep things going. I lent you money and you could go your own sweet way while your wife remained alone to worry about all the details and the finances . . . . Well, one person is different from another. We did things that were not proper . . . then . . . ." But he could go no further, since Douwe took a step in his direction and said, not loudly, but with a voice as hard as steel, "So, she and you! One more word about her and I'll murder you right here in your own house, skunk that you are! Five minutes in which to defend yourself, well, even if you took five days, Wilco Heerema, you still would not succeed!

"When you and I were young we often double-crossed each other, and also as young boers. We were both what might be termed wild; my wildness consisted in drinking and racing, yours in something else about which several girls and women could tell interesting tales. For that reason I had no use for you, and for that reason I considered you a foul, dirty person. The situation continued that way until I gave you a beating on your own land. All of a sudden the thought struck me how sad, how wretched it was that we had to live that way. I invited you to my house. I offered you my friendship and gave you concrete evidence in the form of the horse named Kol, to show you how I trusted you and how happy I was. . . . And you, you coward that you are, you were unable to do what I did namely, to erase your hatred. You remained unchanged, and I can see it now that many a time you must have laughed at me because of what you considered my folly. But I did not see it; I did not want to see it, no matter how often people warned me against you.

"And so, Wilco Heerema, you could have your way. Like a vulture you could circle high above your victim and when the proper time had arrived you were able to throw yourself upon your prey and devour with your destructive mouth the very best you could find in it. If only you two had been able to love each other . . . but that was impossible. You wanted to strike at me and you took Liesbeth . . . you beast!

"We are living in a newer world and everything has to be recorded black on white. In that kind of world I am not so well equipped as you, and even if I did have the necessary tools I would not use them against you. But, Wilco Heerema, had we lived in the days of our ancestors you would have put yourself into a precarious position. Now you can go ahead freely wherever you choose, and you may wait for the Judge of all judges to call you before His throne. How it will go with you there I do not know.

"But how low your character must be that you could continue to associate with us after your unseemly behavior, after you had stolen the most holy possession of another man. To think that you could look into the eyes of your own wife, day after day, take your child on your knees, and come to visit us. What a despicable person you must be!"

Douwe had delivered this oration without excitement, and his voice did not tremble once, nor did he move his feet. But he could continue no longer, and he sat upon the chair offered to him by Wilco, though previously he had refused to take it. And Wilco? What sort of thoughts were in his mind? He rose and walked in Douwe's direction.

"Douwe," he said, "Douwe, I wish we could have a chance to live our lives over again; I wish I could show you how I feel now, but is that worth while after so many years have passed? We have grown older, and must the whole neighborhood start talking about us, and must our children perhaps bear the shame through their lives? What will be said about us who for so many years were friends?"

Those last words embittered Douwe, and he burst out, "*Friends?* You and I *friends?* I have been the friend, and I gave my friendship without pausing to think, without paying attention to the warnings of others. I was the friend, not you! Not you, Wilco. You robbed me! You big thief that you are! How often you must have laughed at me, that idiot of a Douwe! My most precious treasure you were able to take away from me because I was blind and refused to see. . . . There was only one who did see, who felt what you were trying to do . . . . and I . . . I beat him out of my own home!"

He was beginning to lose control of himself and to talk more wildly. "The only one who knew you I beat out of my house, and that, Wilco Heerema, was my own son, my own son. I beat him with the Golden Whip . . . . Why do I remain seated here? I should have given you a beating so that you would no longer be able to see!"

Douwe rose and walked slowly to the door, and when he had reached the outside door he was not sure that he could master his feelings. If he had not thought about Liesbeth. . . . He opened the door and sped away.

He did not know what Wilco would think about this, nor did he know what would become of their relationship, but deep within himself was the conviction that he had achieved a victory.

In this frame of mind he reached home and went directly to Liesbeth. "Are you sleeping, girl?" he asked as he stood at her side.

"No, Douwe," she replied in a soft voice. "No, I waited for you. I have been with you all evening, and I hoped so strongly that you would behave. Come here." When he stood close to her she touched his head and his hands. "Fine," she said. "Fine."

"Nothing happened," said Douwe. "I paid him and told him that our friendship is finished. Nothing else."

"That is a good thing."

"The situation will get still better," said Douwe. "It will get better. You are to spend a few months in another region to get stronger, and in the meantime, girl, I shall become once more a real boer — that I'll show you — a boer on my own place."

He looked at her a long, long time. But why did he suddenly feel sad? What could be wrong?

"When you return, Liesbeth, our fields and all Friesland will have on their summer garb. It will be midsummer, and we shall be harvesting and haying. That will be a double festival. I should like to do just what Dad and Grandpa did — hold a grand harvest festival with tables and benches in the yard, workmen and women, servants and maids, musicians, and eat all night. And when the musicians start the polonaise, girl, then you and I in front, the boer and his wife, and after that we'll join in the feasting.

"I could invite all my people, Keimpe and Auk, Gaele and his wife, our former servant Gelf and his wife, some people from Hantum, the day laborers and others."

He became so engrossed in this plan that he could visualize the entire scene, and he did not observe that everything had become quiet around him the moment his voice no longer resounded through the room. Then he looked at Liesbeth and suddenly he became frightened, though he could not tell why he had that feeling. It seemed as if something warned him.

Liesbeth lay peacefully in her bed. She did not move. Her wonderful, blue eyes were wide open and they did not look at him.

"Liesbeth," said Douwe softly. "Liesbeth. . . ."

Her voice was clear and strangely strong. "If our boy could hear you now, Douwe! If I could see you two together here in this room . . . you and our boy, Ate. . . ." And a little later she said it again. "You and our boy. . . ."

As if in a trance Douwe looked at her, and he went to the kitchen, where Jouk and the new servant were sitting. He looked at them so strangely that Jouk jumped up and said in a voice full of fear, "Is there something wrong with your wife?"

"I don't know, Jouk," he answered, "but I am going to fetch Ate. Help me a minute, Wiggele," he said to the servant, who followed him to the yard immediately.

Jouk paused a moment, deep in thought. Then she went to Liesbeth, who was lying just as when Douwe had left her.

"The boer," said Jouk, "the boer is getting Ate."

Liesbeth seemed to be awakening from a dream.

"Is it true, Jouk? Is it true?"

"Yes, mistress, stay quiet; they are hitching the horses already."

"Ate," she whispered. "Ate is coming. My boy. . . ."

In the yard the boer and Wiggele were busy. The servant took Prince and the new horse, and Douwe carried the harnesses out of the shed. It did not take long to hitch the horses in front of the buggy, and the lanterns were quickly lit.

The thought came to Douwe that he must drive fast. Well, that he could do easily enough. Perhaps this was the last time he would ride over this road, but he and the horses would not soon forget this trip.

He jumped into the buggy, and seized the reins. The servant moved aside, and then, "Gid-up!" The word was like a shriek in the silent night, and at once the horses sped forward. They took the curve so fast that the iron wheel hoops made a strange, squeaking sound as they scraped the stone posts along the dam. Then they raced up the road to Brantgum, to Metserd. Douwe hardly had time to seat himself. He was glad that the top of the buggy was down. He wanted to stand, move, look out, but he must not relax.

"Gid-up, horses," he shouted, "as fast as you can run! We must get the boy whom I have chased away myself." Then he added, "If we don't get there on time I would be doubly guilty. Run, beasts, or do you want me to apply the whip?" He took the whip out of the socket, but the moment he touched it he remembered the frightful scene of the beating with the Golden Whip. It seemed as if the whip were full of fire, and he put it quickly away as he thought, *No whip any more; no whip again.*

Like as the lanterns on the buggy flickering like two eyes, the horses, like ghosts, raced along the dike. Like a storm they sped through Brantgum, then along the road to Metserd, after Ate, for whom somebody was waiting anxiously, and who knew how little time was left?

19

For Ate it had been a step backward, from the Free Estate, where he had been the boer's son and almost as highly regarded as the proprietor himself, to Metserd, where he had to perform some of the most menial tasks, since Uncle Ids made no distinction between him and an ordinary laborer. But Ate was not greatly concerned about this matter; he had more important problems on his mind — problems which would not so easily find a solution. He thought often about the people at home.

Upon his return from the Free Estate Uncle Ids had gone to Ate and said, "Now you must bear this in mind, boy; I don't know exactly what the situation is at your place, but this I do know, that your dad is plenty sorry about what he did to you. He won't talk about it, though. You can stay here on the level of a workman as long as you like, and before long there will be a change." Ate had made no comment, but every day he waited for something to happen, although he had no idea of what it might be.

So far his days had been busy, and he had had no time for reflection, except at night when he lay in bed, and then there were many thoughts . . . Doutsen! He could not understand why he no longer thought about her as he used to do.

Was it a fact that now Doutsen meant nothing to him? How could that be? He had walked with her by the hour, and often he had embraced her fondly. On those quiet Sunday evenings he had been supremely happy in her company. But now he felt no affection for her. That was beyond his comprehension, and the thought made him afraid. On that last evening he had seen her sitting next to her mother, and even then it had seemed as if she had ceased to attract him.

How were things at home? He was eager to know about his mother's condition. Although he was interested also in the others, she was his deepest concern.

Uncle Ids was aware of the situation, but he never discussed it. As a matter of fact, he studiously refrained from the mentioning of Ate's home and family. The name "Free Estate" was never mentioned. It seemed as if Ate had spent his life at Metserd, and more as a workman than as a member of the Wallinga family, for he was kept busy, and if he did not perform each task to the utmost satisfaction of the old man he suffered a severe verbal lashing.

But gradually there came a change, and presently Uncle Ids began to talk about Ate's parents. It seemed as if in the course of time some of the sharpness of the pain had been removed. Other subjects were also discussed in the living room at Metserd. The same evening that Douwe made his settlement with Wilco, the carpenter had brought the portrait of Waling Dijkstra.

Uncle Ids, unlike Ate's father, was greatly interested in Frisian literature and nationalism. He entertained profound admiration for Waling Dijkstra (1821-1914), who for half a century, had labored to raise the Frisians to a higher level of culture. Ids had ordered the portrait, and now they hung it in the living room. Ate had met Dijkstra but twice, and each time the meeting had been a casual one. Judging from the admiration which Ids and the carpenter cherished for the man, Ate concluded that he must be worth studying.

"My good man," Ids had said, "Waling Dijkstra? Posterity will be the first to appreciate his talents and the tasks he has accomplished for Friesland. During his life he was sadly neglected, but for his historical work alone we should be grateful to him. Day after day he devoted himself to pains-taking scholarly labors, recording important events and search-ing for important sources of information which otherwise would have been lost to our people. Popular customs, legends, chronicles and folk tales he described or collected. And what was his purpose in all this? Merely to serve his native land and people. Near the end of his career he was ridiculed by a few young literary pups who had no conception of his marvelous contributions. He loved our country and our language, and he inspired thousands of common people to a higher ideal than the serving of their own bodies and minds."

Uncle Ids had become enthusiastic, and particularly when the carpenter observed how Dijkstra had been accused of hav-ing ridiculed sacred rites or customs, the old man spoke with rare fervor. "Would Dijkstra make fun of holy things? If that's what you thought, you would expose your own dense ignorance of the people in your village. If there is anyone who has the nerve to make that accusation, he had better. . . . Do you know what kind of people he vehemently attacked? The hypocrites, who walked around with God in their mouths and the devil in their pockets. Against those folk he fought all his life. It is especially for this reason that I am hanging his portrait here in this room.

"And do you know what he once said here in this very same room?" The carpenter was a bit frightened by Ids' sudden burst of eloquence. He had not meant to accuse Dijkstra. "Well, what was it?" he asked bashfully. "This. Friesland is like a huge house and the Frisians are the children in that house. Most of them are too small in stature, but they

om Jezus te zien. is geweest, die begeerte is
voor hem het middel in Gods hand die alle
dingen gebruikt om zijn doel te bereiken, om
de stem van den goeden Herder te hooren,
een stem die zoo liefelijk en zoo krachtig hem
in de ooren en in het hart klinkt, dat zonder
verwijl de boom wordt verlaten en hij in de
nabijheid van Jezus is. En zegt de Heere:
Ik moet heden in uw huis blijven, dan is dat
„Ik moet" van het grootste gewicht. Ja, Hij
moet omdat het in de eeuwigheid in Gods
raad was besloten en Hij het op zich geno-
men had om des Vaders wil te doen. Hij
moet omdat de ure van genade voor Zacheüs
heeft geslagen en hij dus moet toegebracht worden tot de Gemeente der zaligen. Hij moet
omdat de tollenaar in een apostel wordt her-
schapen en alzoo de wondere liefde en macht
des Heeren zou blijken. En waar hij komt
wil Hij blijven, blijven met zijne liefde en genade, met zijn Geest en trouw tot in eeuwigheid.

Gij hebt veel goeds bij uwen knecht gedaan;
Hem, naar uw woord, gered uit al zijn nooden:
Leer mij, o HEER! een goede zin verstaan.
En wetenschap, der dwazen waan ontvloden.
Wijs Gij mij zelf den weg der waarheid aan,
Naardien ik heb geloofd aan uw geboden.

Ps. 119 : 33.

Zon	**15**	Nieuwe M 16 Aug
opgang 4 u 43 m		Eerste K 24 .
onderg 7 u 25 m		Volle M 31 .
Maan		Laatste K 6 Sept
opg vm 3 u 30 m		
ond nm 7 u 46 m		

Ik moet heden in uw huis blijven.

Lukas 19 : 5

Jezus gaat door Jericho den weg op die naar Jeruzlem leidt. Maar Hij gaat niet doelloos, maar om te zoeken en zalig te maken dat verloren is, een van de verloren schapen van het huis Israels. Daar op dien weg, in een wilden vijgeboom gezeten was, Zacheüs, een rijk oversten der tollenaren, die daar is in geklommen omdat hij Jezus wil zien, wat hem, daar hij klein van persoon was belet werd door de op een gepakte schare. Om dien Zacheüs was het te doen, die moest gered, van de zonde verlost en ten eeuwigen leven behouden worden. Daarom zegt Jezus als Hij bij den boom is gekomen en Hij zacheüs ziet: Zacheüs kom af, ik moet heden in uw huis blijven. Al hebben zij elkander te voren niet gezien, Jezus kent zijne schapen bij namen en Hij weet wie door den Vader aan Hem zijn gegeven. Jezus roept Zacheüs om tot Hem te komen, en wat ook de reden van zijne begeerte

refuse to recognize that obvious fact. They all want to take part in the discussion about their breakfasts, lunches, about eating and sleeping, but each wants to do it in his own peculiar manner. As a result it looks sometimes as if the devil himself were in charge of human society."

Ate had listened with great interest to his uncle's oration. He spoke fluently, and there was nobody who understood Dijkstra better than Uncle Ids. He had purchased all the books written by Dijkstra, and often he read them.

They accompanied their guest a distance on his way to Holwerd. Returning home, they walked slowly in the late evening. After the first mild days a period of damp, cold weather had begun. The wind blew often from the southeast and then turned north. Presently the uncle and his nephew were walking more briskly than at first, and Ids was thinking again about Friesland's literary hero.

Suddenly Ate stopped and listened intently, with his head raised in expectation of the arrival of a carriage. "Uncle," he said eagerly.

"What do you hear, Ate? Ghosts maybe?" He laughed quietly.

"Listen, Uncle," replied Ate, "it sounds like horses and buggy." Now Ids could also distinguish a sound, but it was still far away.

Ate did not know why it was, but he felt a sudden shock and the thought came suddenly, *From home!* Ate began to walk faster, past the gates of Metserd. He stood still for a moment and then said, "It is a carriage with two horses in front, and I think it is Dad."

The sound came closer. Nothing was visible, but the hoofs of two horses could be heard, together with the squeaking of iron wheel hoops on the gravel road. There they came, the flying horses, and as the lighthouse on the coast of Ameland threw a faint light upon the road, Ids and Ate saw Douwe standing in the buggy. He was frighteningly pale.

"Dad!" shouted Ate. "Dad!" At the same time he seized

Prince's head, and he let himself be dragged along for nearly six feet.

Douwe stopped.

"Are you there, Ate?" It sounded like a cry for aid in a storm.

"Yes," answered the boy.

"Then immediately with me to Mother." That was all Douwe said.

Ate let Prince loose, jumped into the buggy next to his father and watched him make a turn in order to start the trip back home.

But at this point Ids, who had said and done nothing to stop Douwe's strange performance, said in a reproving voice, "Are you stark mad to go without giving the horses a moment of rest? Do you want to kill them? Go up the yard and let the horses rest!"

"No," replied Douwe. "No."

"Are the horses to be killed?" asked Ids fiercely. But Douwe retorted hoarsely, "Must Liesbeth die before she has seen her boy again? Ready, Prince!" He pulled the reins and they hurried away.

"Shall I drive, Dad?" asked Ate, but Douwe, who did not seem to hear him, gave no answer. The two horses ran as fast as they could, and that was fast indeed. There was again that intimate connection between man and beast, and the reins were like a thread along which Douwe sent his thoughts to the horses.

They sped through Waaksens, through Brantgum, and along the curves the two men hung to the side to help the wheel get back on the road. They left Brantgum at such a speed that Ate realized this was to be the limit of endurance for the horses.

Just before they reached Brantgum the new horse stumbled, but with a shout from Douwe and a pull at the mouth it got back on its feet.

There is the road to the Veldbuurt. Thank God! The cramp which had troubled Ate caught at the beginning of the trip was gradually disappearing.

Old Ids had gone into his house. *What madness,* he thought, *to punish those poor horses that way for the sake of only five minutes!* Yet he would have done the same thing. "That poor Liesbeth," he mumbled. "I wonder how she is now." Ids pictured her lying in her little room.

At last they reached the Free Estate. The horses entered the gate. Douwe jumped out of the buggy and started to unhitch the horses. Ate had dismounted on the other side, and he started to loosen the belts. But Douwe said, "Let go, boy. You go to Mother." He took care of both horses. "Quiet, boys," he said soothingly. "I admit that we went a bit too fast, but that could not be helped."

Ate walked through the cow stable to the kitchen, where Jouk was waiting for him. She rose when she saw him coming.

"Boy," she muttered, "how glad I am that you are here!"

"How is Mother, Jouk? Better tell me the truth."

But Jouk did not want to tell him something that was not true. She had done that once, and she had known much regret because of it.

"Not very well," she replied, "but if I must say it exactly, she has not looked so happy in years as she does now."

Ate went to the bedroom. As he opened the door he saw his mother lying there, as small as a child, but with a smile in her eyes.

"Mother," he said, "Mother, here I am already." And she replied, "Wasn't that fast, boy? Dad surely got you in a hurry. Now everything is fine."

Ate did not know what else to say. This was not a death-bed, and yet he recalled the words of Jouk and Dad, which indicated that his mother was seriously ill. Nevertheless, her eyes were so clear, so very clear. . . . Suddenly the thought entered his mind that he knew another person with the same eyes. Who could that be? But then he heard his mother say, "How good it feels, boy, that you are here again . . . you who suffered so for me."

"Be quiet, Mother, and don't let us talk about that, for it is far behind us, and belongs only to the past."

"No, boy, that is just beginning. Look here, when I am gone, yes, boy, my time is up . . . then you and Dad will remain here together, and that is why I am so happy. I wanted to ask you something." Both were waiting in deep silence, but then she spoke again. "How do you feel toward your father, Ate?"

"Dad? Well, I have always seen him as a strong, true and honest man, and in spite of what has come between us, that regard for him will remain."

"Do you know that Dad sold his racing horses to pay Heerema the money for the mortgage loan?"

"No," answered Ate happily. "No, I didn't know that, but it does not surprise me in the least. You could have expected that of Dad."

"Yes," she remarked, "that is true, and now you must go to him, Ate. You must both go to bed. I am also going to sleep."

But at that moment she was reminded suddenly of a message far more important than earthly slumbers. She asked Ate to come closer to her before he left her for the last time. Her life was fast ebbing away, and how could she let him go before she told him about her salvation? To make peace on earth was as nothing compared with making peace with God. So she paused with him while on the brink of eternity. She told him of her thoughts, how she had confessed her sins not only to his father but also to Christ. Ate must never forget what it meant to face a just God.

"Sure, Mother," replied the boy, and he left the bedroom and went to the kitchen, where Douwe was sitting while Jouk prepared a sandwich for him.

Liesbeth looked at him as long as she could; she wanted

to retain this evening always in her memory. "I thank Thee for that, Lord!" She wanted to say much more, but she no longer had the strength.

At two o'clock in the morning she peacefully left this life, she, the mistress of the Free Estate, peacefully indeed. When they found her she looked as if she were asleep.

But for the others there was no peace, no rest. First came the members of the family . . . then the carpenter to measure her body . . . and still later the women to wash her and dress her in the burial robe.

The work on the farm continued as before.

The young life came pushing out of the ground. That could not wait, and every day it required proper care. The cattle also could not wait even a day. In this matter the two Wallingas were hard men.

People who enjoyed criticizing others made bold to discuss the hardness of Douwe and his son, and when those same people were certain that no one could hear them they said, "If a cow had died, or if one of the racing horses had been lost, you would have heard them lament, but now it is only his poor wife, who was slowly murdered."

That was indeed the way in which certain folk did talk about the death of Liesbeth, but it did not disturb the two Wallingas. They continued to plow, to disc and to milk, as if nothing of importance had happened.

Jouk and Janke performed their proper tasks as well as they could.

During the last evening Douwe and Ate sat together with Liesbeth. In the large room she lay in her casket. Ate was sitting in the kitchen reading a book, but he did not get far; Douwe was turning the pages of the newspaper.

Finally Douwe raised his head, looked at Ate and said, "This is the last evening that we are spending with her. If you wish, you can go with me." He rose and went to the room — the death chamber — and Ate followed him.

There they stood, father and son: Douwe, the father,

on one side of the casket, and Ate, the son, on the other, with Mother between them. Here she lay at rest. Her blue eyes were shut, and the long, fine lashes were spread over them like little curtains. The white, cold face seemed transparent.

Her hands lay folded on her breast.

The old clock stood still; the mirror was covered with a black cloth. In the glass cabinet were the prizes won by Wardy, Kol and Prince. The Golden Whip, though broken in pieces, shone in the feeble light that came from the lamp on the table.

It was then that Douwe spoke. "Ate," he said, "here lies your mother, the mistress of the Free Estate, and I, who was to have been the boer of the Free Estate, became no more than the slave of the Golden Whip! That will soon be over with, I hope."

"Will Dad never go racing again?" asked Ate.

Douwe looked at his wife and said, "I have sold the racing horses; Wardy is sold, the new horse is sold, Prince, all of them except Hisk. That was yours, and I hope that you will become a different whip winner than I. I hope that some day you will come home with the very highest prize, for I believe that you will do better with that than I."

Ate left the drawing room. In the kitchen, beside good, old Jouk, he slumped upon a chair, and, his head on the table, he cried a long time, convulsed with grief. Jouk got up, walked up to him, held his head and kept it close to her.

"My dear, dear boy," she said, "go on and cry. Your mother enjoys now the rest that she sought."

Such was the last evening.

The next morning the yard was filled with carriages. Relatives, friends, the pastor, the doctor — all had come to the funeral service in the farm home, where the minister spoke a few simple words of comfort to the bereaved husband and son.

At ten o'clock the old, bronze church bells of Hantum

began to toll, first one, then another, and then together and in turns, singing the Song of the Redemption.

They carried her coffin on a freshly-scrubbed farm wagon, and Keimpe, sitting on the bench, with Wardy pulling the cart, drove her to the church yard. From the Church Path she was borne by the men of "The Last Honor," held firmly upon their shoulders, and followed by her husband, son, relatives and friends, once, twice, three times around the church yard. And then, when the church bells and the people were silent, and only the heart spoke, Liesbeth was gently laid to rest in the earth.

For one solemn moment they stood there in profound silence, and then they returned without Liesbeth to the Free Estate, where a meal was served and the pastor led in prayer and read a chapter from the book of Job.

A month later one more tombstone was placed in the church yard, in the shade of the old tower. Several children were watching to see if the stone would be placed erect or laid flat. A suitable inscription mentioned the date of Liesbeth's birth, the name of her husband and the day of her departure from the joys and sorrows of this world. On numerous occasions friends and acquaintances paused and reflected on the vicissitudes of life. Who could have thought at the wedding of Douwe and Liesbeth that her life would have this sad ending? But one day, desperate in her sin, she had cried, "God, be merciful to me, a sinner," and He had answered. "Without shedding of blood is no remission" — the God of heaven was just — but there was also the mercy of the Saviour's promise, "Him that cometh to me I will in no wise cast out." Liesbeth had beheld "the Lamb of God, which taketh away the sin of the world," and, having believed in Him and accepted Him as her Saviour, had been born again and received life through His Name. In that certainty she had lived; in that certainty she had died. Now she had gone to that land where "they hunger no more, neither thirst any more. . . . For the Lamb which is in the midst of the throne shall feed them . . . . and God shall wipe away all tears from their eyes."

PART THREE

20

SUMMER! Midsummer! All day the glowing sunlight bathed the fields and pastures, bringing the warmth so greatly needed in northern Friesland. In the meadows the grass had turned to hay, and it was heaped in neat little piles, ready to be hauled to the barn. This meant hard work for the men from early morning till late at night.

When in the morning the sun peeped above the horizon, the workmen were busily engaged in their tasks. One could hear the familiar sounds of milk pails which had to be put on the milk wagon, the voices of people who were talking about the crops and the cattle, the lowing of the cows that were waiting anxiously for the milking, and among these sounds were the songs of hundreds of birds which hovered joyfully over woods and fields. The little lark seemed to express most perfectly the jubilation of the birds as it flew into the sky and sang, but no matter how high it soared, its pleasant music could still be heard plainly on the farm.

The men had to work so hard that in the evening their

backs smarted and crackled, and when a thunderstorm threatened, one man would have to do the work of three, lest the hay be spoiled by the rain. But such labor was good for man and beast.

Protected from the rays of the hot sun by a broad-brimmed straw hat, his shirt open and the sleeves rolled up, sweating, the workman toiled. He lost a little weight, but the sun tanned his skin, and to be a bit slender was not necessarily to be lame, for there was power in slender muscles.

On Sundays there was an atmosphere of peace and rest. No work was done in the fields, and on such a day Friesland was a veritable paradise. When one took a walk through the country he felt changed for the better, and wished those with too little courage or with bitterness in their hearts would take a stroll some Sunday afternoon through the fields and the pastures, particularly when the sun played a game of hide-and-seek with the clouds, throwing the shadows upon the land . . . light and shadow . . . light and shadow. . . .

This summer Ate Douwes was no longer his former self. He had grown to be a fine, strong young man, and he had acquired stability of body and mind. Jouk often thought that he would be a duplicate of Douwe. Like his father he carried his head erect. His deep blue eyes shone, and his curly hair refused to stay in place when he ran and laughed — and he laughed often. He had discovered that life outside the farm was also significant, that he must attain proper mental and physical growth, and so, like a young horse, he had entered the arena of life like a young horse. All doors were open to him, and life with all its charms and attractions absorbed him. Each day he experienced new wonders and delight.

Douwe let him have his way in everything. He made certain that Ate had enough money in his pocket, but otherwise he did nothing to check or encourage him.

A few times he had thought about Doutsen, particularly when the Heerema farm was put up for rent and the family moved to Leeuwarden. It was then that he remembered those long winter evenings spent in her company, but it was a fleeting recollection. There were plenty of other girls, and some of them were unusually pretty. There were many from whom he could choose. Where was the girl who could refuse him when he looked at her with his searching eyes and gave her his endearing smiles? He was as handsome a young man as any country could have produced, and his character was as strong and powerful as his body. But Ate did not want to start "steady company." To spend a pleasant evening at the fair, to embrace, to take a girl home, yes, but not to burn with emotion. Not that! Later, perhaps, but not now. When the time came for his father to retire he would look for a boer's daughter who had money, and he would marry her. Such had long been the custom among the Frisian boers.

How large a role would love play in such a transaction? Love? Well, that was a phenomenon exhibited when two young people were violently attracted to each other. Perhaps love might operate also in the lives of two persons who were united in matrimony for many years, and such cases it made little difference if they were together or not. But in Ate's opinion love was to take what you could get, even though you did not know where the girl had come from, but you must always be certain to derive some enjoyment from her company. He believed that one should rise above emotion, and he knew how to apply that ideal to life. He was a pleasant companion, but at all times he subordinated his emotions to his will and his reason.

The innkeepers were delighted with him, and the managers of the fairs and carnivals felt the same way about him, for he could always gather a crowd and keep them interested. The people of Dokkum would never forget the time of the annual fair when there was a small circus on the cattle market. Among the principal attractions was a donkey so contrary that nobody could remain seated on its back for more than a few minutes. The manager offered twenty guilders to anyone who could stay on the donkey for two rounds.

There were some twenty young folks and Ate had made a

bet with them that he would keep his seat for two rounds. When people heard about that bet there was hardly enough room in the tent for the crowd of spectators, and amidst great applause the donkey was led into the tent. Ate jumped confidently on its back. How could he who had tamed Hisk and had mastered the wildest of horses fail to control a mere donkey? But in a few seconds he was sprawling in the sawdust with his legs in the air. Immediately he jumped on the donkey again, and once more with the same result. The crowd was wild with amusement.

Finally Ate became furious, and he said to the manager, "Man, don't stand there laughing like a fool. Who can ride such a rattling skeleton of a donkey? Give me the meanest, wildest horse you can find and I'll show you what riding really is."

The manager laughed heartily. He detected more free advertising, and he whispered into the ear of his stable servant. Then he informed the audience that this gentleman was not satisfied with the blue spot on his back and legs and that he desired to break also a few ribs or a leg.

People shrieked with delight, urging the manager to show his horse forthwith. But he was not yet through with his oration. "We have among our prized animals a young horse which has never been broken in. I make a bet with this gentleman for the sum of twenty-five guilders that he won't be able to remain on that horse for more than five minutes." There was an ominous silence.

Some of the people were afraid that this foolish young chap would be hurt badly, and a few of his companions warned him. But he paid no attention to their well-meant advice. The musicians began to play wildly and vociferously. The spectators were in a state of great tension. Yes, there came the horse!

Two men were holding the animal tightly, and the manager walked behind it. The horse was a mare, red-brown with white legs; her eyes were a bit sharp, but Ate saw no sign of meanness in them. The circus director, wearing a long coat and a rose in his lapel, presented the horse and made a formal bow. Then he invited Ate to mount her. Ate did not even bother to look at him but walked directly to the horse, peered into its eyes, stroked its neck and felt the veins under the skin. Immediately he said to the servants, "Let her go!" With one jump the young man leaped on the horse's back.

The musicians were silent, and the spectators did not move. They all sat spellbound, watching intently the struggle between horse and rider. The two were perfect strangers, and each was eager to win the victory. At first they raced beyond human control. The boy was white, his blond hair disheveled, his muscles taut.

The servants, drivers and artists stood in the path that led from the circus to the stables, and they watched the extraordinary spectacle with marked interest. During the first few minutes they joked and laughed, fully convinced that this clumsy boer would lose the contest. But the longer he rode the better he exercised his control over the unruly mare. After having tried all his tricks he finally became involved in a mighty struggle. The horse galloped, jumped, kicked and danced excitedly, but Ate emerged as the victor, and during his ride of honor which followed the contest the spectators shouted with glee and the musicians played vigorously. It was an unforgettable sight.

Ate dismounted and the servants took charge of the horse. The director showed his amazement and admitted his defeat. He said, "Young man, I take off my hat to you. That is riding indeed! After this I shall have more respect for the young boers of Friesland. For more than forty years I have managed horses, and I must say that you have performed the work of a supreme expert in the field." He shook Ate's hand as if the young man were an old friend. Gladly he offered Ate the money, but the victorious youth refused to accept it.

"You can keep that, for I am no beggar. But hereafter you had better respect the young boers of Friesland. Not alone you but also we here in Friesland have been brought up among the horses, and we love them." Then Ate went to his friends, and that evening they celebrated the gayest night of any fair in Dokkum.

Late that evening Ate took Beth home, the girl he had met one day in Janke's company when they were both working in the field on his farm. Beth was far from bashful; she enjoyed Ate's company immensely. He was hilarious that night and the girl was fascinated by his gay laughter and winning personality.

Douwe let his son go his own way. Sometimes he heard from others reports about his lively escapades, and he thought, "That boy certainly is getting fun out of his young life." But he never discussed this subject with his son. He was happy to observe that Ate had finally overcome his melancholy dreaming after Liesbeth's death. Douwe spent hours and hours in the evening looking over old papers, and when he grew tired of that chatted with Jouk, who had talked about leaving but never did. Although they had not discussed the subject she had become his housekeeper, and Janke had remained as maid.

But it did not take long to exhaust the range of subjects that he and Jouk could discuss. She refused to talk about things that concerned only herself, and she was afraid to mention his affairs. She had enough to do with the housework, and she cared for Ate as if she were his mother. She was always awake when Ate came home at night, no matter how late he was. Faithfully she kept his clothes in order and constantly, although Ate himself was unaware of her diligence, she darned and mended.

Deep in her heart she kept alive the recollection of the mistress and often she thought as she worked, *For you, mistress . . . for you. . . .*

She watched Ate always with great care, and in attempting to discover his associates she exercised ingenuity. Ate often told her far more than he had intended, but the affair with Beth he did not relate, for he could not be proud of it. Beth had not been satisfied with one evening of his time. She had cleverly induced him to ask her to accompany him the next evening on a walk.

Beth had a multitude of grand plans. In her imagination she saw Ate as the boer and herself as his wife. She was so immersed in these thoughts that she could not refrain from communicating some of them to Janke. But poor Janke had to bite her lips in order not to burst into tears; she must under no circumstances let anyone know her feelings toward Ate. . . . In all those years there had never been room in her heart for anyone except Ate. It was always he who occupied her thoughts. She did not recall when first those feelings had begun, but it seemed likely that they had started at the very beginning when they had been in the first grade at school. Since that time they had increased in strength and clarity, although now she did not even have the courage to greet him. And now he was to go out with Beth. . . . Was not that enough to make her shriek? She realized fully what Beth wished to accomplish, and she knew also that Beth was not at all concerned about how she attained her end.

Every day Janke was on the farm, and at night she went home. The boer had objected to her going home, but she had insisted that she must sleep at home. That she had to spend the whole of each day with Douwe was bad enough, and at night she wanted to be elsewhere. Eagerly she longed each evening for her little bed with the red and white pillows and the straw mattress.

Ate once more showered fiery kisses upon a sweetheart, but the one he had now was dangerous. She felt no affection for him, and sought to lead him to his doom with hypocritical words and actions. Her eager mouth and eyes nearly enchanted him, and each evening she felt certain that the moment of victory had come. While he was consumed with physical pleasure she planned and plotted with her eyes wide open. Well did she know how many men in a few minutes of folly lost a fortune or an entire life of married bliss. But each evening had the same ending. Ate never took the fatal step, much to her amazement and chagrin.

She, who believed that she had bewitched Ate, finally came to the conclusion that he was as wide awake as herself. Finally she asked him the question: "How are we getting along now, Ate? Are we engaged, yes or no?"

Ate had been looking up at the sky, filled with sparkling stars. He heard Beth talking, but he did not pay serious attention to her words, for his thoughts were far away.

"Ate," she asked again, and she put her head close to his and acted as if she were deeply in love with him. "Ate, tell me, dear, aren't we really engaged to each other by this time?" Ate looked perplexed and replied, "Do you see all those stars in the sky? Don't they look at us as if they want to tell us something? You are asking me if our relationship is satisfactory. It could not be better, Beth."

But she was not so philosophically inclined as her friend, and stoically she pursued her aim. "Those stars can blow themselves to pieces as far as I am concerned. I want to know where you and I stand. You can understand that we cannot go on like this much longer. Are you coming Sunday evening?" She awaited his answer with much anxiety.

Ate, half confused, looked at her and said, "No, Beth. Get that idea out of your head. I visit the daughter of one of our workmen? No, that would not do. Dad would soon put an end to that!"

That was true. His father would fight to frustrate such a romance.

Once more Ate spoke. "Get that idea out of your head." He tried to pull her closer to him. But now her real intentions were quickly made manifest. Jumping up like a veritable little demon, she shouted at him. "So that's what you wanted with me — to be your plaything. You, young boer, had to have a toy to play with, and you thought that as soon as you were through with me you could cast me aside. But that won't be so easy, boy, as I'll show you, conceited pup that you are." Ate wanted to help her assume a more reasonable attitude; he felt that perhaps he had gone a little too far with the girl, and he said soothingly, "Beth, girl, listen a minute. Come, sit here and let's talk this thing over a while." But Beth refused to accede to his wishes.

"You big bully, do you think you can do anything you please with a girl like me? Others might let you go ahead, but I am not in that cheap class. You must not imagine that you have Janke here at your side. She would be delighted to fall on her knees and scrub the spot made dirty by your feet, but I was not built that way. And I tell you once and for all, if you won't come to my house as is proper under the present circumstances, I shall take my leave."

Janke, thought Ate. *Janke. What makes her say that? I was just thinking about her. How could she know that?*

But he had to make a suitable reply. What was she saying? Oh, yes, she wanted him to come to her house. "No, girl," he answered. "I have no intention of coming to your place Sunday evening." Beth rose. She was so angry that the tears sprang from her eyes, but she did not want to have that fact noticed. Quickly she must speak her mind and leave him. So she said bitterly, "Then I am through with you for good. Good-bye." With tired legs she walked away and with each step she held her breath to hear if perchance he was following her. When she failed to discern any sign of such action on his part, she turned to look at him. There he was, lying in the same position as before, his hands under his head, his legs crossed.

A diabolical hatred had mastered her, and she wanted to seek revenge for her failure. The thought of scratching his eyes out occurred to her, but fortunately she was able to control the impulse. She walked all the way home without further pause, and she refused to spend more time and energy thinking about her misfortune. What would be the use? Nothing would be gained by that.

A few minutes before, when Ate and Beth were still

together and Ate was looking at the sky, he had begun to think about Janke. How that had happened he did not recall now, and yet he did, for this afternoon she was singing, "Do you know how many stars are cleaving to the firmament?" But wasn't it strange that Beth also was thinking about Janke when she realized suddenly how hopeless her position was? Was it so remarkable that he saw her pretty little face in front of him again? "Janke . . . she would be delighted to fall on her knees and scrub the spot made dirty by your feet." He sat up, and everything became plain. Janke's bashfulness in his presence, her blushing, her refusal to talk to him when he entered the room — these assumed another color. He decided to make love to Janke and make her as affectionate with him as Beth had been a moment ago. But did he really desire her to be as Beth was — a girl without love? No, not that at all. What was he to do? If Janke were any other girl he would forthwith go to her and see how quickly she could be won. He decided to wait and try other means at his disposal.

When he entered the yard of the Free Estate everything was still and peaceful. In the living room was Jouk; the servant was in the village, and Dad was attending a meeting.

He sat near Jouk and drank the tea she had poured for him. With a loud bang he put down the cup and asked suddenly, "Jouk, why is Janke always so quiet?"

Jouk looked at him cautiously and wondered what was behind that peculiar question.

"That Janke is quiet must be known only to you," she replied, "for all I know is that she is a pleasant and affable girl, although I am of the opinion" — and Ate felt that she was talking for effect upon his state of mind — "that she is not so silly as to fall into the arms of any young chap that came along."

Ate thought that idea so amusing and so timely that he remarked, "Thank you, Jouk, for that dig of yours."

"I did not mean you, Ate," she said, but he made a gesture

of denial and added, "Let it be that way, Jouk. It might have been intended for me, and that would have been to the point."

"So then it was a direct hit, though I had not meant it that way at all." She laughed.

"Jouk, we should talk about Janke a while. Tell me something about her."

"Well," she observed, "How queer! She is here all day long, and you want some information about her. Are you blind perhaps?"

"Not exactly, but a person sometimes looks too far afield, Jouk. From now on I want to pay closer attention to her."

"Perhaps I could give you a little hint. She likes everybody around here, but she is scared to death of you!"

"Is that so? Well, I am not afraid of her, and one of these days I'll take a good look into her eyes."

21

So Ate opened fire upon Janke.

He tried to shadow her, and to find her alone in places where nobody would see them, but no matter how ingenious he was, she seemed to understand his aim and ran from him. Could it be true that she really was afraid of him? But that did not harmonize with the words spoken by Beth.

Or could it be that she was putting on an act to deceive him? *Of all things!* thought Ate. What a vain little miss she was, what a choosy princess, who could look at one as if he were made of thin air and turned her head as she were the proprietor of the entire place. The daughter of a workman — and proud!

But that would all be changed as soon as he approached her in the right manner. The more he thought about her the more eagerly he turned in circles around her, condemning himself for his folly and yet drawing ever closer to her. And his desire increased.

Janke knew it and she could feel it, and she had to control

herself for fear that she might shout with joy, now that after
so many years of patient waiting her boy was looking for
her. But Janke could not and would not respond, for she
remembered the remark made so recently by Beth, "And now,
girl, he will go after you, but look out for that fellow. If
there was anyone who was crazy about me it was Ate Douwes.
But now we are through, and you can easily guess why that is
the case. When the men cannot have their way they are
through with us." Janke rehearsed in her mind the unpleasant
truth about Ate's affair with her own friend Beth. She would
have to be careful and not reveal too soon her affection for
the young man.

One morning in late summer, just after coffee time, Ate
had something to do in the living room. His father was in
the village and Jouk was preparing lunch. As Ate walked
through the hall he was thinking of trivial affairs, not of
Janke. He opened the door, and he saw Janke in the middle
of the room on her knees cleaning the floor. She was beautiful
in the golden glow of the sunlight.

He did not realize just what was going through his mind,
but before Janke had had time to get off the floor he was
beside her and threw his arms around her.

"Janke," he said. "Janke."

He did not know what he was doing; he was yielding to
an impulse from within. He pressed her hard against his body
and looked at her. He could say only "Janke, Janke."

In a brief moment of emotion she left herself go, as if
she were experiencing the joy of knowing that at last that
long waiting was over — those dozen long years of her young
life. But her surrender was brief. Suddenly she fought against
him, against herself and against her love, and she tried to
break loose. But Ate refused to let her go.

"You little, proud princess," he muttered. "Are you going
to run away from me all the time? And must I run after
you some more?"

"Ate, look here, I don't want to; I'll call people." She

thought she had been shouting, but her voice had been extremely feeble. She felt that she was loosing this battle, for he was much the stronger of the two; and he pressed her still harder against his powerful frame and laughed triumphantly. He was trembling with desire, and he did not know what he was saying.

"For such a long time I have been waiting for you, my darling, and I will kiss you. I will kiss you until you don't know where your mind is. I will . . ." and with his free hand he lifted her head. But as he was searching for her mouth he saw suddenly, though her eyes were closed, large, warm tears rolling down. Those tears were running down her cheeks and were falling on his hand. This was too powerful for him, something against which he could fight neither with his body nor his mind. He looked at them . . . one, two, three . . . and he lost all sense of reality. Then he whispered, and there was nothing left of his triumph. "Janke, why are you crying? Tell me, dear. . . ."

For a few minutes he was in a daze. Every concrete thing had lost its value for him. Time, the world and all things around him were swallowed up in this new experience which was altogether beyond his control and totally unpremeditated. Then Janke lifted her head and looked at him — and hardly had Ate taken one look when he saw in her eyes the same lakes of blue as he had seen many times — lakes without bottom, unending in depth. He gasped. "Mother's eyes."

"Janke," he said, "I did not know that. I did not know that." And he let her go. As if looking for support, he leaned against the table. He had turned his head toward the window, and he looked over the fields. "Please forgive me, girl," he stammered, and then he slowly left the room, his head bent as if he were ashamed of himself.

For a little while Janke remained standing in the middle of the room, wondering what she should do, but then she followed him, as if in response to some inner urge. "Did I cause you any pain?" she asked in a soft voice. "Ate, tell me."

She offered him her hand. Did she want to hold him back? She did not know what she was doing; she seemed to be controlled by certain invisible forces that guided her through difficult places in her life. But he reacted queerly to her tender gesture. As if stung to the quick he turned and said, "You? You? Say, what do you think of yourself and of me? You cause me pain? No, don't you believe that!" As if to show her how little this meant to him he walked back into the room and sat in the big oak chair in front of the cabinet containing the prizes.

Janke went away, and when he saw her no more the tension under which he labored disappeared. He sat there like a child, and he looked around as if a strange feeling had overpowered him — a feeling which he had never known. He tried to analyze his surrender to this mysterious force. It had come to him like a mighty revelation. Like an open book his whole life now lay before him, and a marvelous feeling of jubilation came over him. "Dear God," he mumbled, "this feeling, this glorious feeling, has always been there."

Memories came to him, scenes out of the dim past, days, weeks, months and years ago, and that feeling for Janke hallowed every scene, that feeling which thus far he had always given another name. He relived those scenes, and in each was Janke. Like a flame of fire it burned through his mind, warming and beneficent, permeating his entire being, so that he would never be able to flee from it.

Then came days of exhilaration for both Ate and Janke. She also could not fathom the ties that had bound them together for so many years. One evening Janke felt Ate's strong arms around her, and she lost herself in this ecstasy.

Jouk, old, faithful Jouk, knew it. She whose sole aim in life had been to care for Liesbeth's son — she knew it. She rejoiced in this love of Ate and Janke, but at the same time a foreboding of future trouble came to her. She did everything in her power to prevent Douwe from discovering her new secret. She knew well that if the young people were in earnest they would face a great danger — Douwe Ates. Far from approving of this love he would do all he could to break it. Jouk was certain that this which seemed so true and noble would become a source of enmity between Dad and Ate.

In these glorious days of late summer, in which it had become difficult for the young people to hide their love from Douwe, Jouk knew that they were often together, and she knew also that Ate went frequently to the Soberhoek. As the evenings grew longer she sat by the hour with Douwe and discussed with him a variety of subjects, most of which concerned the management of the farm. But not for a moment did she forget the fact that the young folk were doing something most repugnant to her employer. She felt as if she were deceiving him.

During the following winter she could no longer hide the secret from Douwe. He, who never suspected anything of this sort, was told about it by an acquaintance of his. One evening during a meeting of the Ice Club at the inn, when Douwe was sitting near the stove, a man came to him and said, "Douwe Ates, what do I hear about your son Ate? Has it gone far enough?" Douwe misunderstood the nature of the subject, but he could feel that something unpleasant was about to be revealed which he did not wish to hear. He replied that he need not turn to others to discover what his son was doing. He would first ask his own boy. "Well," continued his friend, "perhaps you will have to get the information from your workman." That remark disturbed Douwe considerably, but he did not wish to show his anxiety, and so he continued the conversation with the other boers. But he could not forget those words about his workman.

On his way home he constantly reviewed the scene in the inn, where several of his friends had laughed at him and asked him embarrassing questions about his boy and the workman. There must be something wrong, for else these men would not have sat there and made fun of him.

Immediately after he reached home he asked Jouk for information. "Jouk, have you noticed anything lately about Ate that I ought to know?" He wanted to add "something wrong," but he did not dare to do that. Jouk looked at him, and suddenly she got the impression that he knew everything. She asked him, "How is that, boer?"

"Well," replied Douwe, "why do you ask me that? I was asking you a question, for I was looking for information." These words showed plainly that the boer did not know the whole truth. She began cautiously. "Well, boer, I believe that Ate is engaged again if that is what you mean."

"Then it is that . . . ." But he got no further. What did it matter if Ate rode a few evenings with Keimpe's daughter? That was not worth worrying about. He continued to look at Jouk. This was an insignificant affair, he concluded, no worse than that between Ate and Beth.

Jouk finally could not stand it any more, that funny stare of his, and she said, "Why are you staring at me so?" "That I don't know," he replied, "except it be that I was thinking about your position here. You are always worrying about Ate, aren't you?"

"True," answered Jouk, "and I have plenty of reason for that."

"Then," observed Douwe, "you might tell him that he had better stop taking out the daughter of my workman Keimpe!" After those words he went to bed immediately.

Jouk was afraid. She surmised that Douwe knew everything. She was waiting for Ate, but still she did not wish to mention the matter that soon. Gradually she would point out to him the danger of his course of action, but not yet . . . .

The two young people were walking home together, Janke and Ate. They did not realize that the world was preparing to give them condemnation, ridicule, contempt. They did not feel the cold air about them; there was for them only whispered words of love which did not go farther than the ear for which they were intended: "I love you, I love you." They repeated them often, those simple words, but always they were precious.

Millions of stars hung like jewels in the sky, and each was so large that it made one marvel. All around them was the winter scene, with the purifying frost. And upon the earth were these two small persons made great through love.

Ate finally said, "Tomorrow I am going to explain it all to Dad."

"No, Ate," she remarked, "not yet, not yet." She felt as if that would mean the end of her happiness.

"Why not, Janke?" asked Ate. "I love you and have always loved you, and I may not keep that a secret from Dad. He shall and must know that you belong to me."

"Well, boy, that will never do. Your father will never approve of it that I, the daughter of your workman . . . . It's not right, either, I know it." Here eyes were full of tears. "It's not right what we are doing. You had better go away . . . ."

Ate stood still and turned Janke so that she was directly in front of him. "Look at me," he said, "straight into my eyes. So, that way. And now I'll ask you a question. Is there nothing, nothing in the world of which you are more fond?"

At first she said nothing, but then she spoke.

"Ate, I have loved you so long, you don't know how long, and I will never belong to anybody else. But, boy, I know that this will mean a lot of worry and misery for you, and for that reason it is better that we separate."

"No, Janke, I don't want to do that. I have found you, too late perhaps, but I am not going to let you go again, even if I have to encounter Dad . . . ." "Keep still," said Janke, and she laid her hand on his mouth. "Don't say it. Don't say it . . . ."

Neither of them could realize how close Ate had come to the truth. Filled with thoughts of their love and of each other, they walked farther down the path to the Soberhoek.

But at the Free Estate on the big bed in his bedroom lay Douwe Ates, and time after time he remembered those words about Ate and his workman. No matter how he tried, he could not get rid of them.

Like a dark shadow they hovered over him. A terrible

threat menaced him, and he was lonely. Liesbeth was no longer there, Liesbeth with her soft eyes. Her dear hand could not care for him any more. Her soothing words could help him no more. All of that was past.

His beautiful horses were also gone, and there was no more racing. What was still worse, Ate was a small source of comfort to him in his declining years. He was fond of the boy, more than he cared to tell him; his boy who was around him all day long but nevertheless lived his own life, reading books, going to meetings, having seemingly no time left to talk with his father about things that concerned them jointly.

Could it be possible that he was keeping company with the daughter of a common laborer? He hoped not, but if it were true, and both were serious about it, he would be obliged to put an end to the whole affair.

That night Keimpe and Auk also could not sleep. They were talking about the same subject that perplexed Douwe Ates, and they also were deeply worried.

Keimpe had said, "The engagement between Janke and Ate must come to an end. You can figure out on your fingers that nothing can come of it, Janke and the son of a gentleman farmer." At first Auk had become angry. "Our girl is worth no less than any other girl." But she began to realize that Keimpe was right after all. The big question did not concern the worth of Janke but the relation between Douwe and his son.

Keimpe continued. "You must not think that Ate is in earnest, and if he were it would mean a quarrel between Dad and him. No, no, it is causing me a lot of worry, you will see."

Keimpe had been correct, for the following morning, while they were threshing oats, Janke walked through the hall of the threshing house and said, "Dad, Dad, you must come to the boer in the living room!"

"I to the boer?" he asked in surprise, but Janke was gone again, and Keimpe detected serious danger. "There you have it," he said to himself. "Now we are in for it." And he walked through the cow stable to the house.

Douwe was waiting for him and said, "I must have a talk with you first."

"Yes, boer," said Keimpe, and he seated himself.

"How long have you been with us, Keimpe?"

"In May it will be twenty-one years," he replied.

"Twenty-one years. Yes, that is a long time, Keimpe, and we have been able to get along fine, haven't we?"

"As far as I know we have indeed."

"Yes," observed Douwe, "and until now there has been nothing to mar our pleasant relationship. Until now. You understand? Now there is something between us that I don't like at all."

"The boer means perhaps . . . ." Keimpe wanted to make it easier for Douwe to discuss the embarrassing subject. But Ate's father, making a gesture to stop him, continued to speak. "I know what you want to say. It is about the children; yes, that's what it is. I have heard, Keimpe, that my son and your daughter are together a great deal. They take walks, go out riding and do other things; isn't that it, Keimpe?"

"Yes," he answered. That was true, of course. The boy was out often with Janke, and frequently he had been at their house on the Soberhoek. "Yes, boer, that is true."

"Very well, then," remarked Douwe. "Now we can quickly finish our business. Your daughter will be dismissed today, and we shall get another maid. And you must take care that this relation between Ate and Janke comes to an immediate end. How you do it is your own affair. I need not say any more, except this, that unless you do at once as I say you lose your position here and the house you are occupying must be vacated by your family. That is all!"

Keimpe was crushed completely by these cruel words, and in his heart he felt a desire to do something foolish. *What a bully,* he thought, and he tried to find utterance for his wrath by striking the threshing floor with all his might as he threshed the oats.

22

IN THE MEANTIME Ate and Janke still had no idea of what was in store for them and their parents. Completely oblivious of their environment, they had taken another long walk that evening. Even Janke had not observed any change in her father's attitude. But when Ate had taken her to the door the news came like a clap of thunder.

As she entered the little room, she saw her father sitting at the table, which had never been his custom. He had taken off his shirt and vest. His wife was sitting under the lamp, darning socks.

"Good evening," greeted Janke. "Has Dad not yet gone to bed?"

"No," answered Keimpe. "He has not yet gone to bed."

"Well," she laughed, "that should be mentioned in the paper."

But as she took off her coat the thought occurred to her that he must have been waiting for her. She remembered the message she had brought him that morning. "Dad must come to the boer in the living room." So now it was going to happen, the dreadful and inevitable thing that would end her happiness with Ate. She could not run from it . . . .

She sat on her chair, and there she waited for the unwelcome news. At first there was a long silence, and then she remarked, "You might as well tell me." Her face was white, and she fingered her dress nervously. Keimpe began, "You probably know what I have to say." "Yes," she replied. "That is fine. The boer asked me this morning how long I had worked here for him. I said it had been twenty-one years. That was a long time, and now, now," for a moment he halted, "now he has dismissed me from his services, and he has fired you, and next week we'll have to leave this house as well. That is your fault, Janke."

"Dismissed? No, that is not true, is it?" she asked. "Yes," affirmed Keimpe, "it is a fact. The boer has taken quick and drastic action. Janke, Janke, you could have figured on your fingers that it would have ended this way."

"So," said Janke in a shrill voice, "so I may not return to the farm, and Dad is discharged? Oh, but that is terrible!" "Yes," insisted Keimpe, "it is terrible, but there is one way out of our difficulty, if you are willing to make a sacrifice for us and understand what your duty is. I can keep my job if you and Ate give up your courtship. You don't have to say anything at once, and tomorrow morning will be soon enough, but remember that your father's job and our whole living depend upon your choice. No matter how hard I should try, I see no chance in the middle of the winter to get another job from any boer. That is what I wanted to tell you, and now I am going to bed. The boer will talk this evening with Ate."

He rose slowly. Then he removed his socks and his stockings. Next he chased the cat from the chair in front of the bed and disappeared behind the doors. He still had something else to say, but when he saw Janke sitting there in profound misery he did not have the heart to add to her sorrow. "It's hard," he mumbled, but a few minutes later he was fast asleep.

Janke did not know what to say. It was useless to talk. Alone with Ate she could say, "I love you," but here in her humble abode it would be mockery.

"Well, Janke," her mother asked, "what are you going to do about it?"

"Break it up," she answered in a voice so soft that her mother could hardly hear her. There was something cold and resigned about her and it was pathetic to behold. She began to take off her clothes, and at the touch of each button she asked herself the same question over and over again: "What is going to happen to Ate?" She knew his father well, his drinking and racing of the past years, particularly the history of the Golden Whip. As she lay in her little bed she wondered about his next move, and her heart was grieved. What if something terrible had happened this evening? That would be her fault perhaps.

"Ate," she whispered, "why must I love you so much?" She had to bury her head in the pillow to prevent her parents from hearing her cry.

Janke had also discovered that love is not only sunshine . . .

Ate had walked through the fields to his home. His love had made him feel strong and energetic, and he was determined not to wait longer to tell Douwe his great secret. That would have to wait until tomorrow, for his father had no doubt by this time have gone to bed. It was ten o'clock. All was quiet in the yard, and he walked softly to the small barn door, which was standing open. He hung up his skates and went through the hall to the cow stable. In the kitchen he found the coffee on the light as usual and his sandwich on a plate next to it. Carefully he pulled off his shoes in order not to awaken Jouk, but when he put them behind the bench he heard a voice. It was Jouk, who whispered from her bed, "Ate, you must go to your dad."

"Is Dad not yet in bed?"

"No, he is waiting for you, but first you must eat your sandwich."

"Then let me go at once," said Ate, and he went to the

door. He heard Jouk say, "I'll stay awake, boy." By this time he was in the hall.

Jouk not only remained fully awake, but she opened the door wide, for she was not going to tolerate another whipping in this house. If something of that sort threatened again, she would come between the two, no matter how proud that boer was.

Ate opened the door of the room. On the threshold he stood still for a moment and looked. Yes, there sat Dad in the big oak chair in front of the cabinet containing the prizes. He held his head erect, and his eyes looked coldly at Ate, who detected in them something sinister and menacing.

The mantle clock ticked methodically as the seconds passed swiftly, and the cabinet seemed bathed in a golden glow. The massive table, decorated at each corner with a carved cow, was bare. Above the mantel on the ledge, were the six blue plates of expensive Makkum porcelain, and below the mantel was the modern fireplace, the somber black of which was relieved by nickel knobs.

In the cabinet hung the whips, and above it were the portraits of Kol and Wardy. To the right stood the porcelain cabinet filled with old china.

Ate saw all of this with one comprehensive glance, and then he asked, "Did Dad want to talk with me about something?"

"Yes," said Douwe, "I have been waiting for you. Sit here." He pointed to a chair close to him.

Ate entered the room, and it seemed to him as if that cold feeling of a little while ago had vanished. "I can hear it just as well standing up, Dad."

"That is up to you," said Douwe. "Remain standing then." He was seeking a suitable topic with which to start his oration, and he was surprised to hear Ate say, in order to expedite matters for Dad, "It must be about my courtship with Janke, I believe?"

The hot words sprang from Douwe's mouth "Courtship,

courtship? If you call that going around with the daughter of Keimpe a courtship, very well, that is the subject I had in mind."

"That is exactly what I had wanted to discuss with Dad right now. So that is fine." And Douwe thought, *Look at him standing there, so cold and proud.*

"Yes, boy, this is the situation. During the past year you have been indulging in some wild escapades, and I shall be the last to make a complaint about those. You are no longer a child and a person must know that he is alive, but the last few months you have gone a bit too far, and I would like to know what your intentions are regarding Janke. People see you two together almost every day, skating at night, walking together whenever you can, going to her house, as if you were actually engaged. That must not continue."

"Why not?" asked Ate.

"Because you are a son of mine," replied Douwe. "You are not to ruin your career by keeping company with the daughter of a common laborer. That's why I have been sitting here waiting for you. I am anxious to see you stop it."

So, Douwe thought, *that's that.* Now it was Ate's duty to speak, and he did not need much time for reflection.

Calmly, almost too calmly, Ate said, "Janke and I are in earnest."

"Nonsense," observed Douwe. "Come, come, don't use such fine words, boy." But he was not certain of himself. "Those are not fine words, Dad. Every evening I have wanted to talk to you about this, but each time something prevented me from finding you alone. Janke and I love each other, and tomorrow I want to talk to Keimpe about it."

"I have done that already," boomed Douwe suddenly. "And you be quiet. Let me have the first say," he added as he saw Ate wanted to interrupt him. "I have fully discussed this matter with Keimpe, here in this same room. And do you know what I told him? No, you don't know that, so listen to me. If he does not persuade Janke, whom I discharged today, to give you up, they will have to leave their house within one week and Keimpe will be fired, after having worked here for more than twenty years. Do you hear, that's what I told him, and as sure as I live I'll carry out that order. We shall see what weighs more heavily with the girl, her flirtation with you or the welfare of her parents. I would be surprised to see you put her father out into the cold of winter without a job."

Those words struck Ate. He looked at Dad and asked, "Would Dad do that sort of thing? Oh, yes, those are fine words about feelings of honor for Janke, but she won't do it. Janke won't make her dad lose his job and his home. It isn't she who will do it but *my* dad, my own dad! To fire a workman and chase him out of his home like a dog, after he has worked here for more than twenty years, because his daughter and the son of the boer are keeping company — that is a mean trick, I think!"

Gone was his calmness. The blood ran to his head, and his hands were formed into fists. There he stood defying his father.

Douwe rose and stood directly in front of the boy. "You shrimp," he shouted, "what, are you going to tell me that I would chase somebody away like a dog? The man would receive compensation. But we must put a stop to this thing. Are you ready to give up this girl, yes or no?"

Like the peal of a church bell came his answer. "No, Dad, she remains mine, forever!"

Jouk was listening sharply, for she had to find out how this contest would end. She was afraid, but Douwe was able to control himself, and she heard him say, "No, no? So you don't perceive how that girl through underhanded means is trying to worm herself into this place? Are you letting yourself get bewitched by a pair of lovely eyes, you nitwit? Man, I have to laugh about that." But Jouk, who had heard every word, thought, *He is lying. To shout and to break things to pieces — that is more his style.* Then she heard Ate say, "Janke has the very same eyes as Mother . . . ." "That's true," murmured

Jouk. "You dear boy, that is true." But Douwe fumed, "That does us little good, even if she had the eyes of . . . of . . ." He was so angry that his words would not flow coherently. "I forbid you to marry a girl of a workman."

Ate was still standing before him, and Douwe realized that he was a true Wallinga, which meant that he would rather die than yield to anyone. Yes, he would go straight ahead, even if something broke to pieces.

"Then," replied Ate, "I have a few more things to say. As true as it is that Mother in that last evening stood here between us, so true it is that I shall never give up Janke. And if Dad, who loved Mother so much, does not understand that a person does not say such a thing without knowing why and that such a feeling does not ask who you are and who I am, then Dad had better do some thinking about it!" Then, breathing deeply, he added emphatically, "If Keimpe is being sent from this farm and from this house on the Soberhoek, then somebody else will also leave."

Without waiting for a reply he went to the door, opened it and was about to leave the room. As he took one more look he observed that Dad, who was sitting in the chair he had occupied before, did not look the same. Ate was waiting now, but for what he did not know, and Douwe said, "Ate, boy, would you leave me alone? Would you then . . . ." But as if ashamed of these words, he changed his manner. Why did Ate want to go away? He had said what he wanted to say, and was that not enough? Ate came a step closer to Dad and remarked, "If Janke said to me, and not to Dad or to Keimpe, that she no longer loves me, all would be finished." But happily he added, "Sooner than that the Free Estate would sink into the ground."

He left the room and went to the kitchen, where coffee and a sandwich were still waiting for him, and like a hungry wolf he devoured them. This fighting had given him a ravenous appetite. The first blow had fallen, and what would come next?

Jouk had taken one more look through the doors of her

bed, but when she saw how calmly he was sitting there, she let her head rest peacefully on her pillow.

In the big room Douwe was still seated, and he continued to look at the spot where his son had stood so haughtily before him. He recalled those brave words which made him feel both proud and sad. A workman's daughter had bewitched the boy, and for good — that was the worst of it. He still heard those words vibrating through the room . . . . "Then somebody else will also leave . . . . Janke has the same eyes as Mother." Yes, the eyes of Mother. But must he lose Ate because of such a trifling coincidence?

He rose and began to walk back and forth through the room. A feeling of loneliness came over him. The proud owner of all this property, who ruled the farm like a king, who knew what he wanted and always carried through his plans, now seemed sadly forsaken. For a long time Ate could hear him walking, pacing the floor and wondering about the future.

The next morning, in the cow stable, Ate rehearsed again and again the events of the previous evening. Regardless of his efforts to think about something else, he did not succeed, for the all-absorbing theme of his young life was still his love for Janke. He wanted to do this particularly because he felt sorry for his father. Perhaps he should not have talked to him as he had done the previous evening, but what else could he have said? He thought, *Our love is stronger than a whole farm, stronger than anything in the whole world!*

When he and Keimpe were giving the calves water to drink, he said to Keimpe, "Last evening I talked with Dad about Janke and myself. Dad had also talked with you, hadn't he?"

"Yes, boy, we waited for Janke."

"The same thing happened at our place," related Ate. "Dad was waiting for me, and I tell you, Keimpe, it went hard against hard. And how did it go in your house? Didn't Janke look surprised when she found you still sitting at the table?"

"Yes, that is true. But, Ate, when she heard what your father had said to me, she nearly died."

"Oh, well," suggested Ate, "you must bear in mind that Dad is that way; he barks more than he bites."

"That may be, boy, but," and at this moment Keimpe had to restrain an unruly calf, "I did insist that. . . ."

"What did you do, Keimpe?" Ate put his hand on Keimpe's shoulder and continued. "You did not tell her that she should give me up, did you?"

"No, she said that herself. 'I'll write him,' she said, and then. . . ." Ate looked as if someone had struck him a blow in the face, and when Keimpe saw how Ate reacted to those fateful words, he said, almost gently, "Listen, boy, you must not take it ill of me, but it is for you both much better that you break this thing up. I like you very much, Ate, that you know, and my wife and I would be happy if you could have each other, but take my advice and stop at this point. You will heap a world of misery upon yourself if you don't give each other up. You people of the Free Estate don't marry workmen's daughters."

"You are right, Keimpe, you are right," he admitted, "but I must ask you one more question. Did Janke on her own account say that she would write me, or did you persuade her to take that step? Tell the truth, man." And as Keimpe was about to answer him, he said, "You might perhaps. . . ." But he could go no farther. Putting down his pail, he ran without stopping to the Soberhoek.

Douwe was standing in front of a window in the stable, and he watched Ate running; he disappeared, and then he was climbing a wall. *Stupid boy,* he thought, *stupid Ate. Will you never believe?* Then to Keimpe, who, confused, was coming his way, "Let him run, Keimpe. He will soon get calmer. He who will not listen must feel pain."

You bully, thought Keimpe.

Through the frozen fields Ate ran to the Soberhoek. Just as the sun was appearing above the horizon, as red as if it had bathed in blood, Ate pushed open the door of the little house, then another, and he had found his people.

Auk was at the table peeling potatoes, and Ate was looking at her without saying a word. Auk was surprised and rose to go to the shed. Janke was coming. Ate looked at the floor, then at Janke. He did not know what to think or say. "Janke," he finally gasped, "Janke, Dad says that you were going to write me and let me go, but that isn't true, is it?" And again, very softly, "That isn't true, is it?"

Trembling from head to foot, with his eyes on the floor, he stood.

"Janke," he asked, "my girl, did they tell you that you should do it? Say it, I can't believe that you. . . ." Then slowly she lifted her head. Two blue eyes, in which a world of pain lay hidden, looked at Ate. "No, Ate, I did it on my own account. It is better that way," Janke said.

Like a drunkard Ate reeled out of the room, and, seeing and hearing nothing, he went back to the farm.

23

FROM THAT DAY it looked as if mountains of enmity had arisen between the father and his son at the Free Estate.

In the morning when Ate had returned from the Soberhoek, half crazed with misery and disappointment but outwardly sullen and taciturn, he saw his father and Keimpe sitting on the bench in the stable. The men had once more discussed the situation, and Douwe was pleased that Keimpe had kept his part of the agreement. When they observed Ate they were both curious and waited in silence to see what he would say. Douwe and Keimpe, both of them fathers, felt keenly how painful this experience must be for Ate and Janke.

His eyes were cold and there was contempt upon his lips. He spoke sharply. "Keimpe, I could expect it from you, for you have nothing in the world except your work, and there are people who may take that away from you because they seem to think that they have supreme power. But I had not expected that my father would have done such a thing without having thought at least twice. I am ashamed of the deed committed by the boer of the Free Estate."

Ate said no more but went swiftly to the barn. Douwe had wanted to jump up, but he had been unable to do so. He could easily understand Ate's state of mind, but the boy had made serious charges against his father, who at all times had desired the best for his son. He was angry, but Ate's great sorrow restrained him from punishing the boy in his present condition. He would no doubt recover soon.

But Ate did not change. Nobody knew his thoughts for he refused to discuss the matter. Even Jouk failed to make him talk, much to her surprise, since she had always cared for him faithfully and she could not bear to see him pensive and morose. He walked through the house, sat at the table, ate and drank, worked in the fields, but except for the most highly necessary directions to the workmen he never said a word. It seemed as if he had been struck dumb.

On the Free Estate there was unbearable tension, and finally Jouk could stand it no longer. She mentioned the fact to the boer, who replied rudely that it did not concern him at all; the boy was old enough to know what was best for him. But Jouk remarked, "Perhaps it would have been better if you two men had flown at each other's throats, for the way you act now is beyond endurance. You torture each other and tear the soul out of the body."

That statement did not improve matters, for Douwe gave her such a sad look that she did not dare to say another word. He left the room with his own sorrow, and no one knew how great that sorrow was and how much he suffered.

Outwardly he had to play the role of the boer, the employer and everyone must look to him as the master and leader. He could not fail to show proper energy and leadership, but inwardly he was torn asunder. The same was true of Ate.

On the Soberhoek the situation was equally serious. Janke's appearance when Keimpe returned home, thoroughly alarmed him. Her heart was filled with pain to which she could not give verbal expression. She walked back and forth as if she had lost all confidence in herself and the world.

One afternoon Jouk said to Ate, "I'll get everything ready for tea time, for I am going to make a call somewhere." She waited to see if he would ask her where she was going, but he showed no interest whatsoever. "That's fine," he replied. "We'll get along."

At two o'clock she left the house. Her head was wrapped in a warm, woolen shawl, and she wore her coat, muff and wooden shoes. She went directly to the Soberhoek, to discover how Keimpe and his family were bearing up under the terrific strain. She wanted to see how Janke acted. Keimpe had told her everything, explaining carefully that Janke of her own free will had written Ate that their courtship was definitely and permanently terminated. But Jouk had her doubts on that score. Was Janke perhaps trying to play with poor Ate? She had better be careful. Two days ago Keimpe had informed his wife and daughter about Jouk's intended visit, and now they were waiting for her. Presently the door opened and Jouk made her appearance.

Janke's mother walked into the hall to meet her. First she was invited to warm herself near the stove, and then she sat in the corner close to Auk. A pleasant conversation ensued, beginning with the weather, which in Friesland was changeable enough to furnish to topic at any time. Clothes, crops, cattle, church affairs and a few bits of choice gossip required half an hour for proper consideration. But suddenly Jouk turned to Janke and said, "I wanted to find out about you and Ate."

"There is nothing more to add," she replied. "We have stopped keeping company, and you need not come here to hear about that, for on the Free Estate that is well known."

"Well," remarked Jouk, "your indifference makes me believe that this means little to you."

"That is a fact," insisted Janke. "It is a fact, and if the boer should have sent you here perhaps, tell him that he can rest at ease, for there is nothing wrong down here. What does that proud Wallinga think anyway? Let him fly in the air like a kite."

"Girl, not so funny," objected Auk. "Remember to whom and about whom you are talking!"

"Mother must not concern herself with this thing," said the girl in a shrill voice. "Let Jouk hear it. She asked me didn't she?"

Auk was ashamed of the girl, and she wondered what Jouk would think of her behavior. But she was pleasantly surprised when she scrutinized Jouk's features. The latter sat listening with great satisfaction. She observed, "Yes, I asked her the question. Auk, let her tell me what she has on her mind; it can do no harm."

"Is that so?" asked Janke, and there were tears in her eyes. "It won't do any harm, so you say. Well, you must know all about it, then. But let me tell you one thing — and as far as I care you can also tell Ate that same thing — I have gotten over it completely, and if he thinks that I. . . ." She was unable to continue. She turned and left the room.

Auk watched her leave. "Such funny tricks," said Auk. "I don't know what to make of it."

Jouk rose and said, "You stay here a minute, Auk." Then she left the room and went to the little shed. Straining her eyes in the twilight, she walked inside and finally saw Janke sitting on a potato crate next to the goat stable, where two goats were standing. Jouk went to her and put her hand on Janke's head. "Janke, girl," she said. "Janke." Janke let her head fall against Jouk and began to cry, unable to control her emotion. Jouk pulled her closer and tried to comfort her with whispered words of sympathy. At the same time she thought, *So, girl, now you are showing your real feelings. Did you think that you could fool Jouk?*

"Now be quiet, girl," she continued. "Don't cry any more. Tell me the whole thing. What you said a little while ago you didn't mean, did you?" "No, Jouk," she replied. "No, I can't help it, and I don't know what to do with myself." Then she asked Jouk, "How is Ate, Jouk? Did Wallinga. . . ." She did not dare to add, "beat him?"

"No, girl, everything is fine on that score. I am so glad to hear what you said, and Ate feels exactly as you do. You can be sure of that. He'll never give you up . . . never. . . " "Did Ate say that, Jouk?" Poor Janke looked at Jouk as if her life were at stake. "That's what he told his father that evening when they had their talk. But you people acted much too fast. You wrote him the first thing, and he refused absolutely to see you again. Oh, what a pair of children you are! Now, wipe your eyes and go into the house; I must go back to the farm."

"Listen, Jouk, you must not tell anybody. Promise me that. I could not do otherwise, for I couldn't let my father be discharged from the farm. You understand that, don't you?" "Sure, I understand that, and I'll say nothing. Come along now."

They both went into the house, and a few minutes later Jouk, overjoyed, walked back to the farm. She knew now what the real situation was: they both loved each other as much as before. That was good, for though Douwe Ates seemed to be the stronger and to have won the victory, he fought futilely against two hearts that beat for each other, and he must at last go down to defeat. When she was home her happiness was complete, and Ate looked and looked at her, wondering where she had been, but he was too stubborn to ask her. There was something that prevented him from relenting, and Jouk knew that. She wanted to help him, but could she do it? He was a son of Douwe Wallinga, proud and stubborn.

How it happened she did not know, but that evening she told Ate a simple story, as if he were a little boy, and Ate listened to that story.

"Hundreds of years ago there lived in Friesland a man named Berend, who was so proud that from time to time somebody had to be there to hold a mirror in front of him to show him how he looked. Berend thought he was very handsome, and it was his wish that everybody would regard him as an important personage and bow before him. He was very rich, which did not improve his character. For every sum of one thousand guilders that he invested in houses and land he felt that people should offer him special thanks. For that reason nobody dared to interfere with him and he could do as he pleased.

"One morning Berend and his mirror-carrier were walking in a field in which grain had just been sown. But don't you believe that Berend was worrying about the grain. He could walk where he pleased! But, look, there came the man whose grain was in that field. He was running with a whip in his hand and shouting at them, 'Get off my field, don't you see that there is grain in it?' But Berend said, 'Let that man come; I'll walk where I please.' The mirror-carrier, on the other hand, saw that the owner of the grain was in earnest, and so he ran away as fast as he could. That made Berend afraid also, and he also ran away. They were unable to reach the gate on the dam, and so they had to jump over the ditch. On one side was a narrow ditch filled with blue mud and slime; on the other side was the wide, clear Mill Ditch. 'Let's cross here,' shouted the mirror-carrier, and he jumped across the narrow ditch. But Berend ran in the other direction, saying, 'I don't want to jump over such a dirty ditch.' He made a running start and proudly leaped. The mirror-carrier landed in the soft mud and crawled up on the other side, dirty and wet, but safe from pursuit. Berend jumped proudly into the middle of the clear water, which held him fast, and so he drowned. And often Berend's ghost haunts the Mill Ditch to remind people of the proud man who was so pleased with himself."

"That is the end," said Jouk.

"Very nice," remarked Ate, "and now I had better go to bed, just as I used to do?"

"No," answered Jouk. "What I should do is to give you a licking."

"Jouk, Jouk, I know why you have told me this story, but I couldn't do anything else. Janke wrote me, ending the whole affair, and that was the finish of it all . . . ." "Just a minute," observed Jouk. "There comes the mailman; he is calling us, so he must have something important."

Ate went to the door and came back with the newspaper and a letter. "From Uncle Ids," he said, "To Wallinga and son." He tore open the envelope and read:

Holwerd, March
When I consult my own feeling and consider what my doctor tells me, I haven't much time left, and soon it will be finished with me. Things may turn out better than expected; perhaps I may have to undergo some repairs for a few days. I would like to have Ate come here to help me, if possible very soon.
Ids Wallinga

"Uncle Ids," mumbled Ate, as he looked at Jouk. "Uncle is in a worse shape than he is willing to admit. I had better go there very soon."

"But not any more this evening?" she asked.

"No, not this evening, but tomorrow after milking at the latest. That uncle! I didn't even know that he was ill."

Jouk wanted to say something. She was eager to see him take care of his own affairs at home before leaving for another place. "Ate," she remarked, "shouldn't you tell Dad first?"

"No, Jouk. Dad can read it for himself."

"But should you go like this, Ate? Oh, boy, that will never do. Why don't you make friends with Dad by being the humbler one?"

"No," he answered. "You need not say any more about it. He wanted it this way, not I."

"And what about Janke?" she asked, but on this point also he did not want to seek reconciliation. "Janke wrote me, and the day before that she said we were finished; so what's the use talking about it any more?" he said.

"Oh, you wretched Wallingas, stiffnecks that you are. You

are a true son of your dad, let me tell you. Have you never wondered about her condition? The girl had no choice in the matter. She had to tell you what she did."

"I know that, but she could have written me that, couldn't she?"

"Such a thing you cannot write; you have to talk about it, and I believe, Ate, that you and she will have to have a talk soon. I found that out this afternoon."

"This afternoon?"

"Yes, I paid Auk a visit."

"Did you then . . . ." Ate came closer to Jouk, and as he looked at her he observed how Ate had suffered. "How was she, Jouk? Tell me now, if only I know that she is all right."

Each of his words and his entire attitude indicated such a longing for the girl that Jouk, who had planned to reveal nothing, told him the complete truth.

The next morning Ate rode his bicycle to Holwerd. He was cheerful again, and all his thoughts were of Janke. He must first see what the situation was on the farm at Metserd, and if he decided to stay, the milkman would bring his clothes.

It was the time of new life and growth. This meant hard work on all the farms, but on the Free Estate the owner would have to get along without Ate and Janke.

Ate looked to the left, toward the Soberhoek, and he wondered when he would go there again. In the meantime his father was standing in the living room at the Free Estate, and he was wondering when Ate would return home. He realized that the boy was glad to get away. He watched Ate, and his hands trembled in his pockets. He was so moved that he turned from the window and scolded himself for being a coward. He left the room, but as soon as he went he saw that Jouk had also been watching at the window. Quickly he went to the barn, where he severely reprimanded a workman for no good reason at all.

As Ate entered the yard at Metserd and put the bicycle

against the wall, he found Gep, the housekeeper, waiting for him. He did not like that. Was the old man perhaps in a serious condition? "How is he?" asked Ate. "Well, Ate, I don't know. He is so queer lately. All winter long he has been suffering from minor ailments, but he did not want to see the doctor until last week, when he became much worse all of a sudden. And what do you think he asked the doctor?"

"It must have been a funny question," surmised Ate.

"Well, boy, 'funny' isn't the word. Terrible! When the doctor had examined him he said, 'Now don't beat about the bush, and give me the facts. How is my condition? Am I sitting in the waiting room, as my friend, Waling Dijkstra used to say? Must I make preparations for the trip? Is my train coming?' "

"Now, Ate, wasn't that a terrible question to ask?"

"And what did the doctor say?" asked Ate.

"If he took good care of himself he would last for years, but otherwise not so long, I believe."

They entered the room, where Uncle Ids was sitting. His mass of red hair was disheveled, and his face resembled a forthcoming storm.

"Here I am, Uncle," said Ate. "How are you today?"

"Fine, boy. Fine. Glad to see you. Better change your clothes and get to work. The whole place is a mess."

Gepke remarked, "The boy should first have some coffee and a sandwich, don't you think?"

"Hasn't he had that yet? You housekeeper without a boer, where are your brains?"

"I don't need anything to eat or to drink, Uncle, but I would like to know what my employer has in his mind regarding myself."

"You are to act as if the whole farm is yours, and each evening we can discuss matters together. I can't manage the place any more. I have to be treated like a child. I cannot go to the fields, and there are other things besides. He even wanted to put me to bed for good, but that I refused to do."

"Why isn't your dad here yet?" he asked Ate, who did not care to play the hypocrite and said, "I don't know. During the last few days I haven't talked with him." Ate left the room and Ids smiled. *Are they at it again?* he wondered, and Gepke glared angrily at him.

"They are all alike," she thought. "Wallingas, that is all you have to say."

24

DAYS PASSED and Douwe Ates did not appear. Uncle Ids often directed the conversation to the affairs on the Free Estate. There was something amiss, he could feel that, but he did not know what it was until one evening Ate told him the whole story. The old man had finally been able to pry loose Ate's great secret.

"Now I'll tell you, boy, why I have fished these words out of your mouth. I knew how hard it was for you to reveal this to an old man." Ids paused a few moments and then continued. "You must give your heart some air. You must talk with somebody about this thing. I know how trying it is to keep a secret. You want to think that it is nobody's business, and you want to hide it from all your friends. This is particularly aggravating when you won't even tell your nearest relatives, who are involved the most of all. Nobody knows that better than I, boy, because my own life has been almost exactly the same as yours.

"My dad, your great-grandfather, also a Wallinga, was just

like your dad. I was keeping company with the daughter of common working people who lived here in Holwerd. We separated and I never visited my girl again, while Dad and I remained enemies, Ate, like you and your dad." Ids was silent for a few minutes, as if he had to bring back to his mind the events of a remote past. Ate thought, *Well, such things occur more often than I had realized.* Then he heard again the voice of Uncle Ids. "Don't keep still, I tell you. My dad died before he and I were able to effect a reconciliation. The girl could not stand our separation long, and one day her dead body was found in a canal."

"Now you go ahead, boy, and do what you please." Ate did not dare to say a word. He had great respect for that man of seventy-nine who could be faithful after so many years. The next morning the mailman on his way back to Holwerd had a letter for Janke. He threw it, with other letters, into his mailsack, and in Holwerd it was put into a white linen pouch as if it were of no particular value, but each word in it was worth a dollar, even though not for the postal service.

> Janke:
> Jouk told me a number of things, but to tell you the truth, I did not intend to visit you again. You had written me about your stand, and your four lines which came to me like a cold shower I soon had learned by heart; they deprived me of all hope that some day we might come together again.
> But today I heard a very sad tale from Uncle Ids which I must tell you some time, and that has made me change my mind. Janke, would it not be better if we gave up all false shame and showed the world that we are ready to face all the results of our reunion rather than let our love be brushed aside by another person?
> Do you dare? I do.
>
> Ate Douwes

An answer was not long delayed. It was written in simple language and again only four lines in length, but it contained a volume of good hope for Ate, who was happy now, although he did not publicize his feelings, partly because he was so busy with farm work. He must also watch Uncle, who, according to the doctor, might leave them any day. No, he did not have much time for talking, but his heart sang, and he longed for the evening when he could have a talk with Janke.

"So it will be Janke after all," was the refrain of his song.

He performed his duties at Metserd as if the farm were his own, and no one knew that better than Uncle Ids.

One morning the doctor arrived again, and again Ids asked, "How long, Doctor? I must know it. I must know it."

"Well, old stiffhead," answered the doctor, "if you want to know it so badly, it will depend on how you behave. If you continued to act as you do now by refusing to stay in bed, I'll give you five weeks."

"That is a short end," said Ids. "That is a short end."

"But if you will obey my orders the situation will be very different. One should let such patients alone, for they pay no attention to what I advise them."

"Come, come, Doctor, boy, don't be angry."

Two days later he called Ate and said, "Next Sunday you must hitch the old black horse to the buggy and take your girl to our place." "Fine, Uncle," replied Ate.

Gepke muttered in the kitchen, "Listen to those blockheads: 'You must hitch the horse to the buggy,' and 'Fine, Uncle.' That's all those people can say about such an important matter!"

But on Sunday afternoon Ate fetched Janke from the Brantgum Road. He saw her coming far in the distance. Her light-blue dress was bright in the spring sun. When the happy couple was seated side by side in the carriage, Ate told her the history of Uncle Ids.

Janke was not easily frightened, but she looked forward with some trepidation to the meeting with Ids. Although Ate was with her and he was his uncle, she felt ill at ease. Ids Wallinga was known far and wide as a peculiar old fellow. The fact that he remained a bachelor had led to many stories, with the result that no mother would ever want her girl to serve in his home as a maid, notwithstanding the fact that absolutely nothing could be found to prove that he was not a thoroughly respectable gentleman.

When they were seated together in the living room, Uncle Ids as usual in his old chair, with Janke and Gepke on one

side and Ate on the other, Ids said to Janke as he looked
her straight in the eyes, "So you have bewitched this ape of
a boy, have you?"

Gepke thought it her duty to say, "Boer, boer, remember
that she does not know you, and don't scare her with your
funny talk." Ids paid no attention to her and continued. "Now
you expect me to go the same way? Well, you had better get
that idea out of your head, for I don't have any use for women.
You have brought enough quarrels into the world."

Janke looked at Ids, but he laughed and laughed. Suddenly
she burst out, "Wallinga, I don't know you very well, but I
do know that you have had many experiences, and it may be
that women have caused you grief. I doubt, however, that I
have been guilty, since I have never done you any harm and
I see you today for the first time."

"You went after a boer's son," said the old man, but at
the same time he winked at Ate, "and that is not proper."

"Boer, boer," gasped Gepke, raising her hands high in the
air. "What kind of talk do you call that?" But Ids replied
bluntly, "Talk with which my housekeeper need not concern
herself."

"So it goes here all the time," said Gepke to Janke. "Whatever happens, Gepke is always at fault."

"Then you must be at fault," declared Ids, and it seemed
to Ate that Uncle was a bit queer today. Janke hardly knew
what to make of his peculiar speech.

Gepke jumped off her chair. "I am going away, you with
your nonsensical talk!" Angrily she left the room, but Uncle
Ids was laughing heartily.

"Janke," he remarked, "I want to have a talk with you.
Come here a minute." Desperately afraid but seemingly calm,
she went to him.

The old man was completely changed. His voice sounded
like that of a child as he said, "You must pay no attention
to what the old man has said so far, child. Bear in mind that
one kind of person thinks he learns to know a flower by smell-

ing it and throwing it away, whereas another admires its colors, is amazed at its beauty and lets it grow. I don't know if you two can grasp that so quickly, but that does not matter. Janke, I know that you love the boy. Will you, no matter what happens, stay at his side and not leave him alone? For we, especially the Wallingas, cannot exist without someone who cares for us always."

"If I can find a way to do it," replied Janke.

"Every way, girl," asserted the old man. "Everything that you can do!" Janke was almost at the point of tears, but she was still able to say, "My whole life is his, Wallinga, and I hope that I may be permitted to suffer for him." That was all she could say, and she left the room. Ate wanted to follow her, but Ids restrained him with a gesture.

"Come here, boy," he said, and as Ate came closer to him, he added, "Show her the farm buildings and the land. I have seen her and listened to her, and I believe that she will make an excellent mistress on a farm. . . . Now go. I want to be alone and think about. . . ."

Go now! said his gesture.

Ate looked for Janke. Quietly they walked over the fields and inspected the buildings, wondering about Uncle Ids' behavior. They were very happy this evening, partly because now they could enjoy each other's company again, and partly because of the marked interest shown in them by Uncle Ids. His fields and orchard promised to bear an abundant harvest, and it was a pleasure for the young people to survey the fruit of wise management. When Janke returned home that night the relation between her and Ate was so perfect and pure that words were superfluous.

Monday morning at ten o'clock the notary public visited Ids Wallinga. Tuesday morning, while Ate was mowing the grass, Douwe Ates made his appearance. Only a few words were exchanged between uncle and nephew, but each was significant.

"Before I undertake the long journey, Douwe, and because

you can't find Metserd any more on your own accord, I have
sent for you."

"Here I am," answered Douwe.

"I know what there is between you and Ate, Douwe!"

"That female," replied the nephew.

"No, your hard head and your pride — our pride, we might
well say. You know how it went with me, Douwe, why I
never married, because I preferred to listen to my dad rather
than to my heart."

He paused a while to note the effect his words might have
on his nephew. But the latter showed little interest in his tale.
The old man continued nevertheless.

"That girl has, but, no, I won't discuss that. . . . She rests
in the church yard at Holwerd. And now I shall have to leave
this earth after a long life in which nobody cared for me and
in which I did not know the privilege of being a dad and a
man. Look, boy," and the old man was beginning to speak
with great difficulty, "that must not happen again among the
Wallingas. You two should meet each other half way. . . ."

"Uncle does not know her." "Oh, yes, Uncle does know
her," interrupted Ids. "She was here, right here, I tell you,
quite close to me, and I studied her carefully. She will make
an excellent boer's wife."

"But not on the Free Estate," grumbled Douwe.

"I happen to own a farm myself," was the unexpected
reply. Douwe rose. "Will Uncle then. . . ." "Yes," remarked
the old man, "that's what I am going to do. Yesterday the
notary public wrote my will. Now you perform one good deed,
Douwe, and give them your permission. Then next May they
can get married, and everything will be in order." Douwe
had walked through the room, and in the distance he saw
Ate mowing the grass. He felt a throb of pain as he realized
that Ate would be lost to him, but he said bravely, "I'll do
nothing to interfere with their plans. When he lets me know
the date of their forthcoming marriage I'll have the papers
made up at the courthouse."

"Will you make that declaration in black and white?" asked Ids.

"Black on white?" Douwe turned angrily. "I am no cheat. My word is always good. But I'll never go inside their door, if that's what you mean."

"Thank you, Douwe," said Ids. "That makes me feel good — 'My word is good.' As for the rest, you go your own way, back to your farm which my brother gave to you, and think about your deeds. That was my last wish for you."

He gave Douwe his hand. "Douwe," he remarked, and Douwe, placing his hand in that of the old man, replied, "Uncle." Then he turned and went.

In the door stood the housekeeper, who shook her head in disdain as she witnessed that abrupt and rude parting.

When Douwe rode back home he was angry. The thought that Ate would disappear completely from his life caused him intense grief, and in his house he snarled at Jouk, who asked how Ate was. "If you ever say another word about Ate, you had better find yourself another job. I am through with Ate. *Through!*"

In his confusion he forgot to take off his good coat, and he walked through the fields to Keimpe, who was weeding. "Say, Keimpe," he shouted, "your daughter is still flirting with my son!"

"Yes, boer," he answered, "but I would not call it flirting. I can't help it."

"It's a good thing, then, that I did not hire you again for another year. This week is your last."

"But my good man, I am not in a position to stop this thing. The boer should listen to reason." But his appeal had no effect whatsoever. Douwe was immune to reason and good sense. "What I have to listen to is none of your foolish business. That is your last week. Finished. Do you hear?"

With the same heavy steps he returned to his house, but he could find no rest there. Everywhere the stark truth confronted him. He had lost Ate! That hurt him. He could not get over it. *Who knows what the end of it will be?* so thought Jouk. Everything was again in confusion.

The following week Keimpe vacated his home on the Soberhoek, and Ate rented a house for him in Holwerd, and assisted him with the moving of the furniture. Keimpe became a laborer at Metserd, and Janke received a position as maid at the house in Holwerd.

Summer returned, and it seemed as if the boer had been rejuvenated. Although his condition in the past few weeks had been deplorable, he suddenly revived. He was able again to discuss at length the management of the farm, as if he had been at work himself.

The two men sometimes had arguments about the system of crop rotation and the most efficient use of fertilizer. Gepke often had to shake her head disapprovingly, for Ids would never yield on any issue, nor would Ate. In many details Ate wanted to introduce a change, particularly in the planning of fertilization. He had a diploma from the agricultural school, but there was no use in mentioning that to the old man. "That book knowledge," he would argue, "what good does it anyway? So many pounds of this stuff and so many pounds of that, plus some outlandish kind of salt or soda — what utter nonsense!" Uncle Ids would spread the manure while it was still warm, plow it under and then raise potatoes!

"And on the pastures you are not to throw fertilizer, do you hear? I don't want you to poison my cattle. Look through the window at those fields of grass. You cut it yourself, you remember? Wasn't that some hay you got there? Never has there been put one cent's worth of junk!"

But at other times the old man sat for hours, and meditated, and it appeared as if he were soon to die. On such days Ate came two or three times to Gep to inquire. He went into the bedroom and asked Uncle Ids for advice which he did not need at all. Would Uncle tell him where the cows should go this time, or should they hire another workman for weeding? Ate's sole purpose, however, was to look at the old man.

Slowly his old uncle declined, for he fought against death until the very end.

The young summer grew into full stature, and the villages of Friesland were like doll houses among the tall trees. In the fields there was much commotion, and in the barns were the familiar sounds which foretold the beginning of another harvest. The rattling of the milk cans, the singing of the girls in the fields and the grinding of machinery and wagons were heard everywhere. Here and there a young wife was taking a walk in the warm sun with her first baby. It was a pleasure to see the contented cows in the pastures and the waving grain in the fields. The tall flowers were swaying gently in the breeze, and in the ditches the gay rays of the sun were reflected brightly. Was not all of this like a festival?

25

I**T WAS IN THIS** summer, on one of the most beautiful days,
that Ids Wallinga departed from this life at Metserd. "Not
even in his bed," so babbled the gossip-mongers. "No, not in
bed, but like a dog in the middle of the living room!"

True, not in his bed. It was not yet six o'clock in the
morning when he wanted to get out of bed, and the housekeeper experienced great difficulty in trying to keep him under
the covers. When she cautiously looked around the door —
one had to be careful for he was so weak — she heard him
say, "My clothes. I want to get up."

"No, farmer," she muttered good-naturedly. "Don't do
that. It is only six o'clock; please stay there." She thought,
If only he is down again first. The doctor had warned her
that Ids was no longer in a condition to get out of bed.
"Where is the boy?" he asked.

"He is eating bread just now," replied Gep, "and Ate said,
'Make as little noise as you can, for the boer must not be
awakened.'"

It seemed as if these words satisfied him, for he lay down again. The housekeeper resumed her work, but she was worried about her employer. No matter how queer he seemed at times, she was fond of him.

At ten o'clock, when she was busy with her work, she heard his voice again. It seemed as if suddenly he had a spasm, for he shouted wildly, "Gep, Gepke, come here!"

She ran to the bedroom and asked him, "What's the trouble, boer? Can I help you with something?"

"Yes," answered Ids. "Get my clothes."

She objected. "You know very well what the doctor said, don't you? You have to obey his orders."

But nothing could make Ids give up his plan. His two legs appeared over the side of the bed, and groaning with pain, he tried to raise himself to a sitting position.

"I don't want to stay in bed any more, woman. I don't want to," and Gepke gave him his clothes. How could she stop him from getting out of bed? When once he had made up his mind to do something no amount of talking could make him desist. She put on his stockings and socks, helped him don his trousers, shirt and vest, and then, frowning, the farmer started to walk, step by step — far too slowly to suit him — to the big chair which was standing near the window. Panting, he seated himself.

"Well," remarked the housekeeper, "are you seated comfortably?" He did not answer. "Would you like to eat something?" Again no answer. He was looking through the windows, and he seemed completely satisfied. With a gesture he told Gep to remove herself, and she left the room, fully determined at lunch time to warn Ate. She did not like the boer's queer behavior.

Quietly, and erect, Ids Wallinga sat in his chair, and a great peace entered his heart.

His eyes were not sharp any more, and he could not see very far, but nothing escaped his attention. All morning he sat there, quietly, peacefully.

Near lunch time Ate entered the room to inquire about Uncle Ids, but he also received no answers to his questions, and he was also told to leave the room. That caused Ate plenty of misgiving, and near milking time he went back to look at the old man. When he entered the room and stood next to the chair in which Uncle Ids was still sitting, the old man still refused to talk. But he could tell that Ate was there, for suddenly he said, "The cows . . . . for me . . . . in the barnyard . . . . I want to see them . . . ."

He tried to stand, but that he was unable to do. He pointed to the land. Ate asked nothing more but went immediately to the yard, where Keimpe was about to leave for the pasture with the cart. He heard Iepe coming home with the cows. He was shouting at the cattle, which were going far too slowly for him.

"Keimpe," said Ate, "open the gate of the barnyard, and I'll open the gate of the pasture. The boer wants the cows in front of the window." Keimpe executed his orders without asking him the reason for it. Ate went to the pasture, opened the gate as wide as possible and shouted to Iepe, "Drive the cows through; they have to go to the barnyard."

"What?" asked Iepe. "Why should those cows start grazing again just before milking? Somebody around here must have lost his head."

"We are doing that to please the boer, Iepe. He wants to see his cattle once more, and if you were to ask me I would say that this is no doubt the last time that he will see them."

Iepe objected, but softly, so that Ate could not hear him. He was thoroughly disgusted, but he would not say anything about it, though he saw clearly that the cows were confused by this strange arrangement. The cattle were finally led across the yard into the plot of grass near the barn.

"You'll have to milk without me this time," said Ate, "for I must go back to the boer."

"Is your uncle worse, Ate?" asked Keimpe.

"Yes, if I must say so, it looks very bad." He entered the residence again. In the living room he felt that strange atmosphere caused by his uncle's unusual behavior.

The old man continued to look in the direction from which the cattle were to come. He tried to sit a little higher, and Ate took a pillow from the bed and shoved it behind his uncle's back. "Is that better?" he asked. But there was no answer. The old man was waiting.

Then they came, the handsome, shining cows, one by one, and some in pairs, with the men behind them. Iepe made Bontje II halt in front of the window, for that was the famous cow that gave much milk and whose descendents are to be found in many foreign countries.

Iepe and Keimpe were milking some of the cows, while the others were grazing. Ids was sitting in front of the window. The scene was unforgettably beautiful. The cattle's tails were swaying and occasionally they shook their heads to get rid of the flies. Behind them were the cultivated fields of wheat, oats, flax and other crops. In the meadows the hay was ripe for the mowing, and in the rows of beans and potatoes the workmen were weeding. In the background was a large windmill whose four arms divided the sunlight into four parts over the fields and pasture.

In front of the window sat the dying man, portioning his breath among his lungs, his cattle, and his land. Like a king he sat there immovable, and Ate did not dare to utter a word. That impressed Ate, but it was painful to behold. There sat Ids Wallinga. He had known one great experience of love, but it had not been permitted to unfold. Now there lay before him the only thing he had left for his affection. He knew the complete history of his cows, the strength and weakness of each piece of land, the various kinds of plants and their respective requirements . . .

The housekeeper was also in the room now, for she knew that this was a parting scene, another queer phenomenon, with touching and tender aspects, and she found it difficult to restrain her tears.

Who can tell how long this lasted? Was it an hour, half an hour perhaps? But suddenly Ids stretched forth his hand to Ate, and he grasped it. "Uncle," he whispered . . . Ids squeezed Ate's hand, and then it seemed as if he wanted to stand. Ate and the housekeeper heard him say clearly, "For you . . . and . . . for Janke."

Then, with a slight nod, his head fell upon his chest. Ids Wallinga, the boer of Metserd, had closed his eyes for the last time. He had died in the midst of his cattle and the Frisian fields; in utter peace and contentment he had spoken his parting words. Ate carefully released the old man's hand and motioned to Gep, who was about to close the shutters, that she must send for the doctor. He opened one shutter, which had just been closed by the housekeeper and said, "Uncle shall lie in the light as long as he can."

The doctor arrived while Ate was helping with the milking. Iepe pressed his lips tightly, for he did not want to be seen weeping. Nevertheless, he realized that he was almost over-come with emotion. He would miss the old boer.

"I extend to you my sympathy, Ate," said the doctor. "He died as he lived — a great man."

The short period between Ids' death and burial was for Ate a busy time, and he was unable to do much thinking about himself. Letters of mourning had to be sent, funeral arrange-ments must be made, and the work on the farm, disorganized by the sudden passing of the owner, also required much atten-tion. Ate did not feel like a person who had just lost a relative. On the contrary, Uncle Ids seemed to be with him and helping him. The workmen had little to say; Iepe was silent. His rough voice, which used to boom far afield, was heard no more, and suddenly he looked old.

When the relatives arrived on the day of the funeral and Ate saw his father, there were moments of suspense. Each wanted to raise his hand and show some sign of friendship, but neither did so; they passed each other without saying a word.

Then the men wearing the black caps carried the casket out of the house across the yard, where Ids had walked back and forth from day to day, for years and years.

In the golden sunshine, while all plant and animal life

seemed motionless because of the intense heat, and only in the farthest distance men and women were working in the fields, Ids was carried to the lot in the church yard, a lot that he had bought for himself, not in Hantum, where all the Wallingas were buried, but in Holwerd, next to the grave with the wooden cross. That ancient relic was already half decayed, and it is difficult to decipher the name: — Goukje Hemminga . . . the girl who could not live without him. Ate did not know if among the people around him there were any who were thinking about that girl, but he assumed that there must be a few.

On the way home his thoughts were with her and Uncle Ids, and in his heart there was great respect for him. At the same time he felt a strong desire to give expression to this love and faith. He longed to shake hands with his father, who was walking at his side, but Douwe would not look at him, and after the meal he was the first to leave.

Three days later, Ids Wallinga's will was read. The cousins, nephews and nieces, and other relatives listened at first with hope for themselves, then with amazement and disappointment, which turned to intense hatred as the notary proceeded. The latter, looking at them from beneath his glasses, saw all too plainly their feeling as it was registered upon their angry faces.

Douwe Ates followed the perusal with cool indifference, but Ate was profoundly interested.

The notary public read:

I, Ids Wallinga, boer of Metserd, have this day, the 18th of June, made the following provisions concerning my property:

I bequeath to Gepke Vriezema, my housekeeper, the house No. 36 in Church Street, with a weekly pension of twelve guilders until her death, in gratitude for her faithful service.

I bequeath to Iepe Walstra the half acre of cultivated land near the railroad dike.

I bequeath to Johannes Hemminga and wife the house in which they are now living.

I bequeath to my nephews on my mother's side each 200 guilders.

I bequeath to Ate Douwes Wallinga my farm Metserd near Holwerd, consisting in residence, barn, cow stable, small stable, shed; together with my land, consisting in thirty acres of cultivated fields in the upland district, twenty acres of land in the drained district called *polder,* forty acres of pasture in the upland, and twenty acres behind the woods. Further, all my cattle, carriages, wagons, machines and all horses — on condition that next May he marry Janke, the daughter of my workman Keimpe.

This I have provided in order that some day happier persons shall live at Metserd than I was.

That it may be so.

The notary public will make the proper arrangements.

It was deathly still. The relatives who had hankered after the money of the man whom they hardly knew, with the exception of Douwe and Ate — those relatives had listened with immense surprise. One after the other made ready to leave, but one of them from the district far to the south called the Wooded Country, a half-nephew only, could not keep still and remarked, "What you think of it I don't know, but it seems queer that all the property has been given to a person who during the last few weeks has had control of the old man." That remark called forth other comments, such as the following: "You are right man, and don't forget that marrying of a daughter of his workman. You should think that a boer who does such funny things must be . . . ." He was trying to find a suitable word with which to express his hatred for Ids, but he was interrupted by Douwe Ates. Like a piece of granite he stood there, his eyes flashing with contempt. Ate was afraid of what might follow, but eagerly he awaited his father's words.

Douwe Ates looked them all straight in the eyes and said, "You cowardly hunters, if this time you did not obtain any prey, it is not because of the victims but because of the man who is now dead. If any of you says another word about his choice in the matter, you shall have occasion to remember this day."

Ate was about to jump up and thank his father. So Dad was with him! But just as he wanted to go to Douwe he heard these cold words: "I am greatly displeased myself, but we have to abide by his decision."

With those parting words Douwe Ates left the place. "Good-bye to you all," he muttered on his way out. Ate heard all the others go away, but he paid little attention to that. Douwe's last words were a hard blow to him; first he had had the happy feeling that his father stood behind him, but immediately after he had heard those bitter remarks, his hope had been taken away again.

Ate had to digest all of this. As if to make up for lost time, he labored with all his might on the farm, his farm. Physical activity enabled him to suppress remorse for his feeling toward Dad. During the autumn Janke and he were often together, and they talked about the great event that lay before them. It would be the consummation of their love.

In the long winter evenings Ate studied many books and magazines, that he might be a deserving manager of the valuable property left by Uncle Ids. But there were also happy hours spent in the little house at Holwerd, evenings on the ice with Janke, visits with old friends, especially with Gelf, who was acquiring much property, and with old Jouk, whom he could not visit on the Free Estate. He said to Janke, "It is up to Dad." But she felt uneasy about it.

There were, however, some other things which occupied Janke's mind far more at the moment. Her absorbing theme of interest was that overwhelming event which was drawing ever closer, filling her with awe and wonder. At first it seemed as if the month of May would never come, for their marriage loomed so large that all other affairs were dwarfed. But gradually the days and weeks sped by with increasing tempo, and when the wedding was almost at hand they were still in a daze, from which they did not awaken until after they were living at Metserd as husband and wife.

Even then they required some time for adjustment. Iepe, Keimpe and the new maid sometimes shook their heads with wonder, as Ate had another spell of confusion. He would be working with the men in the field and suddenly jump on his bicycle. "I forgot that a certain person was coming to the house!" he would exclaim. Then Iepe would urge him to go to the house again with, "Yes, you had better hurry!" As he left, Keimpe and Iepe would watch with subdued amusement. Iepe would ask Keimpe, "Now we have gotten ourselves in a mess. Does that condition last quite a while?"

"One week, according to the almanac," Keimpe would say as he laughed.

26

THE LEAST that could be said was that Ate and Janke were happily married. Ate had the girl he wanted, and Douwe had not sought to prevent the marriage. At the courthouse he signed the necessary papers, as he had solemnly promised Uncle Ids. Now they had a farm which produced a handsome income. But there remained one thing which caused much uneasiness, though this might be assuaged in time . . . yes, perhaps in time . . . .

It was easy to wish for the best, but Douwe Ates was a proud man who did not readily change his mind. He kept his promise, that was true, but he had also declared, "I shall never enter their house." That prediction also was well conceived and executed. Ate had the same blood as his father, who was usually calm and quiet, but on particular occasions extremely passionate. It was that blood which now perpetuated the old feud. Father and son acted in different ways and used various means by which they achieved their purpose, but they were nevertheless alike.

On the Free Estate the atmosphere was almost unbearable. The day laborers enjoyed their work, for they could well afford to ignore the peculiar behavior of their employer. They received higher wages from him than from any other, and was not that what they wanted most of all? Nevertheless even the most callous person could not always suppress his anger when he was reprimanded for a nonexistent offense. On such an occasion one felt as if he should give the boer a sound thrashing, jump on his back and beat him into a more reasonable state of mind. But if one did that, he had better go to a distant region, for no boer in the neighborhood would give him a job after such behavior.

It was enough to drive a workman to distraction. In all sorts of weather, in all sorts of places, near the house or far away, Douwe Ates was always spying, his head in the air, his mouth closed tight, his thumbs in the armholes of his vest. The wisest procedure was to say nothing at all, otherwise he would swear at one, for the boer was always supposed to be in the right, and anyone who thwarted him had better prepare yourself for the worst.

Gradually there came also that other thing that Jouk had feared. His intense love for racing returned; he led almost exactly the kind of life again which had characterized the early years of his marriage. People began to gossip about him again. His old cronies welcomed him back in the inns, and they pointed to him as they said to the younger associates, "That man there, Douwe Ates Wallinga, is the greatest expert on horses in Friesland. He won the Golden Whip!"

That pleased Douwe immensely, and he was the hero at fairs, races and carnivals, though he had never expected to be seen there again. He tried desperately to forget his sorrows, some of which could never be forgotten.

For nearly two years he and Ate had not talked to each other, although it had been difficult at times for them to get out of each other's way. That is what made the situation so much more unpleasant. One day this occurred in the office of the boer's bank at Holwerd, where Douwe could not have been expected to appear for any reason. As he opened the door he came face to face with the boy, who opened his mouth to express a greeting, formal though it be. But Douwe was in no mood to make peace, and with his fists swelling as if for a fight and his old heart filled with rancor, he walked past Ate without saying a word.

When he returned home again his anger knew no bounds, as Jouk readily saw. She could tell to the last detail what he would do next. He would first walk back and forth in the living room, then slump into the big chair and stare at the walls or ceiling. If that became too boring, as was frequently the case, he would go to Dokkum or Ternaard and carouse until he finally had to come back in the middle of the night, swearing and scolding and dirty and fatigued besides.

This state of affairs merely increased his misery. Old Jouk saw that and felt pity for him, but she could not say a word about it, for she knew in advance that he would burst out in a flood of curses and complaints. For that reason she tried to serve him in silence and by her company help him forget his loneliness. She realized only too well that he did not act this way because it pleased him. Oh, no, he was driven by a force beyond his control!

Life on the Free Estate became ever more unbearable for Douwe. He could not take one step without being reminded of Ate, always Ate! When a little boy, Ate had walked hand in hand, the boy asking question after question and the father proudly explaining to him the mysteries of the big farm. Finally the boy had become tired and his father carried him home on his broad shoulders. Later he went to school and learned the farm work from Gelf. He could still hear Gelf say to him as the two were threshing the oats, "That boy stands there like a big man, boer. I have to work hard to keep up with him!" Ah, how proud Douwe had been then, but he had always been proud of Ate, and for a good reason. Ate Douwes was his boy and Liesbeth's. There was no change of importance until that wretched girl had come to plague him. She had wormed her way into Ate's heart and caused the fatal separation. Then Ate had left Douwe in the lurch, and henceforth he meant nothing to him. He did not want to talk about him to anybody except in terms of derision. Away with that memory! Burn it out of existence as the blacksmith burns away a sore on a horse's leg.

A horse, a horse he thought. "I want another horse," he said. He jumped up, went to the prize cabinet and laid all the prizes on the table. The magic power of racing overwhelmed him again, and in imagination he saw Wardy, Kol and Prince; they were with him in the room. They swept him along in their train. In the middle of the room he stood, his eyes ablaze with fire, his hands trembling with emotion. He could conjure up visions of himself racing along the track, behind the horses, one by one, his eye watching back and head, his body reclining in the soft feathers of the sulky, moving up and down with the rhythm of the horse's legs.

To return to the scenes of enchantment — that was his glory and his solace. And why not? He was not yet fifty, and he was fully able to jump over a horse, let alone riding one.

One morning he paid a visit to the man in Leeuwarden who knew everything about race-horses in Friesland, the man who could tell one the history of each horse and all about the relation between horse and man.

"Well, well," he said. "Douwe Ates is back in Leeuwarden! Come inside, man. You have no idea how happy you make me with your visit." When they were comfortably seated in his living room, Douwe said to him, "Do you know of a good horse for me?"

"A horse? Are you planning to go racing again, Wallinga?"

"Sure," he replied, "that is, if I can do it yet."

"Oh, I was not worrying about that, friend. You stay here with me today, and after lunch we'll go looking around."

Two days later Douwe picked up the paper at home and began to read. Suddenly he said excitedly, "Now listen to this, Jouk!"

Jouk almost became frightened. "Did something happen?" she asked.

"No, no, just listen to this":

> After having spent years on his farm in seclusion, the famous expert on horses, Douwe Ates Wallinga, has decided to compete once more on our race-tracks.
>
> The Frisians cannot fail to be happy about this, for he will reintroduce scenes of beauty and tension when he returns with horses like those of old: Wardy, Kol and Prince, of which the last-named won the Golden Whip in Leeuwarden. We learn that Wallinga has bought from the stable of Van der Wal the three-year-old mare "Darling," which has often demonstrated that she possesses true racing blood.
>
> It is Wallinga's intention to train this horse, in which, as we all remember, he applies a unique system. "Darling" will appear next summer under the name of "Marja."

"What do you think of that, Jouk?" asked Douwe Not only once, but time and again he asked her the same question: "What do you think of that? The Golden Whip farmer is going to race again."

In all the towns and villages of Friesland a similar question was heard: "What do you think of that? Douwe Ates is going to race again." Those who knew him well and did not like him said mischievously, "What do you think of that? Douwe Ates wants another whip; with the first one a few years ago he beat his son half to death."

In the living room at Metserd that question was also asked, but there it came almost as an answer to other questions. Ate understood the reasons why Dad had made this decision, for he himself had felt the magic of horse-racing. He did not dare to discuss the matter with Janke, but when he read the announcement he had wanted to go to his father and offer his help till suddenly that awful pang of enmity shot through his startled mind again. Dad would see him coming. No, Dad would not want to have him around the place.

During the summer Marja entered the race-tracks, and there

was no contest without her appearance. Some were skeptical about Douwe's methods and said, "He is going too fast with that horse." But others contended, "Douwe Ates knows his business." The latter were right. Douwe's aim was to gain complete control of the horse; he must familiarize himself with all her faults and good points.

What pleased Douwe in particular was the joyous fact that he had lost little of his enormous physical energy and his con‐ summate tact with horses. Marja was to run in such a manner that she would not be using any extra energy; her gait would show no strain.

In those days Janke gave birth to a baby girl, and her mother insisted that she call her Liesbeth, but Ate, realizing that this would be interpreted as a conciliatory move on their part toward Douwe, made another decision by saying, "We are not beggars; I don't want to break an old tradition to please a proud father. The girl is to be named Auk, after your mother." That is exactly what happened. A letter was dispatched to the Free Estate, and for days they lived in a state of suspense, that is to say, Auk and Janke, for Ate realized that his father would never yield an inch to his adversaries. When Jouk, as gay as a child, had shown the letter to Douwe, he had snarled, "Even in this respect he has shown that he is no longer a Wallinga." He threw the letter at Jouk. She had read the news herself and said, "A girl! How glad I am. Say, boer, wouldn't you like to go there?"

"I wouldn't know what for," he replied sneeringly. That was all he said. When Jouk told Ate about that during her visit at Metserd, she explained to him that Douwe's words did not come from his heart. He had said them to cover his inner feelings.

"Perhaps so," admitted Ate, "but you would like to take him by the neck and give him a sound thrashing. Perhaps he might then tell us what those words of his mean. What does the fellow think, anyway? 'Even in this respect I am no longer a Wallinga.' Well, what have I done to cease being a Wallinga? Have I hurt our good name? Must this thing between us always continue?"

This is the shadow that fell across Janke's heart. There was always that hatred between Dad and Ate. She knew well that her love had caused this tragedy. Her hope had been that the baby would be a boy, for he would have been named Douwe. But that also had not been permitted.

Fortunately for her the presence of the child removed these doleful thoughts, and whenever she looked at the pretty little head and the blue eyes she felt rich and happy. Silently she thanked Ate for his precious gift to her, and they continued on their way to a useful life of harmony and sympathy. They could do very well without Douwe Ates Wallinga.

The knowledge of that unpleasant fact increased Douwe's fury. He had been driven from home because of it, but he sought solace in the knowledge that his name would be honored again in all Friesland. His name appeared regularly in many of the local newspapers, and he was welcomed in numerous circles.

But not seldom his bad temper caused serious offense to high and low. Often he involved Ate in his discussions. When heated with liquor he would lose his senses and talk with the utmost contempt about his only son. "That nitwit of Holwerd, who inherited from his crazy old uncle the farm called Metserd, and now lives there as the husband of a good-for-nothing laborer's daughter. Women, my friends, are diabolical creatures, and I would suggest that we put them all into boats and drown them in a lake, especially that sort which steal our boys. With a pair of pretty eyes and a cute little head they bewitch such a nitwit as my boy is, and now he is stuck forever. They have a baby girl besides, and not even a boy. Among us Wallingas it was always the custom to have boys first and then girls, but this nitwit has failed me also on that score. He can go with his wife and child, and jump into the river."

Everybody applauded and added further contempt to the father's denunciation. But no one knew the true cause of

Douwe's behavior. No one comprehended all these words of fury were merely answers to burning questions that continually troubled his aching heart. He took great care to keep those questions buried deep and made certain that he could always master them. For that reason he kept busy with his racing, drinking and carousing. Only on rare occasions did he spend a few days at home, and then he was involved in many urgent operations because he had so sadly neglected his most important duties and obligations.

Ate could not fail to hear about his father's escapades and the slanderous remarks he so often made about the young man and his wife. One Friday, when he was coming home on the train from the market in Leeuwarden, he suddenly heard his name mentioned and he listened intently.

"Yes, that is the reason," said one man, "that Douwe started racing again. It is Ate's fault, for he humiliated his father with his love affairs. Yes, a workman's daughter; she was living right there on the place, and in no time at all she had him in her power. And then he with his mad head rebelled against his father."

"He did not have much fun in his life to begin with, did he?"

"Very true, my friend; he is a widower! No, you must have respect for that man!"

"He does quite a little talking about his boy, doesn't he?"

"Yes, indeed," continued the other. "You can imagine how that hurts a father. Douwe sometimes accuses him of all sorts of crimes, but only when he is under the influence of liquor."

"But then, you know how that is; when you are drunk you give utterance to thoughts that are in your mind before you get drunk."

"You should hear him say, 'That nitwit of Holwerd!' I heard him talking that way the last time in Dokkum."

Ate became livid with rage, but he calmly asked the two men if he might join them in their compartment.

One of them said encouragingly, "Of course, man, come

here and sit with us. Have you been to the big city?" But the other examined him closely and said nothing.

"You were talking so loudly about Ate Douwes that you made me curious, for I want to hear some more about him and his father."

"Do you happen to know him?" asked the second, and Ate replied, "Knowing and knowing are two things. I thought I knew him, but after what I heard you say I am not so sure about it."

"How do you mean that?"

"Well," continued Ate, "the man whom I thought I knew was not the sort of person to talk that way about his own son. You say that you heard him call the boy the 'nitwit of Holwerd'?"

"Yes, I did," said the other.

"Are you sure that he meant his son?"

"Absolutely he meant his son. Ate lives in Holwerd, doesn't he? And didn't he marry the daughter of his father's laborer?"

"That is a fact," replied Ate. Then he got up. The train was near Holwerd. "Now I would like to ask you one favor, gentlemen."

"What is it?" asked the first.

"When you meet the boer of the Free Estate, Douwe Ates Wallinga, give him my compliments and tell him that nobody will be able to help him in his present condition. If I ever meet him again it will be a fight to death."

The train stopped, and the conductor called, "Holwerd! Holwerd!"

"But who on earth are you then?" asked one of them.

"I?" said Ate with a bitter laugh, "I am the nitwit of Holwerd. Good-bye to you both."

27

A T METSERD, Ate spent hours and hours during which he did not dare to look at his wife. A burning hatred had overpowered him, and he did not pause to ask himself what this might produce.

The thought of that trip on the train and the knowledge that Dad had slandered him and his wife when they had no opportunity to defend themselves drove him nearly insane. This was going to lead to some terrible outburst, for although in some things he might have ceased to be a real Wallinga, he remained one in his desire to ask for justice. His father no longer wanted to acknowledge him as his son, and he had to ask him the reason for that, as well as for his refusal to attend their wedding. But when Douwe talked about him as if he were the worst bandit of Friesland and his wife a wanton wench who had in a dishonorable manner made herself mistress of a farm, that was serious indeed! He would show his father what kind of nitwit he was!

He wondered how he could most effectively strike at Douwe

and teach him a lesson that he would never be able to forget. That proud man who wanted to rule like an absolute monarch must be properly humbled. Ate did not believe in half measures; no, this time he would hit his father in his most vulnerable spot.

On the Free Estate, Douwe lived in a daze. Marja was doing very well, as the trainer explained to him. Moreover, Douwe had perfected a technique all his own by studying every part of Marja's anatomy. Her whims he catalogued and studied with deep interest, and he succeeded in building up her reserve energy.

But no matter how proud Douwe was of Marja and how much time he spent with her, he did not forget Ate and he continued to ridicule the young man and his wife. There sat his son at Metserd, playing the part of the goody-goody husband, instead of maintaining the high traditions of the Wallingas. Why could not Ate imitate his father and train a race-horse? If only that wretched girl had not intervened, his son would now be a credit to him.

Jouk knew all about that. As a matter of fact, she knew something of great importance. While visiting Metserd she discovered that this autumn Ate was almost never at home. Suddenly he had become transformed from an exemplary husband and farmer into a vagrant. Who could have expected that of Ate? Poor Janke had no conception of what this meant. She had asked Jouk if this were perhaps her punishment. But then she had added, "I know that he is trying to do something about the trouble with his dad. He said that things could not remain as they were; a change had to come, and Janke must have faith in him as they made that change possible." That statement puzzled Jouk tremendously. Suppose that hatred which had been fostered by these two men for nearly three years were to get the better of them. What would be the outcome then?

Shouldn't I warn Douwe and try to find Ate before they go too far? she thought. What was she to do about it? She worried day and night, but she found no solution to the problem.

But Douwe had little time left for worries. In the spring he showed Marja to his friends and let her trot. He must register her for the races, for now, with the admiration of his friends to encourage him, he knew that Marja could win. The names of Douwe and Marja would be favorites this summer; a horse with such style and technique would be unbeatable in Leeuwarden and the other cities of Friesland.

In the midst of his happiest dreams a rumor arrived to the effect that a certain ghost horse, black in color, victor in many races in the province of Holland, had been purchased by an unknown person in Friesland. The rumor was whispered from one ear to another, and the picture of the horse could be found in some of the Frisian newspapers.

One evening in the Hotel Lijbering in Dokkum a group of men discussed openly for the first time the ghost horse, and Douwe was among them. They had been in the town of Wolvega, where many races were held, and now they were about to take leave of each other. They were sitting in a wide circle, and Douwe did most of the talking. Had he not won their confidence and could he not count on the winning of the Golden Whip? Never had Marja run better than today. The horse had been brought back in a truck, and she was resting in her stable, but her owner continued to boast about her forthcoming victory in Leeuwarden. Not only he but many others felt that his chances were extremely good.

Finally enough had been said about that subject, and now one of the men, Tjalling by name, struck the table with his fist and said, "I am not too sure about this dream that the Golden Whip will go to Hantum, for I don't trust that black ghost horse! Nobody knows who bought that horse, and what is even more remarkable, nobody knows where the horse is!"

A brief silence ensued, broken by Douwe, who shouted wildly, "Well, let me tell you that this sort of talk sounds to me more like fairy tales, and only children believe them. 'Ghost horse,' you say? Don't forget that we are living in the twentieth century. What kind of talk is this anyhow? Among all the horses in the world there is none for which Douwe Ates entertains any fear!"

Late that night Douwe returned home, as drunk as a man of his class ever was. He could hardly stand, though his mind seemed sharp enough. Jouk heard him but said nothing; she knew it was useless to talk to such a person. The next morning at nine, Tjalling came to ask if Douwe would like to go with him to Groningen, where the ghost horse was to run. Douwe refused. He swore vociferously and ran from the yard into the house and back again, trying to escape his misgivings about that mysterious ghost horse. But he did not succeed fully.

The next evening he began to study the reports about the leading races. He jotted down the figures concerning the black horse in question which ran under the name of Mr. X. To his amazement he observed that this horse could run at least as fast as Marja. He could not hide that very unpleasant fact. How was this possible? There was no better horse than Marja, for yesterday did she not beat Henriot with flying colors? Henriot was beaten by Mr. X. in Groningen, the distance being two meters, which was greater than that achieved by Marja. Even that grand horse Athleta was no match for Mr. X.!

A brilliant thought came to Douwe. Strange it had not occurred to him before. His beloved friends, the owners of Henriot, Athleta and Walter Scott — they had jointly bought the black horse in order to defeat him. As in warfare the smaller countries ally against a powerful state, so his competitors had allied against him. Very well, let them have their fun. If they thought that he would move aside for them, they would get a surprise, those cowards!

Douwe Ates laughed at those weaklings. As usual, he registered his horse for the races that preceded the grand finale in Leeuwarden. First came the contest at Drachten, where Marja won the highest prize, and Douwe proudly covered the round of honor. Then followed Holwerd, where victory was easily achieved. But when later he studied the figures he uttered such a terrible oath that Jouk was alarmed. She could no longer hold her peace, and said, "But boer, keep still; be calm. The last few days you have been all up in the air; come down to earth and use your head." But he, forgetting for the moment that Jouk was not familiar with the details of racing, shouted at her. "They are holding him in reserve, the big rats! They are planning to murder me in Leeuwarden. Let me find out who is back of this thing. Let me find that out!"

Jouk let him shout; she did not know what to say in reply to such mysterious talk, but she did decide to talk this matter over with Ate.

Jouk did not know, but it was clear to Douwe that Mr. X. was kept out of the local races in order to save his strength for the grand show in the provincial capital. He determined not to register Marja for any more of the local races until the last moment, so as to mislead his opponents. But even that ruse brought no change; the black horse never ran against Marja.

One evening a large advertisement appeared in the *Leeuwarden Courant*. As soon as people had read the paper a large number of them attempted to discover who had placed it, but no one could tell except Douwe Ates and one of the officials on the staff of the paper. The advertisement read:

> A certain person who loves horses and racing would like to know why Mr. X, or the ghost horse, as it is called by people who still believe in magic, never appears on the race-track where Marja of Douwe Ates takes part. The owners are not afraid that this famous ghost will be defeated, are they?

The next day appeared the answer, also in large letters:

> The time is not yet ripe. N. N.

Yes, the time was not yet ripe, but soon it would be. Did those people think they could frighten Douwe Ates with such childish pranks? In Douwe's opinion they were idiots. He rushed from one town to another, and everywhere he caused a sensation. Suddenly he would make his appearance in a group of imbibers, and towering about them like a giant, he would shout, "N.N. — I know what that means. I know it.

Would you like to hear it? Listen well, people; open your ears." In his heart he knew that they were trying to deceive him, but he would fix them: "N. N. — that is . . . . that is nothing, double nothing, double zero!" His laugh reverberated through the inn and was repeated by the others, so that some of them were impelled to write on their plates, "N. N. is less than double nothing. N. N. is double nothing, double zero!"

When Douwe was beside himself because of his drinking and boasting he gasped, "N. N. double nothing is Ate!"

He realized that if Ate had not left him in the lurch the Wallingas would not have to fear anyone; in that case there would have been two to gird themselves for the contest. Douwe actually was afraid of the race, while at the same time he longed for it. At Leeuwarden he was to be smashed by his opponents. Ate had forsaken him. When he thought of this his anger became so fierce that he would not even listen to Jouk when one afternoon she wanted to tell him something.

"Boer," she said with marked excitement, "now you will have to go there, for Janke has a . . . ."

"Shut your mouth," shouted Douwe. "I don't care what goes on at Metserd; I have other things on my mind."

That was true, for Marja had been registered, and in great suspense Douwe lived through these last days. He had to weigh each portion of feed for the horse, supervise the training and attend to the arrangements for the final race in the capital. Douwe could not deny that his advancing years had reduced his vigor, but he would grit his teeth whenever symptoms of physical weakness clamored for attention. Every morning Marja made the rounds in the meadow, the trainer behind the horse in the sulky, and Douwe with the chronometer in his hand, watching intently to see if Marja made a slip. But no matter how long he watched, the horse did not fail him in the slightest detail.

Three days before the last race the trainer and Douwe put the horse in a truck. The trainer went with Marja to Leeuwarden, in order to run with the horse in the track on the

Westersingel. Meanwhile Douwe made the necessary preparations for his own trip. He must be calm, for the victory depended as much on himself as on Marja. But that evening he was greatly disturbed by a notice in the newspaper which read:

Who is N. N.? Who is Mr. X?

Although many foreign practices have lately been introduced among us Frisians, some of which have been reprehensible, it has never happened that a horse ran whose owner was called N. N. We are of the opinion that this feat is contrary to the hallowed customs of Friesland. In short, before the last series takes place we insist that the owner of this horse inform us who he is; otherwise the series cannot be arranged, since we shall withdraw our horses from the contest.

Below this notice the names of three owners of far-famed horses appeared. Douwe approved of this advertisement, and for a moment he had to admit that these three men were not among those who wanted to thwart him. Nevertheless he began to wonder immediately if perhaps even these men had some mean trick up their sleeves, as was often the case among horse racers.

He examined the list. Twenty horses registered for the opening prize; fourteen horses for harnesses; parade of carriages; driving of an ancient mail coach; harnesses of Frisian horses before sleighs with compulsory Frisian garb; prizes for the most beautiful span of horses. Then . . . the race for the Golden Whip. To honor an old tradition the list gave the names of those who owned horses which were to participate in the grand finale. Yes, indeed, as if done on purpose, these names directly followed each other: Marja, four-year-old mare, famous winner of prizes, owner Douwe Ates Wallinga, Hantum; Mr. X., six-year-old black gelding, imported from East Friesland in Germany, and, after having been a favorite for one year in the province of Holland, sold to N. N. in Friesland.

There it was again, that mysterious N. N. Well, Douwe was not afraid of anybody, but one had to be careful with an opponent whom he did not know. What would the management do about that request to have the name of this person made known to the public? The answer was not long in coming. Twenty-four hours later the following notice appeared in the same newspaper:

> N. N. will reveal his identity before the grand finale for the prize of the Golden Whip.

What more could one expect? Douwe would discover after all who this queer person was. In victory or defeat he was eager to face his opponent.

But it would be a distinct disadvantage to prepare for a fight against a horse which one had not seen in action on the same race-course. Douwe would wait . . . and when the contest was over . . . . He would not repeat; tomorrow he would race for the last time, whether he won or lost. But regardless of everything else, Douwe Ates would ride with honor. Let people say what they pleased, none would be able to prove that he had been a coward. Tomorrow he would ride as he had never ridden; he would be like a king, and then that glorious feeling, the pride of his ancestors, would course through his body. That storm of emotion would overpower him once more in the great race. So did those heroes of primitive times venture forth against their enemies of old!

He took the train to Leeuwarden, a queer boer from the country who said hardly one word to strangers. He walked from the station without paying any attention to people or vehicles past the cattle market to the stable where Marja stood. He and the trainer carefully examined every detail, and at an early hour Douwe went to bed.

As he lay there he was reminded of that other night, many years ago, when he had been here, and the next day he had won that grand prize. But how different things were then! Liesbeth was still alive. Little Ate had played and romped on the floor. Gelf had still been with him. . . And now . . . Liesbeth was dead . . . Ate was as good as dead. What a mean trick Ate had played on him by leaving him in the lurch like this! But away with such thoughts. He must think about Marja; yes, Marja. . . His thoughts were darkened by the appearance of a huge black ghost.

28

THE DAY OF Leeuwarden began to take first place on all the calendars of Friesland. It was the day of the Golden Whip! In every village and hamlet, people who were interested in horses all talked about this day as if it were a matter of public concern.

Among the horse trainers the discussion was professional only; they made their living with this business, and they were interested almost entirely in the question of the bets on the favorites. For them, however, it was difficult to tell who was the real favorite this time.

Strange though it may have seemed, all Friesland was affected by the outcome of the race. Everybody was eager to see which of those two horses would win the race, Marja or Mr. X. Few seemed to believe that any other horse had a chance to win.

Whenever Douwe Ates was mentioned he was spoken of merely as the owner of Marja, Marja the fast one, the pure one, the gypsy horse that ran like a hare and was as proud as a princess. Women in particular were partial to Marja.

But next to Marja there stood that black ghost horse which had caused even more speculation because one could not find a trace of it. The public was not satisfied with the way in which this horse was treated. In the first place, it was not known who the owner was, but people would soon discover that secret. In the second place, nobody could tell where the horse was taken after each race. A car with a trailer behind it appeared the moment the last round was finished. At once the horse was shoved into the trailer, the harness into the car and the sulky on top. Then the car rushed away.

Another cause of speculation was the fact that Marja and the ghost horse had never appeared together in any of the local races, and when people discovered that Douwe had spared no pains to make such a meeting possible, the conclusion naturally followed that someone was endeavoring to play a trick on Douwe. This conviction increased the feeling of suspense. Furthermore, the advertisements in the Leeuwarden newspaper had attracted the attention of many thousands who were determined to obtain a select seat on the grandstand.

Then came the news that Douwe had challenged the mysterious N. N. to a fight. He had frequently boasted about his own honesty and integrity, and if it were true, he shouted, that a certain person had bought the black horse for the specific purpose of defeating him at the race, then let this person beware of Douwe Ates Wallinga. It would be a fight to the death! N. N. was a double nothing, but if he were also a cheater, he had better be prepared for a terrific punishment.

These facts were widely discussed throughout all Friesland. Everyone had to go to Leeuwarden on that particular day, and early in the morning the carriages and automobiles came from all directions. Many rode their bicycles, others came by train or steamboat, not a few from the province of Groningen and to the south of Friesland. What a day it would be for the people of Leeuwarden!

The weather was perfect and everyone was cheerful. Families which for years had not been in the city together were here now. It was a pleasure to hear the intelligent conversation of the people from the rural districts who in the eyes of the city folk were often considered semibarbarous. Occasionally one could detect some who were dressed in the garb of their grandparents.

At ten o'clock the grandstand on the Westersingel was crowded with spectators. The men at the ticket windows were exceedingly busy, and those who sold the programs had the best trade they had ever known. They did not shout as usual about the names of the owners and the horses but only, "Programs with the latest news about Marja of Douwe Ates and Mr. X. of N. N. Who will win the Golden Whip? Programs! Programs!"

First came the race for the opening prize in which twenty horses participated; they ran in groups of five for a distance of sixteen hundred meters. They made a gay and colorful scene. Douwe looked at them also, but naturally his thoughts were elsewhere. Neither he nor any other of the spectators could detect the black ghost horse! Would the owner again refuse to let his horse run against Marja?

This question did not long remain unanswered, for suddenly, unnoticed except by Douwe and a few others, the black horse arrived. The trainer was from the province of Holland, and although he was courteous, no one was able to extract from him a single word about Mr. X. Almost immediately the announcement was heard, "Get ready for the final race, the contest for the Golden Whip!" The horses were to run in the track of eight hundred meters, thirty-six of them, in groups of six each. Now the crowd would at least learn who N. N. actually was, and what sort of horse he owned.

Marja had to run with the first group, and the moment she was put in her place a loud applause came from the entranced crowd of spectators. Hundreds of them shouted eagerly, "Douwe Ates!" The men showed rider and horse to their wives and children, and all were full of happy anticipation of the moving scene at the end of the last round.

The automatic starting signal was given, the rubber bands in front of the horses were neatly removed, and away they went, six handsome animals, well trained and perfectly managed. But only one of them could win, and that was Marja, two lengths ahead of the nearest rival. Douwe had shown what could be done with Marja, for she had not yet been forced to use much of her reserve energy.

The victor of the second group was Paul Kruger, of the third, was Spyk, of the fourth was Winny, and of the fifth was Stanfries. Then came the black ghost horse to run in the sixth, or last, group. Douwe stared fiercely at that one animal. Hatred for horse and owner consumed him.

Loud was the noise that came from the grandstand, for here at last was the height of excitement, the appearance of the veritable ghost horse! One could distinguish hundreds of voices all saying, "The ghost horse of double nothing!" Some cried encouragement, but many others were averse to thoughts of approbation. The atmosphere of mystery that had so long surrounded this particular horse did not endear it to the popular mind. It did indeed look like a ghost, so calm and dignified it seemed, exactly like that man in the sulky, the man from Holland, frozen as it were to his seat. What a sight that was!

The usual sign was given and the six horses sped onward, with the black one passing two of them before it had gone far. But wonder of wonders, it could not overtake the others, notwithstanding the coaxing words from the men and women in the stand who had come partly to witness the supreme struggle of giant against giant, and now wanted the ghost horse to win so that it might run against Marja in the final round. But they were not doomed to disappointment, for at the very last moment the horse passed the nearest competitor and won the series by only a few inches. That in itself caused intense excitement, since the crowd did not want to see a stranger in these parts beat the Frisian mare Marja and her owner from Hantum!

"As far as I can see," said one of the boers, "Douwe Ates won't have to worry a bit about that horse."

"But that means nothing," hastily replied another. "This is only the series, remember. Only a preliminary show, that's all."

"Very true," remarked the first speaker, "but didn't you see how that Hollander used up all its energy while Douwe Ates held his horse in check? I keep my opinion that Douwe Ates won't have to worry a bit about that ghost horse!"

There was much to make the scene beautiful. First came the English mail coach of a century ago, with two, then with four, and finally with six horses in front. The band played lustily, the sun shone brightly, and all was well with the crowd. During the intermission, people left their seats to get refreshments. There was much gay conversation about people and things, but presently the all-absorbing theme was the forthcoming race between Marja and the ghost horse from Holland. That reminded the people of the great contest between Holland and Friesland, ages ago, when the count of Holland had conquered their country. Since the last quarter of the nineteenth century a wave of nationalism had swept through the rural districts and the Frisian language has been accorded the standing to which it had long been entitled. Should it be Holland against Friesland, or was there a Frisian who owned the ghost horse and wanted to humble Douwe Ates Wallinga? That question would now be answered . . . .

The people returned to their seats, and the six horses took their places for the grand finale. Paul Kruger was there, the winner of the first series, with the rider in his sulky, dressed in a black shirt with a golden collar and horseshoes of gold on his sleeves. Next was Spyk, a handsome horse with white legs, whose rider wore a green shirt with a black stripe and a black cap. Winny was a brown horse, and her rider wore a purple shirt and brown cap. Stanfries's rider had a black shirt with red buttons and red cap. Finally came Mr. X., the black gelding, whose rider wore a black shirt with silver buttons and a black cap with a silver cord, and Marja, the gold-brown mare, whose rider had a green shirt with red buttons and a red cap.

There they all were, and everybody in the arena wanted to get the place which would best enable them to see the exciting action. Not a few were trembling with suspense, and nobody dared to utter a sound. The riders were preparing for the race. What a beautiful sight — the colors and the finest horses man could find!

Suddenly there was a question from one of the spectators. "Names," he shouted. His request was repeated by many others who clamored to know who owned Mr. X. There they came — Paul Kruger, owner and Oosterhof, Wirdum; then the other three, until the last two were named: Marja, owner and rider Douwe Ates Wallinga; and Wodan, owner and rider Ate Douwes Wallinga!

Ate Douwes. That revelation shook the spectators. It meant that Douwe Ates would run against Ate Douwes, his own son. Father against son? And son against father? What an extraordinary coincidence!

Gone was the thought that Marja would automatically win or that she should deserve to win. The young chap had dealt his father a diplomatic coup by withholding from him the knowledge that would have prepared him for such a contingency. Now it would be a fight that no one would be able to forget. How were people, knowing the history of the Wallingas, to remain calm under such circumstances? A great drama was about to be unfolded before their very eyes. The young man planned to use the race for the Golden Whip to settle a quarrel well known to thousands in the capital.

Douwe Ates almost jumped into the air when he heard Ate's name mentioned. He did not dare to look around, for he had to pay close attention to Marja, but Ate . . . and for a moment the thought flashed into his mind, *Give up the race,* but only for a brief moment, and presently he felt a grand realization of old hopes fulfilled. He had found happiness at last.

Naturally. Why had he not thought of this possibility

before? What else could one expect of a Wallinga? Ate challenged him to a duel and wanted to strike at the dearest thing in his life. *Now I feel,* he thought, *that I have my son back again. Now I know that the Wallinga blood still courses through his veins. And now we shall fight, boy! I am not going to spare you!*

Ate, who during the intermission had slipped quietly into the rider's seat, now controlled his own horse, and he felt that it was a vital part of his own life. The horses were to run with almost equal speed, side by side, rider next to rider. The rules were strict, and one must exercise great caution. How exhilarating this contest would be! He forgot all things and all people around him except his horse which must achieve the victory and those which would have to be passed. He overtook them all, one by one, until he had reached Marja. First five meters, then four, then three, then two, then one, then side by side . . . and now they flew through the air together, father against son.

To the side was the great mass of excited spectators, who were thrilled almost to distraction.

Douwe's voice was clear and commanding as he urged, "Marja, my gypsy girl, keep it up. You wouldn't want to let that imp of a boy beat us, would you?" And Marja did her utmost to please Douwe, whose patience and skill deserved a high reward.

But not for nothing did Wodan bear the name of the ghost horse. When Ate finally saw that he must call up the latent forces still unused, Wodan increased his speed considerably. One could count the ribs under his hide, and he developed such terrific speed that the reins were taut. The remaining meters were devoured, and no matter how hard Marja tried, her effort was in vain. She could not keep up, and amidst deafening applause Ate won the Golden Whip in the great race of Leeuwarden.

The spectators were not to be kept outside of the track, but there was one who ran faster than all the others, and that was Douwe Ates, who entrusted Marja to his servant, ran furiously, looked at Ate with intense admiration, shook his hand, and said, "An honorable fight. My congratulations to you!"

Then Douwe disappeared, and no one in Leeuwarden would see him again that day. Like one in a daze he left the arena, changed his clothes and hurried to the railroad station. He recalled dimly how when he had looked back at the boy he had seen the crowd raise Ate in the air and carry him on their shoulders to the tent of the manager, and this, he knew, had been followed by the round of honor. But Douwe did not belong there. No, he must go home as fast as possible. He was barely able to catch the four o'clock train, and an hour and a half later he reached the Free Estate.

Jouk looked up with amazement, for such behavior was most unusual. Hastily she tried to prepare some lunch for him. She was worried about his early return. *The boer must have lost,* she thought. *He'll probably be beside himself with rage.*

But imagine her surprise when Douwe spoke gently. "Jouk, Jouk, do you know who N. N. is? He is the owner of the ghost horse."

"No, boer," she replied, "no, boer, but hurry and get yourself something to eat and drink."

"Eat? No, Jouk, I have eaten enough today. Listen, Jouk! N. N. is Ate Douwes . . . our Ate!"

"Our Ate?" Jouk trembled with emotion and asked again, "Our Ate?"

"Yes," continued Douwe, "that nitwit of Holwerd, as I used to call him. Jouk, today in Leeuwarden he paid me with double interest everything he owed me. Today he won the Golden Whip and chased his father in royal fashion from the field of honor. Wouldn't that make you laugh? And you would expect me to eat? Oh, no!" Douwe went to the living-room, but suddenly he turned and said, "What did you want to tell me the other day?" And Jouk, thrilled by his change of heart replied proudly, "That they have a little Douwe."

"Then he has shown in this also that he is one of the Wallingas!"

29

ATE DOUWES did not recall with how many persons he had
shaken hands. He could not even remember distinctly
how he got home. None of those things mattered to him in
the least, and he would never be able to describe the events
immediately after the race.

From the moment that he started his round of honor with
Wodan, with the Golden Whip in the socket, his hands
trembled as he held the reins, while the people shouted with
glee and the band played the victor's march, from that moment
until he put his head under the pump and dashed cold water
over it, he had been in a daze.

Now he dried his face with a rough towel until his cheeks
were as red as beets and he was able to think coherently
again. Suddenly he realized that it was milking time, but must
the owner of the Golden Whip help with the milking? Why
not? To win the Golden Whip was joy, but now that the
evening hours had come, he must go back to work. He took
the old blue shirt off the hook and went into the field.

To sit in a banquet hall with lights so bright that at first one had to blink his eyes, to talk at length with gentlemen who wore shirts and collars so tight and high that they could not be comfortable, to converse with beautiful women in silk dresses with pieces of fire instead of eyes, fire which burned you with a flame of false love — that was all right in its place, but to come home to one's own little wife, to embrace her fondly, and to whisper, "You, my girl, and nobody else," and then to be drowned in a sea of true love — that was real life! Ate was so happy that he was almost overwhelmed and he needed time to think. He began to sing and to jest with everybody, for he had finally won his supreme victory. His proud father, who for years had been unwilling to talk to him, who would not recognize his daughter-in-law, who refused to look at his own grandchildren, and who hid himself behind a wall of stubbornness — this man, king in his little realm, he had driven from his throne and pierced with the dart of retribution.

It was clearly a matter of up or down, and no one realized that more than Ate himself. But the arrow went straight to its aim, to the heart of Douwe Ates. . . .

All those thousands and thousands of people knew what he was doing. This Frisian nation of workers who knew also how to think seriously grasped fully the impact of his extraordinary action. They saw as well as Douwe did that no amount of words would have had a worth-while effect, and where years of searching and planning had produced no change of heart, only a deed would accomplish the desired result. Yes, a unique step was needed — a step which signified overwhelming power, both physical and mental. It was a matter of power against power, and the son had won through his superior power!

Neither Ate nor Janke could adjust themselves in a dignified way to so much happiness. They started early in the morning with their frolicking. First a game with little Auk, then a race with Douwe on his arm till the little fellow began to howl. Janke asked, "How can he know what's in your head, you lummox?" Then Ate tried to lift her and carry her around for a while. Like children they ran around the table. The situation became so comical that Iepe said to Keimpe, "We had better get out of here." Out in the yard he said, "You told me when the boer had just been married and he had to go to the house every hour or so that this condition would last only a short time. But, my dear man, they are starting all over again, as frisky as ever!"

But Ate did not hear that. He even wanted to seize the maid and race with her through the room, because she had just remarked that perhaps the honor offered to him by the management of the race course in Leeuwarden had gone to his head. Finally both women shoved Ate out of the house.

Ate had a reason for his jubilation. He was positive that this time his father was pleased with him, for he had played fair with him, exactly as the best of the Wallingas would have done.

Janke, the daughter of a workman, who had played well her new role of mistress on a large farm but had lost none of her simplicity, did not know how to express her joy. Thus far she had had a feeling of guilt, for it seemed as if her love had caused the separation between Ate and his father. Often she had remarked that it would have been better for Ate if he had listened to his father, but each time Ate had embraced her fondly, saying that she was entirely mistaken. One day he said, "I am fond of Dad, and I wish I could regain his affection, but to give you up would not be the proper way, for that would show I was not a Wallinga."

Yes, he was a true son of Douwe Ates, and he had felt so strong and certain of himself when he told Janke that he had bought Wodan and was training him for the race in Leeuwarden. He used fields and meadows, chiefly those back of the dike that were off the beaten track, where the waters of the North Sea flooded the flats at high tide, and where few persons ever came to watch them. Janke then understood what a Wallinga he really was!

That was all past now. There was no longer the need

for secrecy, and like wildfire the tale of the race for the Golden Whip spread through the homes of Friesland. Those who had not been present soon heard all the exciting details. The last remark was usually this: "What men — Douwe Ates and Ate Douwes!"

The day after the great race was not an unusual one. The sun rose in its usual fashion and followed its appointed path until it sank beneath the horizon. The men and women garnered the fruits of the earth until twilight warned them that their day's labor was finished. Then they went home.

But on the Free Estate the situation was confused, to say the least. All day Douwe had been in the fields, and Jouk had difficulty making him eat calmly. His thoughts were not clear. Quickly changing his clothes, he went into the living room. There he sat and meditated and when at eight o'clock Jouk brought him his tea, she saw him sitting there with his head on his hands, and his elbows on the table. The old family Bible lay open before him.

Jouk's hands were trembling when she put the tea on the table. She was eager to say something, but what could she tell him that would have the desired effect? Quietly she left the room again.

'Douwe remained seated a long, long time. Finally he said, "Ate, son of Liesbeth and Douwe," and again, "son of Liesbeth and Douwe." He had reviewed the whole course of his life, all the good and all the bad qualities of his character and all the events of the past twenty-five years, both good and bad. . . .

He had been sitting there for hours, alone and yet not entirely alone. In the middle of the night he went outside. Like a huge lake of silver Friesland lay before him. Occasionally he heard the doleful voice of an owl, and once the lowing of a cow, but aside from these all was silent. In front of him he saw the light from the lighthouse on the island of Schiermonnikoog, and to the left those of Ameland and Terschelling, and still farther to the west that of Texel. Those

ancient Frisian islands encircle his native land, the land which
he had loved so long.

Douwe, strong Douwe Ates, wanted to cry and pray, so
small he felt. Finally he went to bed, and Jouk heard him
no more until his voice rang clearly through the room, "I am
coming tomorrow, Ate!"

At last the proud man had come to a realization of his own
personal guilt. Throughout his life he had failed to reckon
with spiritual laws. Only on rare occasions, when face to face
with the mysteries of birth and death, had he thought about
God and his soul. But now a great shock had come to him.
He saw that his standards of life had been all wrong. The
mere fact that he had been defeated in a horse race by his
own son was not the sole punishment for the injustice he had
inflicted upon Ate and his charming wife. What he had needed
all along had come to him now. He understood his own faults.
He had sinned not only against his children but even more
against God. That is why he suddenly felt small and mean,
and that is why he wanted to pray like a little child. He must
humble himself before a just and merciful God, and in doing
so he became worthy of Ate and Janke, who thus far had been
greatly superior to him.

The next morning Ate knew that his father was coming
to Metserd. He had a premonition early during the milking,
and he had told Janke three times to keep everything in
readiness. When at ten o'clock he went with the mud cart,
drawn by two horses, with the plow on it, he said to Janke,
"Be sure to have things ready for him," and then he left.
He started to plow a field in which early potatoes had grown,
and now it was to be prepared for a second crop. The young
boer was in ecstasy, for he knew that his wish for reunion
and reconciliation would be granted soon. As the plow cut
through the moist and heavy dirt he listened attentively. Yes,
the noise of a horse and a carriage could be heard plainly.
Only one horse could trot like this and that horse was Marja!

Like a storm Marja approached Metserd, and a voice sang in Ate's heart, "There comes Dad."

But not once did he look. He must plow, plow! Marja turned and entered the yard. Ate could feel that, and it seemed to him as if his father was calling to him. "Here I am. Away, horses!"

Ate had waited years for this. Something tremendous must have happened to his father, for now he was small and humble. Perhaps one could apply that well-known proverb, "In the small lies the great." With heavy steps Douwe Ates walked along the intervening field, and he waited for his son, who left his horses and turned to meet Dad. For a brief moment they stood there face to face; they felt their burning love, their desire for each other and their happiness. No one could see that except God. Then they shook hands and ground to pieces all the evil forces that had stood between them during all these years of sorrow.

"Dad," said Ate. "Boy," replied the father. This is all they said. Neither of them could or wanted to add anything. They had said enough.

Douwe swallowed something in his throat and acted as if nothing had happened between them. "Boy, you are behind your plow rather early, aren't you?" asked Douwe. "Yes," answered Ate. "The early potatoes did very well, and now we must fix the soil for the turnips!"

"Everything all right at home?" asked his father.

Ate answered readily. "Dad had better go there; Janke has the coffee ready."

"Then I'll go," said Douwe, and turning, he went to the dam. When he observed that Ate was about to start plowing again, he asked, "Aren't you coming to drink some coffee?"

"Yes," replied Ate. "Twice around, and then I'll come over." Soon he had finished, and he took both horses with him to the yard, where Iepe relieved him of his care. Iepe wondered what had happened, for Ate was trembling like a child and his voice was strange. He asked, "Is there something wrong, boer?" But he received no answer. Ate ran through the cow stable and into the kitchen. The first person he saw was Janke, who had been waiting for him, and who was overwhelmed with joy. A warm ray of sunshine fell through the kitchen window and made her hair shine like gold, and her blue eyes were bright. Ate saw that tears had been rolling down her cheeks. *Just like that day,* thought Ate, and with two long steps he had reached her and pulled her close to him.

"Girl," he mumbled, "my own little wife . . . . quiet now . . . ." And Janke let the tears of joy come. Ate said, "What have we done to deserve so much happiness, Janke? Quiet, girl." He lifted her head. "Come along," he beckoned as he went to the door of the living room, where they could hear two voices singing. It was the heavy voice of Douwe and that of a little child, and they were singing three lines of an ancient Frisian melody:

"Ride, ride, ride, with Grandmother in the sleigh,
With Grandfather in his new wagon,
So we flew to Leeuwarden."

On the chair sat Grandfather with little Auk on his knee. It was the beginning of a holiday which would pass too soon.

That evening Douwe took the Golden Whip and walked back and forth with it through the room. Ate and Janke were wondering what he would do next, but they did not need to fear, for Douwe was about to make his confession.

"Children, I must tell you how I feel; there is someone who impels me to do this, but I don't know who it is . . . ." The young people waited in suspense as Douwe continued, "I had desired all my life to win the Golden Whip. I sacrificed everything for it, and when I had finally won it I lost my wife, my reason and my honor, because I did not deserve to have the Golden Whip under such circumstances. . . But you, Ate, you have taught me how one must behave to become worthy of it. You have won, boy. You have performed a deed so great that I can't find words with which to describe it. And you, Janke, child, I misjudged you. Will you be so kind as to forgive an old man who would love so much to live in peace and harmony with you hereafter?"

Janke looked at him. "Certainly," she said, and her voice was filled with deep emotion. "Certainly, Dad, everything is all right."

"Now I would like to go home," observed Douwe, and they accompanied him to the yard, where Marja was ready for him. The maid was holding the horse by the head.

Douwe Ates said no more. He seized the reins, climbed over the wheel and went through the gate to Brantgum. The two young people watched him, and their hearts beat with the rhythm of the racing legs of Marja. Hand in hand they returned to the room where little Douwe lay, one hand under his head and the other near his mouth, sleeping as soundly as a fish.

"Our boy," said Ate, "and our dad . . . little and big Douwe . . . . What a man!" He turned, for he did not want to weep. He experienced a grand feeling of admiration for that father who had many faults, but was yet so great, so strong.

On the Free Estate Jouk, the old, faithful housekeeper, was waiting, and she sat quietly in her chair. A moment ago she said, as if Liesbeth were standing at her side, "You should have been there, mistress, there in Holwerd!"

Outside on the road near Brantgum a buggy bounced along with a brown horse in front of it and a boer inside, a proud boer, strong and keen, but none of that strength and keenness was visible in his features. He smiled quietly, and out of his heart came words which were simple and rather monotonous, but what did he care about that? He repeated those three lines over and over again: "Ride, ride, ride, with Grandmother in the sleigh . . . ."

In the meantime two young people in the farmhouse at Metserd were filled to overflowing with their happiness. The Golden Whip lay shining upon the oak table, a symbol of victory well won and well deserved.

The story of the Golden Whip is finished.

They are sitting in the big room on the Free Estate — Grandfather, Douwe Ates Wallinga, and the grandchild, Aukje. He sits in the big oak chair and the little girl is in her little chair a short distance away. With her blue eyes she has bewitched him.

Did he tell her the story? Well, what of it? Perhaps it did not come smoothly and coherently, and Grandfather may have told it somewhat differently, but we have put the pieces together like beads on a string, and it has spoken to our hearts. What does it matter whether we are an employer or an employee?

Once more Grandfather gets up and takes little Douwe on his arm, and then he goes to Hantum, where he is living with Jouk in a little house, from which you can see for many miles over the fertile fields of Friesland. He walks with firm steps, for he knows that his recent days have been filled with righteous living. Metserd has been rented and Ate is living on the Free Estate with his wife and children. Jouk is waiting for him; she has never left him and will remain with him until the end of her life.

At the house his meal is waiting for him, but first he must satisfy Jouk's curiosity, and tell her all about the children of Ate and Janke . . . . Then he begins to eat, reads the paper and gets ready for a meeting in the village. He has become the director of a society and he enjoys these meetings, so says Jouk. "Do you remember that evening?" she asks him, and he replies, "I should say so." Then Douwe drinks some tea, takes a comfortable seat and holds forth with great gusto. . .

Stop for just a minute, boer!

Shall we leave them now? But be quiet; we might break something.

PRINTED IN THE UNITED STATES OF AMERICA